About the

P. J. Whiteley was born in Bradford, West Yorkshire, in 1962, but attended schools in different parts of the UK. He has been a professional writer since summer 1988, working initially in trade magazines. Since 1997 his journalism and, latterly, non-fiction titles have been on the subject of business management, with a focus on research that supports an enlightened alternative to treating people as 'resources'. His first novel, *Close of Play* (Urbane Publications, 2015), was described by the *Church Times* as 'well written and above all well observed'. *Marching on Together* (Urbane, 2017) received a cover quote from Louis de Bernières.

A Love of Two Halves

A Love of Two Halves

P. J. Whiteley

unbound

This edition first published in 2019

Unbound
6th Floor Mutual House, 70 Conduit Street, London W1S 2GF
www.unbound.com

© P. J. Whiteley, 2019

This book is a work of fiction and, except in the case of historical fact, any
resemblance to actual persons, living or dead, is purely coincidental.

ISBN (eBook): 978-1-78965-054-9
ISBN (Paperback): 978-1-78965-053-2

Cover design by Mecob

Printed and bound in Great Britain by Clays Ltd, Elcograf S.p.A.

Super Patrons

Helen Armitage
Felicity Baker
David Baker
Alejandro Cendoya
Sue Clark
Andrew Crofts
Sarah Crouch
Katy Diggory
Anne Foster
Caroline Foster
Rebecca Galley
Johnnie Gallop
Bob & Sally Garratt
Fiona Gell
Nigel Girling
Jules Goddard
Eamonn Griffin
Sue Harrison
Paul Harvey
Sue Jennings
Nicky Kemp

Dan Kieran
Tim Kitching
Marilyn Lawrence
Yvonne Lee
Jenni Lloyd
Ann Lyon
Teena Lyons
The Management Shift Consulting
The Margate Bookie
Ian & Anne Martin
Chris McCoy
John Mitchinson
Jung Park
Justin Pollard
Tess Rosa Ruiz
Katharine St John-Brooks
Catherine Sutton
Katrina Tolley
Jacqui Trowsdale
Mark Vent
Robert Welbourn
Roger Whiteley
Peter Whiteley
Philip Whiteley
Rose Whiteley
Marian Wilde
Max Wiseberg

1

Waking up is like dying

I had the House Dream again. It was the best yet – which is to say the worst, the most vivid. I sensed, even at the most serene moments, that I was condemned to waking up. *No! No! I don't want to wake up! Waking up is like dying!* I wanted to watch Bronte playing, sunlight glinting on her black, shiny hair at the top of each swing, giggling. In the dream she was seven again. She jumped off the swing, rolled in the soft, green grass and white and yellow daisies, picked up my hand and said: 'Come on, Mum! I want to show you the rooms we've never been in yet.' She led me in, up one set of stairs and then another. Nothing was like our real house and yet, in the dream, it was familiar to me, until we reached the second set of stairs. 'Why have I never noticed this before?' I said to her. 'A whole extra storey that I've never been in!' We were both giggling by then. 'Come on, Mum, these are the best rooms.' The light streamed in through elegant dormer windows, lighting up deep, soft settees and four-poster beds; Axminster carpets and oil paintings. 'It's like a palace,' I said. 'It's our palace, and I'm the princess,' she replied.

I knew I was dreaming before awakening. It was too strange. I fought against waking up – fought hard. I woke up. There was no second staircase, no extra rooms, no swing, no lawn; indeed, no garden, except for a front yard so small that if I were to sit on the window ledge and stretch out my legs, I could almost rest my ankles on the front fence. The sun was shining, at least. It shines on the rich and the poor alike. Bronte is fifteen, not seven; sixteen in two weeks' time. But she was lovely: my treasure – kind, clever, funny, artistic, with a great singing voice and good taste in music, for the most part. She was there at the breakfast table when I went down, eating cereal and listening to music on headphones. It was Danny who had wakened me and I'd helped him get washed and dressed, complaining. Him, not me. Three years old and already with a mind very much his own. I hoped he wasn't going to turn out like Darren. Bronte, fortunately, is beginning to resemble Terry: soft in manner, artistic and kind, with high cheekbones and a beautiful face.

Danny would be with grandma the other side of Beeston today; Bronte hanging out with some friends 'til some point in the afternoon. Then, in the evening, we'd all gather together for the telly. It was Saturday, but I didn't have a weekend shift. I'd saved up £20 for myself, and I planned to go by buses to Headingley, shop in the charity stores there for designer brand cast-offs – my little secret, and gather some house details – my guilty obsession. As it was a nice day I didn't even mind if the buses took a long time. I would sit on the top deck, and watch the world as we went by.

It was early afternoon when the number sixty-four returned to Holbeck Moor, where I got off. Don't be fooled by the term 'Moor'; it's not like Brontë Country, more like a rec. But, anyway, I was well pleased with my purchases: a beautiful, green designer top for a fiver, nearly new, and a small handbag, plus half a dozen estate agent colour brochures for north-west Leeds, nice houses near the Otley Road. The brochures were all free, of course. The staff all cheerfully handed them out to me, as I was scrubbed clean, well presented and gave a warm smile. I didn't have to confess that I was skint. I couldn't afford any of the houses; not even a garage, probably, but that's not the point, is it? I was the happiest I'd been for a while, and looking forward to the pizza and wine, with cola for the kids, that evening.

Bronte wasn't back. I texted her, and she texted straight back, which was a relief. She was still in the arcades, and would be back around five. I called Mum to check Danny was OK. He was playing with toy trucks. She'd bring him back for his tea. I had around two hours to myself. I pulled out the house details. One caught my eye immediately: a gorgeous period cottage in Headingley, nicely photographed, beautifully decorated. Just under £250,000. Only two bedrooms, mind, though they did look nice; one of them en suite. I often dreamed of just wandering in from the bathroom naked, or just a towel wrapped around me, on smooth, polished wood floors, from luxurious shower room to deluxe bedroom, natural light pouring in through skylights or dormers. Still, quarter of a million for a two-bed house in Headingley! What was the world coming to? But a nice garden, mix of patio, plants and a bit of lawn, south-facing. All handy for the shops, pubs, restaurants, bars and cafes. And the cricket and rugby ground. You're never far from sport in this part of the world. Might be appealing to a future Mr Lucky, my imaginary Mr Right, as elusive and out of reach as a spacious semi or cottage. Dream on, I told myself, but dreams can be pleasurable, especially when they're all you've got.

3

I pulled out my lottery ticket. Luckiest number between one and ten; luckiest number between eleven and twenty; and so on. That should do it. I kissed it, and placed it back in my handbag. Then the sun, or rather the reflection of the sun, lit up the room, a vivid, bright yellow in a flood of light. I looked out of the window. It was shining off the large, sloping windscreen of a low sports car, parked just outside; actually, immediately outside next door, which was empty and up for sale, but all the houses are close by each other on our street. That was different. Some sporty cars are not that expensive, really, but you could sort of tell that this one was, just by the aura it gave off, and the confident air of the man who stepped out of it, looking around, like he was suspecting a thief or a mugger, before stooping back into the car, seemingly to search for something. I walked over to the window for a better look. I know car makes well, thanks to our Kevin. I recognised the circular emblem of a Mercedes Benz.

What was he doing here? A kind, but worried, face, yet also handsome and confident. He took out a white scarf with blue and gold edgings. Rich White, I thought; Southern White, maybe. That explained it. He was probably only worried about getting to the stadium. I looked at the time on my phone. Eleven minutes to three already. He'd be missing the start, unless he were to run. Yet he didn't run. Here was someone educated, with self-control, used to setting his own agenda. Yet even guys like that still followed a football team; something I would never understand. Curious and amused, I walked out into our front yard. Rather to my surprise, given his air of assurance, he asked me the way. There was a sense of decency about him. He was courteous; well, he was unintentionally a bit rude about the neighbourhood, but apologised immediately. He had a low, calm voice and kind manner; dark brown eyes that shone briefly as they met mine. For the first time in months, I felt the tiniest flicker of something like desire. This was absurd. I scolded myself and my body. We spoke a little. I hoped I hadn't blushed. The accent was hard to place: not local exactly, but not cockney like *EastEnders*. I had glanced down at his left hand. No ring.

After Mum brought Danny round, I watched a cartoon with him as we snuggled together on the sofa. Then he fell asleep, and I made sure he was comfortable before getting up to make myself a cup of tea. I texted Sharon, mostly chat about kids. Then I texted Bronte, worried because I hadn't heard from her for what seemed like days but was probably only two hours. She was on her way back, and had done a bit of shopping, not too much, promise, Mum. I had saved up £50 for her to spend. It had taken weeks, without wine or anything else for myself, and I was proud. I would have my first Chardonnay in four weeks that evening.

It was coincidence, I told myself, that I just happened to be outside in the small front yard again at ten past five, quarter of an hour after final whistle: a coincidence. It needed tidying up, a task that took all of six or seven minutes, but more if you include pulling out a weed or two. The man turned the corner, and I could almost hear his sigh of relief upon seeing his car.

'You've got three wheels left, not bad! Only one short!' I said, cheerfully. 'Told you that you could trust folk round here. You got far to go?'

'Surrey.'

'Surrey, like, near London?'

'Yup.'

'So, you came all this way, to spend the afternoon in Beeston, for a footie match? I hope we won.'

'Lost two–one.'

'Oh dear, I am sorry. You could have spent your afternoon by your own swimming pool, or whatever.'

'Nah, boring! Anyway, there was some funny banter from the crowd. Better than your average stand-up comedian on Channel 4.'

He then lost me completely, making some comparison to his situation and a Spanish film, or it might have been Argentinian, or maybe Hollywood after all. He apologised again and made to leave. Just before he got in his car, Bronte came home, carrying her latest painting back from getting it framed. He noticed this and paid her a compliment. This was not unusual. Bronte was always getting praise for her paintings, and she was brilliant at not letting it go to her head. This was different, though. He seemed more than usually impressed, he was more than usually knowledgeable, and I was more than usually grateful for the interest. I quickly realised also, as he and I stood shoulder to shoulder examining the work, my thumb pressed close against his on the edge of the stretched canvas, that it was more than gratitude that I was feeling.

2

The hosepipe of the vanities

Like most educated men, I have an uneasy relationship with
my satnav. It pits two of my most cherished values –
maximising use of technology and pride in personal autonomy
– at war with one another. In favour of its use, I reflected that
the time spent studying the route in advance of a car journey
was time I could be earning: best to outsource and automate
anything that's not core business. On the other hand, preparing
and memorising a route was mental exercise: sharpening
cognition, enhancing one's geographical awareness, and would
mean avoiding taking orders, which I find irritating. What
is the point of setting up your own business only to end up
taking directions from a humourless automaton who thinks
she has a better sense of direction than me? My satnav had
a steady voice with a rather posh accent: calming when she
was right, extremely irritating on the few occasions she erred,
or was ambiguous. I called her Maggie, in honour of our
former Prime Minister: bossy, but necessary; usually sound in
judgement. I alternated between relying on my own route-

planning and turning it back on: month on, month off. I did miss her, sometimes. She was, after all, the only female voice in my private world, unless you count my sister. Sometimes, I turned the voice on even when I knew the route well, just for company.

On this occasion, running late for a Saturday 3 p.m. kick-off, she messed up – big style. It was a familiar route, and normally I would have dispensed with either map or gadget, but an accident had closed a short section of the M1, taking me into the back streets of Beeston, along with hundreds of other cars, and a few coaches from out of town. 'East Kent Whites' said one of them, with an address in Deal. It was reassuring, I reflected, that some fans were mad enough to travel even further than me to a home fixture. As the traffic ground to a halt I punched in the postcode to the stadium, assuming that for the car park to be the same.

'Keep to the right,' asserted Maggie, confidently, after a right turn at the end of a block.

'Are you sure?' I replied, out loud. 'The stadium's more to the left.'

'Keep to the right,' she repeated. After a pause, as the traffic speeded up, she added: 'Then keep to the left.'

'What??' I said. 'Too late!'

I was in the wrong lane, heading over the motorway, which had reopened leftwards, and into another suburb of red-brick terraced houses. 'Maggie, you have completely lost it! At no point at all was the right-hand lane correct! What were you thinking of? A completely imaginary slip road?' After a pause I muttered more quietly. 'Maybe the map's not up to date.'

Talking to yourself had become less obviously a sign of creeping mental illness, I reflected, since the advent of Bluetooth. I always wore an earpiece, as cover. Where the hell was I now? The streets looked vaguely familiar, from my pedestrian route to the stadium many years earlier. I had not ventured into these streets by car before, and I had a memory of requiring a pedestrian bridge to cross the motorway. I pottered slowly along in second gear, nervously, on the lookout for car thieves, drug barons and other criminals. I reflected upon the nature of acclimatisation. When I was young and a Leeds local, these streets would have felt like home, even though they were a touch downmarket from Dad's home. Now, after years of management conferences, five-star hotels and with a home in the stockbroker belt, they felt strange and unsettling. I also felt guilty, and worried that I had become a snob. Of more immediate concern, however, I wanted to find a parking place and arrive at the stadium on time. A U-turn looked tricky, but there was a turning to the left. I could try to go through the back streets, worm my way along, maybe with Maggie's help, if she was full of remorse. But she kept wanting me to U-turn.

'That's not going to work,' I explained. 'It'll take way too long now. I'm going to have to park up and walk.' Angrily, I turned her off.

I took a left turn, and pulled over to the side, got out my phone, opened the map and zoomed in. There was no obvious route to the stadium, under or over the motorway, at least by car. But a thin line on the map over the motorway probably indicated the footbridge that I recalled. And there were no yellow lines on these streets. I pulled up the handbrake, got out, looked around. Would a £75,000 Mercedes Benz convertible be safe on this street for two hours on a Saturday afternoon? If I drove to the car park now, I'd miss the first ten minutes; if I were able to walk from here, maybe I'd just get there for kick-off. Would those extra ten minutes, in all probability drab and goalless, be worth risking the theft or disappearing wheels of a motor probably worth more than a house in this district?

What the hell, it's insured, I reflected. Covered as long as I

A Love of Two Halves

closed the doors and locked it. I bent over to grab my scarf off the passenger seat, stood up again. I paused to wrap the white, blue and gold woollen garment around my neck – silly, really, like being a schoolboy again, I know – and took another look around me before walking down the pavement, still unsure of exactly the correct route, but confident of my sense of direction. After I had taken a few steps, a young woman came out of her house and to her front gate, perhaps to watch the tourist go by, or perhaps just to call her kids in. She was pale, dark-haired, beautiful and exhausted. It was as though her body reached the fence first, only for her soul to take its time in catching up. It seemed a while since her symmetrical face had been creased by a smile. I caught her eye, and wasn't sure if this was involuntary or not. Since my diversity training, I tried to make it a policy, when asking advice or directions, not to approach the most attractive woman, and, if so, certainly not to flirt. But in this case she was the only individual at hand, and her countenance seemed genuine and friendly.

'Excuse me,' I said. 'Can you get to Elland Road by turning left at the end of this street? I think you can. Years since I've been here.'

'Not in your car,' she replied. 'But there's a footbridge over the motorway. Once you get to the other side, you're on Elland Road. Stadium's a few hundred yards to the right.'

'Ah, I thought there was a bridge, just forgot where it was. Thank you so much! Um, will my car be safe here?' I felt bad about asking.

She gave a cynical look. 'Tell you what. I'll ask my professional-car-thieving teenage sons to give yours a miss. They'll be disappointed, mind. They're on for a bonus if they hit their targets.'

'Listen, I'm sorry. I'm so sorry. I didn't mean to be rude about your neighbourhood, it's just I'm in unfamiliar territory.

10

It's all a bit disorientating. Anyway, you're not old enough to have teenagers!' I scolded myself. That was flirting, wasn't it? A bit. Still, can't get into trouble with HR out here.

'Run along, love,' she replied, in a motherly fashion, as though I were her son; she was actually probably a few years younger than me. 'You'll miss t' kick-off.'

As it turned out, there were many other fans heading towards the match, so I found the bridge and the stadium easily enough, just getting into my seat for the start. The first ten minutes were indeed rather drab and goalless. For the remaining eighty things perked up, and there were even a few goals, but one more for the opponents than for our side. The large stadium, graced by international players in Euro '96, was only half full. It was, I reflected, starting to look shabby at the edges after its upgrade two decades earlier. I was ill at ease for the first half, and not only owing to the frustrating patterns of play by the home side: the passing moves that never quite worked out, the crosses that sailed over the attacking players in the box, the shot from distance that went closer to the corner flag than the goal; plus the late challenges, shirt-pulling, dives and yellow cards of a typical mid-table clash in the English second tier. It was a late season affair, with neither side bidding for promotion, nor at risk of the drop, so there were no high stakes or great anxiety.

Normally, I liked to arrive early: to go to the club shop, wander around the ground, smell the burgers and fries, listen to the excited chatter of the children as they posed with their parents for pictures in front of Billy Bremner's statue by the stadium shop, perhaps have a beer before ascending to my seat, usually high up in the stadium. I didn't live close enough for a season ticket to be worthwhile, and I was often travelling for work on the weekend, but I came whenever I could. When I couldn't attend, I would check the score every few minutes on a sports website, and be genuinely upset for hours when I learned that Leeds had lost. Following a team is more like a social virus than a hobby; an irrational obsession punctured by brief periods of collective joy. In most aspects of my life, I insisted upon a rational justification, so this tribal affinity was my one exception, my little neurosis. And perhaps it did serve a purpose: creating a haven of working-class normality that kept me grounded, I would tell myself, or stuck in my boyhood, a psychologist might say, or just giving me the excuse to shout at people without fear of an employment tribunal.

I was late because I had agreed to an 8 a.m. call with one of my consultants, Luke, who said it was important. It wasn't, and he annoyed me. His main objective – though I admit I wasn't paying full attention, but rather was wondering about the line-up for that afternoon's match and checking the traffic situation on the M25 – seemed to be to rubbish the record and the plans of a colleague, Tony, who I rated. Luke probably saw himself as a rival for when I was to be moving on, which was not in my plans, given that it was my company – well, in spirit, at least. If you're going to play internal politics, don't pretend you're talking strategy, and don't involve your boss. Especially on match day. Except that, technically, I was no longer sole shareholder, something I had to remind myself almost daily. Still, I was the founder, and still the CEO.

Were the headaches of being full-time in the business still worth it? I wondered as I joined the dejected fans trickling out through the gates. I could afford to retire, or at least semi-retire. The main problem was that I did not relish the idea in the slightest: for me, work was not a means to an end, it was all that gave my life purpose. Almost every activity associated with leisure filled me with a suffocating sensation of boredom and futility: golf, gardening, the theatre (surely only of appeal at the end of a working week, and with a date), a round-the-world cruise. The purposelessness of 'leisure', the undoubted tedium and, of course, the lack of anyone to share the moments with was a prospect that filled me with dread. Old age was not an illness to insure against, it was simply an inconvenience to be mitigated. I would still want to work in my eighties, just maybe start at ten in the morning, do four days a week. As for seeing the world, I had clocked most sites worth viewing on days off between overseas assignments. On the few occasions that I encountered the backpacking fraternity, their ambition to do little more than tick off the next glacier or ancient ruin, a routine clocked as progress, struck me as banal. The Instagram generation seemed to be taking such sensation-seeking quests to new depths, or rather shallows.

I could write a book, perhaps – or have it ghosted; writing anything more than 800 words seemed like a chore. Something along the lines of a memoir; or 'thoughts on leadership', that could get me some TED Talks or even an invitation to Davos. I didn't need the money, or the work, or even the networking, but I might finally become attractive to the opposite sex for some quality other than my earning power, if I managed to time the jokes well and get a few thousand hits on YouTube.

I had drafted a book proposal, based on my experience in the run-up to the financial crisis, and I showed it to a publisher friend of mine. He told me it was too technical, and lacking in drama. But wouldn't the public want to know the real reasons for the crisis and the austerity that followed? I asked him. His reply was that even the political class weren't that interested. They had identified their preferred scapegoats based on who they fell out with at uni.

She was in her front yard again when I returned to the car. It was April, still broad daylight. She raised her thumbs, smiling in triumph, ready with a quip about there being very nearly the requisite number of wheels remaining on the car. At least I had made her smile, even if only with my verbal gaffe from earlier.

I still felt bad about asking if the car was safe. 'Sorry again,' I said. 'I was a bit rude earlier. I was just thinking, you see, that my situation was a bit like *The Hosepipe of the Vanities*. You know, the movie.'

'The *what*?'

'I mean *The Bonfire of the Vanities* – sorry, the wrong title of the movie sticks in my head. It's quite amusing, actually; I made a translation error all those years ago. *Hoguera, Manguera*, they're similar words in Spanish, you see.'

'Um, yeah. Still meaningless.' But she said this in an amused fashion, not mocking.

'*The Bonfire of the Vanities* is a movie in which a Wall Street guy drives into a New York neighbourhood he doesn't know by mistake and, well, it all goes wrong from there.'

'Why was it in Spanish, if it's set in New York?'

'It wasn't. I was watching it in Buenos Aires with subtitles.'

'Long way to go. Wasn't there an Odeon nearby?'

'I was working on reward strategies for a multinational company's South America division. First posting abroad. Loved it. Bit of a collapse of the currency when I was there, but good to see history happening, I guess. Great experience. Really good opera and tango as well.'

There was an awkward silence. 'Listen,' I said. 'This seems a really friendly neighbourhood. I really didn't mean to cause offence.'

'None taken,' she replied, sharply, but not unkindly.

'That's a terrific picture. Is it a painting or a print?' I asked suddenly, noticing a teenage girl carrying a large framed picture, a boldly coloured image. She was about to enter the young woman's home.

14

'It's a painting,' replied the girl, tall, slim and confident, afro hair in cornrows. She had high cheekbones, and a startlingly intelligent face.

'This is my daughter, Bronte,' said the woman.

'Who's it by?' I asked.

'Me,' said the girl, proudly.

'Wow, that's impressive. In the style of Frida Kahlo, kind of magical realist.' The painting was of a tree supporting palatial rooms, the interiors of which were visible through a missing wall, like an opened-out doll's house. While the composition was a fantasy, there was extraordinary realistic detail in the rooms' interiors: rich woven carpets, standing lamps and an elegant four-poster bed in one of the two rooms. At the base of the tree was a silver-coloured antique car, and a silhouette of a man in the driver's seat.

'Thank you,' she replied. 'I'm going to do A-Level.'

'So you should. That is most impressive.'

The girl seemed to switch quite sharply from pride to modesty, and bowed her head a little before turning to proceed indoors, clutching the frame underneath her arm, taking exaggerated care to avoid catching the corners on the door frame.

'Hold on a minute, love. May I see it properly now?' the mum asked of her daughter. 'You wouldn't let me yesterday.'

'OK.' Coyly, she held it for her mother to view.

The mum appeared quite moved and stunned, even more impressed than I. 'That's like my dream,' was all she said.

'I know,' the girl replied promptly.

'May I look at it more closely?' I asked.

'Sure,' replied the girl, who handed it to her mum, beside whom I was standing. I moved a little closer, with the pretext of examining the painting. Our shoulders touched briefly. I thought she would step aside, but, if anything, she nudged

15

herself slightly closer to me, maintaining the contact. A tingling sensation of physical euphoria ran through my body for the first time since... well, probably the first time ever, in terms of intensity.

'The technique is very advanced,' I said, striving to keep my voice calm, and concentrate on the painting, not the woman holding it. 'Some young artists think that originality of concept is enough, and they skimp on the execution, but here you see real detail and craft.'

'I spend ages getting the colours right,' said the girl.

'How do you know which colours?' asked the mum.

'I just know,' she replied, as if it were obvious. 'Are you an artist?' the girl asked me.

'No, but I have a friend who's an art professor. I would like to show her this work.' There was an unexpected silence between them. I added hastily: 'Sorry, I don't know you.'

'Don't apologise,' said the mum. 'It's a kind offer. My name's Karen.' She returned the painting to the girl, who tucked it under her arm and went indoors, and then she turned to face me.

My gaze met her blue-grey eyes, but I worried that my overflowing desire would be too obvious, so I glanced down. 'I'm George,' I replied. 'Your daughter is very talented.'

'Thank you,' she replied. 'She is rather brilliant, isn't she? Gets it from her dad, I think.'

At the mention of 'dad' I felt acutely deflated, but was determined to remain polite. 'Do they work together in a studio?' I asked.

'No. Actually, he's not on the scene. But he's not a bad guy at all. Long story. Very long story.'

'Listen, I didn't mean to pry. So rude. I'll be on my way. So sorry.'

'Really, nothing to apologise for,' she said. 'Um, are you serious, about having her work assessed?'

'Of course,' I said. I felt extremely uneasy about proposing an exchange of phone numbers, fearful of scaring Karen by being too forward or flirtatious. 'Perhaps I could call in after the next home match?'

'OK,' she replied.

There was a hesitation, as if she were considering inviting me in. With no invitation forthcoming, I said: 'I'll be getting on my way.'

'Bye then,' she said. 'Nice talking to you.' There was brief eye contact once more, and a jolt of electricity through my body. She disappeared inside. After I had got into the driving seat, I sat still for a while, too agitated to concentrate on the dull mechanics of driving. It was not a warm day, but the sun on the windscreen had heated the car and I was sweating. I gripped the steering wheel with both hands, and took three or four deep breaths. I started the engine, more for the relief of the air conditioning than with an immediate desire for motion. I pretended to be looking at a message on my phone, so that Karen or a passer-by wouldn't be wondering why I was staring at nothing, like someone who was mentally ill. After a good few minutes, I put the car in gear and moved away.

3

Life's a lottery

I paused for a very long time in the tiny front yard, just looking at the front door, breathing rapidly like I'd just seen a unicorn. I could hear George's car still running, and I wanted to turn around and start talking to him again, but I guessed he was answering a message and I didn't want to intrude. My heart was beating at twice the usual rate. I eventually managed to take some deeper, slower breaths, calmed the heart down, and went inside. Bronte was waiting for me.

'So, there's this posh car outside our house, and you start chatting with the driver,' she said, as I poured her a cola and myself a wine.

'It wasn't like that. Just some Leeds fan who were lost, trying to find the stadium car park. He asked me the way to the ground.'

'And then you just happen to bump into him after the match as well! Still, he seemed nice. Liked my picture. Had you been chatting long?'

'No, he was just asking the way.'

'Not seen a Mercedes Benz on our street before.'

'Sure we have.'

'He's not from round here, then.'

'No, he's from Surrey.'

'I thought you said you hadn't been chatting long!' Bronte was giggling, both eyes wide open with amusement. 'Smart guy in a sports car shows up, and you run out into the street, start flirting.'

'It wasn't like that at all!' I protested, though I could feel my cheeks warming as I blushed.

'Go on then, what's his name? Piers? Guy? Does he know David Beckham?'

'George, but we didn't exchange phone numbers. You've got the wrong end of the stick entirely! He was offering to help you!'

'Is he married?'

'No. I mean I don't know! Not like I checked.'

'You so did. You're busted! You're a terrible liar. Did you show some cleavage?'

'That's an outrageous thing to say, Bronte. We just had a little chat. He asked if the car would be safe round here, then he apologised for being rude, which he wasn't really. And he admired your painting. If he gets you into the Royal College of Art you'll be thankful that I flirted with him. Chatted, I mean! Friendly chat!' I corrected myself too late, blushing furiously. She just laughed and rolled her eyes. 'Now shall we watch the lottery, then? After that, we'll turn the telly off for music hour.'

'OK, Mum, change the subject.' She rolled her eyes again, but friendly like. She was grinning from ear to ear, and then giggled a little more. Cheeky girl, but clever, so clever. From her dad. Well, maybe from me a bit as well.

'Are you going to paint my dreams again?'

'Maybe,' she replied. 'If they're interesting enough.'

'I'll try my best. Right, let's get the card out.'

'All the lucky numbers?'

'All the luckiest, each kissed three times, for luck.'

The programme began, and the cheery presenters started their patter, all upbeat like we'd all won. I suppose they get well paid, for that gig, so they've won the lottery already. No wonder they were so cheerful. The coloured balls whirred in the tombola, before the machine picked out one, then another, and another, until all seven were in a row, then rearranged by the TV special features guys into ascending order. We had two; only two.

'Oh well, Mum, never mind.'

'Indeed, never mind. One day you'll be a famous painter. Or not famous, just successful.'

'So will you, Mum.'

'No, I think not. Opportunities have passed for me, I'm afraid.'

'You could go for promotion then.'

'Certainly not! Not after the last time,' I paused, shuddered at the memory of the awkward pauses and clumsy mistakes of my last interview. I drank a big glug of wine, which was having a particularly dizzying effect after the long, dry period. 'Humiliating. Then they promoted that lad who were about twelve.'

'Even so, you should try. You're smart.'

'No way. Management's not for me. There's more chance of some millionaire moving in next door, falling madly in love with me and taking us all off to his mansion.'

'No, there isn't, Mum. There's lots you could do.'

'More drinks anyone?' I asked, taking another big glug and getting myself up.

Danny claimed to be wide awake, and wanting to watch the telly, but I could see that his eyelids were drooping. If

I suggested too soon that he should go to bed, he'd protest and it would all backfire. Maybe another twenty minutes, but no more cola. I brought back just the two glasses. It was lovely to be sipping wine again. Curled up next to my lovely girl, Danny starting to doze on the other side, we watched the talent show, and, with the calming, numbing sensation of the wine seeping into my body after weeks of laying off the booze, I felt good about the world again. The disappointment of yet another lottery loss well forgotten, and still thinking, late into the evening, more often than I'd expected to, about the tall, dark, handsome stranger, who wasn't all that tall or handsome, at least in the Hollywood way. Though he was kind of cute, with his steady confidence, kind smile – and the way he looked at me, all wise but still yearning. Was he confident because he was successful, or successful because he was confident? Which way round did it work? Unless he wasn't successful, just pretended to be, and was in debt. Men sometimes borrow silly amounts for a certain vehicle. Cars are their hairdos – it's all about image. Of course, that sort of thing would never make a difference to me. It was always the personality and the values, for me.

Yet still, where would I find a man? I would want one, eventually, and probably not the type of lad who goes by bus or skateboard.

4

Imperfect, tense

I was there three weeks later, for the last game of the season. It was a lunchtime kick-off, and so an even earlier start 250 miles away, in leafy Surrey. The alarm went at 6 a.m., a high-pitched ringing, followed by Radio 4 starting itself on the backup. I had been very deeply asleep, in an intricate anxiety dream that involved becoming lost on assorted types of transport, and with each decision ending up further away from my destination. I became aware that I was in the middle of my absurdly large bed. For a few seconds I contemplated skipping the long drive north and the match, but I was too far away to hit any snooze button, so I forced myself awake. Also, before fully awakening, Karen's kind face and blue-grey eyes appeared in my mind; incentive enough for 500 miles of driving. I felt a tiny thrill inside my soul that increased as I awoke; just the very chance of seeing her, I thought.

I had a coffee machine in my bedroom, as it was so far to the kitchen, but I was out of pods, and the water tank was nearly empty. Cursing at myself for such basic lack of planning, wearing nothing but pyjama shorts, I became even more awake as I made the long walk down the stairs, across part of the large hall, to the kitchen, feet becoming colder and colder with each step on the cold stone floor around the island (how did the fashion begin for kitchens that were the size of a swimming pool?). I topped up the water tank I had been carrying, then collected some coffee pods from their holder on the side. I was going to want more than one.

Within twenty minutes, I was setting off. I loved the satisfying crunch of the broad tyres as they moved over the gravel drive, and the efficient whirr of the automatic gate as it slid open. These were among my top-five favourite sounds, other than music; the others were the joyous yell of the home crowd as a goal went in, the swish of skis on a freshly groomed piste and I suppose I should add birdsong. I have my sensitive side.

As I drove through the narrow country lanes, at 7 a.m. in the morning, past the farmyards and the gated communities, the mansions and country hotels tucked behind mature oak and beech trees just coming into leaf, I wondered if there were any other Leeds United supporters ahead of me in the same lane, worrying about the traffic, the first-team line-up and whether the popular manager would avoid getting fired in the close season. The M1 was clear, until near the stadium again, when a bit of match day traffic built up. I had the same decision to make, I reflected as the engine hummed and I crawled along in the queue; but I was making it consciously this time, without help from Maggie the satnav. Should I proceed straight on towards the stadium car park, or head over the bridge to the quiet street, near the footbridge to the ground, a free space on the pavement, perhaps parking, once more, out of familiarity, close to the house of the enigmatic, friendly young mum with the talented daughter? I recalled the promise I had made to call in, with a view to discussing the young girl's work and her prospects. Would they hold me to that promise, or had they forgotten it? Would they consider me intrusive for knocking on the door, or neglectful for not doing so, having raised their hopes? I preferred the risk of finding out, to not finding out.

On the slip road, I noted a black bit of plastic, seemingly just a bag, but, as the nearside front wheel hit it, there was a bit of impact, and a quiet thumping sound I did not like the sound of. But the car behaved itself as I found my way to the same street, glancing indiscreetly, but not too often, I judged, at the house of the family I had briefly encountered three weeks before. There was no sign of anyone in the tiny front yard, so I headed on to the ground, in time for kick-off.

It was early May, but grey and bitter. There was high cloud, little wind and the air was tasteless. I buttoned up my winter coat as I walked down the short street, not bothering with the northern English habit of defying the cold with shirt sleeves or going topless, a tendency that seemed to increase in proportion with the girth of the men keen to display their torsos; not that there were any such exhibitionists on display that chilly midday. As I turned the corner, to a larger street, I was joined by other fans, some in coats, some in white replica home-team shirts; couples, families, groups of three or four or ten; and then more of them as we crossed the bridge and proceeded down the main road. Most groups were quite subdued, murmuring, chatting; just one was slightly beery, chanting the hymnal club anthem 'Marching on Together'. The English need a drink before they sing. The small groups combined to form a larger throng as we neared the stadium, joined by others from side streets. All were heading in the same direction, as though by gravity: from Holbeck to the north, Wortley to the west, Beeston to the east and south. I was reminded of the flocks of egrets heading to their roosting place in the Pantanal in

Brazil; just a few small knots of birds in late afternoon, growing to bigger and bigger flocks as dusk fell; from miles around, heading to the same area, until tens of thousands created a premature dusk as they flew in close formation above, before settling in a handful of trees that became more white than green. And they chattered, chattered, chattered away until it was quite dark.

I wondered how, amid this crowd – the ground would be nearly full, for the last game of the season – there was probably no one I could call on as a friend, with whom to have a drink and chat about the game. The one schoolfriend I had contact with was Jeremy Baird, who delighted in sharing the same surname as one of the star players of the day, but who was mocked by the rough lads for his 'posh' first name. I marvelled, then and since, at the ingenuity that teenage children will deploy to invent a pretext with which to exclude and taunt a blameless peer, for the satisfaction of making their waking life an utter misery. Jeremy and I at least had each other, but then of course we were teased for being a gay couple. He had been a sports fan of the nerdy variety: remembering dates, names, scores, players. We had been to a few games together, standing on the terraces. He was pleased when, after two decades without meeting, I contacted him on social media, but always had a reason for not attending a game with me: he lived in Lancashire now, had young children, cost was too much (he bristled when I offered to pay), didn't like the way the game had changed and so on. I had given up inviting him, though he did come to the cricket once. All my other friends were from various parts of the south – London, Surrey, Uruguay and so on. My colleague Tony the Chelsea fan accompanied me once, which was heroic of him, and he pretended to support the home side, at least for ninety minutes, but I could see the effort it took. To return the gesture, I accompanied him to Stamford Bridge – for a European tie, so I could support the English club.

The game that early afternoon was dull. How much carbon dioxide had I emitted from my beautiful sports car in return for such meagre entertainment? Then again, the journey was equally polluting irrespective of the game's quality. I thought about buying an electric car again. I walked back up the main road, past the queues for the taxis, and over the bridge, into the streets of tightly packed houses.

As I turned the corner into the street where the car was parked, there she was, the cute mum. My heartbeat quickened when she glanced up. I looked into her blue-grey eyes, and there was that look again, radiant and full of inquiry. The sun emerged, and shone brilliantly; I felt it upon my shoulders and saw it light up her face. Actually, it probably only did so in my imagination. The day was still overcast.

Her look changed from apparent pleasure at greeting me to one of concern and guilt as she noticed, before I had, that the front nearside tyre was soft. It wasn't vandalism, she promised.

'That's fine, that's fine!' I assured her, 'I felt I hit something as I came off the motorway – thought it was just a plastic bag so I hadn't swerved to avoid it.' I was secretly glad at the pretext to stay for another hour or so. 'Yes, there it is, embedded in the tyre – bit of sharp plastic, probably a chunk off a rear bumper or an industrial part or something.'

I was hoping to be invited in for a cup of tea while we waited for the repair van. I had been wealthy enough for long enough to have people do stuff for me, and I was unused to getting my hands dirty. She then astonished me by offering to help me change the wheel herself. 'We could be waiting ages for them,' she reasoned. 'Might as well get started.' She informed me that she used to help her older brother, a qualified car mechanic, do all manner of repairs. I noted her use of the imperfect tense, and a wistful, pained note in her voice.

5

The perfect stranger

I wasn't sure if I would see him, or that car, again, but I had checked when the next home game would be, when he said he would visit. I had awoken early that Saturday morning, by the noise of next door's vacuum cleaner. Rita was very tidy, but did she have to start cleaning before breakfast? As I awoke, I was on the edge of the bed, and misjudged how near I was, almost falling out as I got myself up. I looked at the clock; it was only 6.15 a.m. I nipped downstairs to make myself a quick cuppa and I brought it back up. The children had still been asleep and I had a quiet half hour, during which time I treated myself to a long fantasy about George, and whether he liked me, and whether he would visit.

Bronte was spending the day with me, rather than seeing friends. It was chilly, and we were indoors. She had a large pad of A3–sized blank paper, some charcoal and some coloured pencils.

'What are you going to draw?' I asked.

'A woman lost. She's in the desert, but there are loads of

criss-crossing paths, and she has to find the right one. She keeps asking for water but she's only got some wine that makes her thirsty.'

'That's my dream again,' I said.

'I know.' It was always the same, her two-word reply. She would have thought it strange to discover that there were mums whose teenage daughters did not guess their dreams and draw them. I sat and watched, mildly dazzled. She never seemed to mind if I watched or if I did not, and was just wrapped in her own creative zone while she painted or drew. I said I had to get up and tidy the window boxes.

She teased me, of course. 'Two hours past kick-off. Wonder who'll be coming up the street?'

He turned the corner, and marched briskly to his car. He returned my look; that look again. I trembled inside. He removed his football scarf, rolled it up neatly and stuffed it in his coat pocket. 'Hello again!' he said.

'Hello there. Can't stay away!' I replied.

'Still got all four wheels?' he quipped, cheerfully.

'Yup,' I replied. 'Checked on them every half hour. Now I'll just kick the tyres to... Oh. That doesn't look right. Front nearside is flat.' I stared down at the item. He did too. 'There hasn't been any trouble here, any vandalism. I'm sure I would have heard!' I felt vaguely guilty, and crouched down to inspect the damage. He explained that he thought he had hit something as he left the motorway. Sure enough, there was a bit of hard plastic stuck in the tyre.

'I'll help you fix it,' I suggested, and he looked amazed. He was all for calling the breakdown van, which to me was like calling them to switch your headlights on. It had always been a matter of pride for Kevin and me that we could fix just about anything, except some of the electronics, and I was only wearing a sweatshirt and tracksuit bottoms, so I didn't need to change. 'I haven't done this model before; it'll be fun!' I said.

'No, I'll do it!' he protested. 'I'm sure I can work out how. I did it for my dad once. Years ago, mind…'

He wandered around to the boot and opened it. It was a classic car; not a very old vintage but not brand new, and it had the old-style jack and spare. I stood beside him, quite close, looking in. It amused me that I located all the spare parts before him.

'I really don't mind helping! It's easier with two,' I said.

'Well… If you're absolutely sure?' he said, as he pulled out the spare, bouncing it pleasingly on the pavement as a test.

'Absolutely!' I assured him.

'Whoops!' he said. The tyre's second bounce was at an unexpected angle, and he almost lost his balance as he stepped to his left to catch it, just about staying upright, maintaining a semblance of dignity, and laughing a little to himself. His slight clumsiness made him appear more normal, and quite endearing. Steadying the wheel, he managed to place it carefully on its side. Then he placed the jack, correct way up, to be fair, under the side of the car near the wheel arch. Immediately, he started turning the handle around, vigorously.

'Stop!' I said, giggling a little. 'You have to loosen the wheel bolts first, or there's no resistance!' It was reassuring to learn that he wasn't in control of everything, that there was stuff I could do that he couldn't.

'Of course, of course!' he muttered, reversing the direction of the turns on the jack's handle to lower the car back down. He looked up at me. He might have been irritated at my little smile of triumph, and showed a bit of wounded pride that a girl was better than him at mechanics, but instead he just returned a gaze of kindness and admiration. I felt the flicker of desire again and he seemed to notice as he looked down.

I knew what to do to remove the nuts, but I lacked a little strength as I pulled down on the spanner. He placed his hand firmly close to mine, touching it briefly, and I felt a thrill run down my wrist, upper arm, shoulder, and then heart and lungs, as we both pushed down hard until the bolt began to yield.

'Sorry, I'm not hurting, am I?' he asked, as part of his hand pinched mine with the downward push. He was taking great care to avoid placing his body next to mine, which was considerate. I admired his restraint but I felt a little bit disappointed at the same time…

'Not at all,' I replied, and between us we removed the nut.

There were four more. When the new wheel was in place, and the nuts tightened onto the bolts, he fretted whether they were on securely.

'I'll show you where the nearest garage is in Beeston,' I said. 'Just drive at thirty 'til you get there, be on the safe side. Run by a bloke called Alan. They'll check it for you.'

'Thanks,' he said. He appeared a little warm, sweating a little with exertion, despite the chilly air. He had removed his coat to change the wheel, placing it on top of the car after carefully transferring his smartphone to his back trouser pocket.

'Do you want a cup of tea?' I asked. I pointed with my head towards the door, as if there'd be some doubt as to where I'd fetch the drink from.

'A glass of water will do fine,' he replied. He rolled up the sleeves of his casual, white cotton top, and dabbed a little perspiration from his brow with the back of his hand.

I went inside and returned with the glass. 'There you are.' I wanted to invite him in – wanted to wash his shirt, make his tea, massage his shoulder and neck. These thoughts just sprang up out of nowhere. I tried to push them back, deep into my subconscious; then again, perhaps he wanted these things too.

'Thank you so much for your help,' he said. 'Do I owe you anything?' He crossed his arms, then uncrossed them.

'Of course not,' I replied. The fingers of my right hand curled a lock of my long, brown hair, twisting it round.

'It's so kind of you – to help a perfect stranger,' he said.

'It's what we do – how I was raised,' I said.

There was a prolonged, nervous silence, which caught me unawares. Was he itching to get away? I tried to think of something to say that was friendly but not too forward. For a talkative person, I can get stuck sometimes.

'Where's that garage again?' he asked.

'Oh, nearly forgot! I wrote the name, street and postcode for you. Here you are,' I offered him the scrap of paper. He reached for it, and took it, brushing his fingers lightly against mine as he did so, setting me off again.

'Again, so kind. Well, I'd best be on my way.'

'Going all the way back to Surrey then?'

'All the way back.'

'Was the game worth it? What was the score?'

'Nil-nil.'

'Oh dear. Hardly worth coming all this way for.'

'Oh, I don't know…' he said, and then stopped, as though someone or something had interrupted him, and he gave me a look, which I couldn't quite read. 'Well, thanks again, maybe see you next season!'

'Yes, bye!'

He glanced up one last time, looked at our house, then at next door with the estate agent's sign, turned and walked towards the driver's side. He was about to get in when I called out: 'Wait!'

'What?' he asked, looking up, curiously, almost with hope.

'Don't drive off with your coat on the roof!' I giggled a little, and so did he.

'Oh! What am I like?' He tapped his palm against his forehead. 'I was miles away.'

'Somewhere nice, I hope.'

'Oh yes.'

'Safe journey, then.'

'Thank you. Thank you again!'

I waited while he gathered his coat, stuffed it onto the passenger seat, started up, and drove away. I briefly considered waving, then thought I might look like a silly schoolgirl. So, I just gave a little smile, mostly to myself, before turning and heading back in.

Bronte had been watching from the front window. She gave me an amused look. 'Did you let that tyre down on purpose?' she asked, eyes circled wide, grinning, speaking quietly, but with exaggerated lip movements.

'No!' I protested.

'I bet you did!'

'I did not! He said he drove over something he thought was soft but it hit the tyre with a bit of a thump. We found it – sharp bit of litter, stuck in the tyre.'

'Did you ask him about his art professor friend?'

My heart froze with panic. 'Oh my God I forgot! I'm so sorry, Bronte. It was the drama with the punctured tyre, and fixing it and everything. I'll… I'll call him.'

'You have his number?'

'Oh. No. He's called, er, George.'

'You have a second name?'

'Um, not as such. No.'

'So, he's called George, and he has a house in Surrey. Yea, well, should be easy to track down.'

'I'm so, so sorry.' I avoided eye contact with her; couldn't bear to see her disappointment.

'That's OK, Mum. We just have to hope he fancies you as much as I think he does. Then he'll be back.'

6

Two up, no garden: the ideal third home

'Yes, that's still on the market. Fifty-seven thousand five hundred pounds but he'd probably take fifty-five, I reckon.'

'And that's for the whole house, not just the basement?'

'Yes, love, the whole house.'

'Freehold?'

'Freehold.'

'What's the catch?'

'It's in Beeston, love. Would've cost twenty thousand pounds seven or eight year ago. Will you need a mortgage?'

'Oh, no.'

'Maybe you can put it on your Amex.'

'Oh, you accept American Express, do you? That's useful to know.'

'Um, sorry, I wasn't being serious. Though, yes, maybe the vendor would. I do ought to advise you that rents are only about four to five hundred pounds thereabouts.'

'Per week? Sounds high to me.'

'Per month, love.'

'Oh. Well, it's not buy-to-let, in any case.'

'You going to *live* there?'

'Well, use it, weekends. Handy for the ground.'

'Ah. Southern White.'

'I was born in Roundhay. But yea, I live in Surrey.'

'Why don't you buy a nice semi in Horsforth? I've got a lovely one coming on the market for just under two hundred and fifty.'

'Well, what's the point? I'd still have to drive to the game. The whole point is to be walking distance.'

'Well, as I say, price has more than doubled in a decade, so I doubt there's any future capital gain.'

'Well, this is a first.'

'What's that, love?'

'An estate agent trying to talk me out of buying a house.'

'I'm not, love, I'm trying to move you upmarket as you've obviously got brass. Only thinking of my fee.'

'That's reassuringly honest.'

'We all have families to feed.'

'Well, I don't, actually.' I blurted this out, not aware of how self-pitying I may have sounded. I felt strangely nervous, passed my phone from right hand to left. I was keen to return the topic of conversation to the house. 'Um, so, two bedrooms. Small front yard. How big is the back garden?'

She actually laughed a little. 'You haven't really looked round t' block, have you, love? There's no garden. It's back-to-back.'

'Oh.'

'Oh indeed.'

'Didn't know there were any left these days. Well, that's all right. I hate gardening anyway. It'll be low maintenance.'

'So, you'll be making an offer?' She sounded desperately disappointed.

'Yes, probably. I'll get my PA to get in touch with you, and I'll put you in touch with my law firm.'

'Takes all sorts.' She sighed. 'Still, no mortgage, cash purchase, no chain. Low maintenance for me too.'

'Have a nice weekend.'

'You too, love.'

It was a Friday in mid-May. Mid-afternoon. The only point of a working day I didn't like very much; the energy seemed to dip. I'd created a half hour to myself for personal matters. I worked enough at weekends and evenings, so I could make personal calls without a pang of conscience at any time. It wasn't that we lacked business. I had a couple of contracts awaiting my approval, and other inquiries in the inbox. The social responsibility side of the consultancy that I had set up, to implement living wage policies in the non-profit sector, with our fees set at no more than break-even, was gaining in reputation and custom. It had the unintended consequence of boosting our image so that demand was soaring for the ridiculously profitable high-end reward consulting also. To offset this further, we had set up a charitable foundation. Given that the non-profit side helped people, our philanthropic arm was dedicated to nature conservancy, helping restore wetlands in East Anglia.

I pondered whether to work at the weekend, or take some time off. I could stay in the tiny apartment near Fleet Street, that I'd snapped up in the early 2000s before the prices went crazy; or the lonely, spooky mansion near the M25, with its indoor swimming pool, all gloomy and echoing with no one there, and the deep, spacious garden with blackbirds and robins and occasionally a woodpecker, but never the sound of children playing. I no longer had the pad in Alicante, but I could book an Airbnb and jet out, given that the weather had turned nice, if I could get an early morning flight. Soon, I'd have the choice of staying in another house – a whole house, freehold, in the north of England, close to such attractions as an urban motorway, a recreation ground and a convenience store, and, of course, the home ground of a once-great football team, more recently the butt of jokes. Next door to the sexy, smart, funny young woman. Not that that was the reason for the purchase, obviously. And she probably had a husband, or a boyfriend, with tattoos, who worked on building sites, played Rugby League and had biceps bigger than my thighs, who would beat me to a pulp for so much as offering her a cup of tea over the garden fence – not that there would be a garden fence, that's a figure of speech. But yes. Put her out of your mind, idiot, I told myself.

I should really have been cutting down further on the property portfolio, I reflected that afternoon, not adding to it. The operation necessary to keep them all shipshape and legal was effectively another small company, replete with paperwork, taxes, regulations, employees and a supply chain in the shape of caretakers, security companies and the like. For the most part, I was comfortable with this; I didn't do leisure, or have hobbies, other than watching Leeds United games, and I didn't have a girlfriend or that many friends. Running a business was something I enjoyed, the only thing I had and the only thing I was good at. I didn't want it removed from weekends, too, but maybe two properties would suffice, not three. And I didn't have a family. Well, strictly speaking, I had an ex-wife and the eighteen-year-old step-daughter, Amelie, who rarely called, but whom I had persuaded to support Leeds. They were living in Manhattan, Upper East Side. But I didn't have a family, at least, it didn't feel like it, most of the time.

I informed Vicky, my PA, that I would be going out for a run. I changed into tee-shirt, leggings and expensive trainers, and set out for a three-mile circular loop along north and south Thames embankments, across the Millennium Bridge, down as far as Hungerford Bridge in the west. The tide was fairly high, but the ebb was picking up speed; the swirling, brackish currents reflecting the restlessness of the city. A giant floating H-shaped contraption caught rubbish in the ever-turning tides, and a family of moorhens had made their nest in one tip of the construction. Throughout the spring and early summer, I observed the parents' plucky fight against the currents, made fierce by embankment construction that had narrowed the capital's river over the centuries. As they energetically fought their way, heads jerking enthusiastically forward with each paddle, towards their chicks, now almost fledged, I marvelled in the tenacity and ingenuity of nature. From time to time a cormorant would fly by and, on one occasion, I spotted a kingfisher, low, fast and tiny, the vivid turquoise back and wings lighting up the landscape as it caught the afternoon sun, like something ephemeral and other-worldly, not of flesh and blood.

It was good to smell the outdoors that afternoon, with the faintest hint of seaside brine in the air, amid the more familiar fragrances of falafel, burgers and fries from the profusion of riverside restaurants. I went for a run two or three times a week, and visited the gym also. I had done so throughout my adult life. I watched my diet, and never drank to excess, protecting my intellect, my sole attribute. Despite this, my body retained this stubborn pudginess, a lumpy weight in my walking and running gait and a lack of trimness at all the edges. No matter how much I exercised, on runs, on bike machines, with weights, my naked appearance never came close to resembling that of David Beckham or Rafael Nadal. The God of Pudginess was always in the corner, laughing with his devilish smirk, throwing lumps of flesh, the consistency of Play-Doh, at my waist, confident it would always stick.

Nonetheless, I still felt refreshed after returning to my luxurious chief executive's office, with its en suite bathroom and kitchen, for a hot shower followed by a half pint of water, large orange juice and fresh croissant. I phoned my solicitor, resolved to get the house purchase bureaucracy under way. In two to three weeks, I could be completing; certainly, I'd be in time for the start of the season in early August.

7

Everybody needs good neighbours

When I turned into our street, he was there. I walked towards our house, curious, looking at him to be certain. I didn't follow football but I knew enough to know the old season had finished and the next one hadn't started. So, could it be... surely not? The estate agent had only changed the sign from 'For Sale' to 'Sold' a week or so earlier, so it was quick to be all sorted, and I never imagined that the rich (or very possibly the heavily indebted) southern chap would be purchasing, despite his glance at the sign a few weeks back. He was getting out of a car – not the smart, sporty one, but a more ordinary hatchback, probably a Volkswagen. Maybe he was moving down in the world: had had a big bankruptcy or summat. Was it definitely him? Yes, it was him.

He was just putting the key in the door as I reached ours.

'Hello,' I said keenly, but trying not to sound overeager, or stupid, or both. 'Didn't think we'd be seeing you back here.'

'Oh, hello,' he replied, really friendly. His face seemed to light up as he saw me.

I had worried that he had been keen to leave at our last meeting, so his bright welcome brought me a surge of joy. 'You the new landlord?' I asked. 'Hope the first tenant's going to be nice.'

'No, I don't plan on renting out; not to begin with at any rate.'

'You moving in?' I asked, trying to sound only moderately welcoming, not showing the secret inner excitement that I was beginning to feel.

'No, I'll still be based in the south for now.'

'Your weekend home, then?' I asked.

'Yea, maybe. Something like that.'

'You have family down south?'

'No, I live on my own, but the office is in London and I'm busy most weeks. I'll come here mostly when there's a match on.'

'Are Leeds really worth it? I thought they were rubbish, these days. That's what everyone says. I don't know why folk keep going on about it or keep going to see them, as it seems just to make everyone unhappy. Why don't you support Chelsea?'

He just looked at me, too appalled to say owt.

'I'll never understand men,' I said with feeling. 'They'll change girlfriends if you put on a couple of pounds, but never change which team they support even if the players start playing like the Teletubbies.'

'Well,' he said. 'I guess it's a tribal thing. Emotional. Something you grow up with.'

That was all he said. There was a pause. Then I asked: 'So you moving in already?'

'Not tonight, there's no furniture yet. I'll just check the windows and doors are secure then go see my dad in Harrogate, then drive back down south, after ten when the roads are quiet. I've taken a week off so I'll get it all kitted out over the next couple of weeks. There'll be someone in to do up the kitchen and bathroom, satellite TV, security systems and other electrics, and so on. So, I hope they don't bother you. Vans in the road and all that.'

'No, fine,' I said. 'Nice to see the area moving up. You got enough in for a cup of tea?'

'Oh, yes, no problem.'

'There's a convenience store just a couple of blocks away: left, then second right.'

'Thanks.'

'Listen, um…'

'Yes?'

I paused before beginning my sentence, fingers trembling so I played with my hair with one hand and placed the other on my hip. 'Um, George, we're having pizza and wine and cola later. Come and join us if you like, as you're the new neighbour. About seven. It's just me and my two.'

He looked like I'd just proposed some satanic ritual or something. 'Really?' he said. I worried that I had made the most terrible mistake, but he quickly added: 'Sorry, I'd love to. So, folk round here just get to know each other as neighbours?'

'Welcome to the north.'

I wasn't sure that he'd really call by; but he did, right enough, and brought a bottle of wine and some garlic bread, which was thoughtful. I could tell from the wine that he'd gone as far as the Morrisons or the Asda – there's one of each about a mile away – as it were quite posh; not the sort you'd get from the local store. It was French. Very nice, anyway.

As he arrived he said he'd bring up more wine from his cellar next time he was heading north. I wondered if he was exaggerating; if it was just an expression. Then I wondered if he was being serious. This chat was all very quick after we said hello at the front door, so we quickly moved into the sitting room, a distance which was not, of course, very far.

'This is little Danny; and you've already met my pride and joy Bronte.'

'Will you be moving in with Mummy?' asked Danny, as cute and embarrassing as any three-year-old could be.

George laughed – a little too much, for my taste, as though the prospect of me as a successful man's partner were faintly ridiculous – but I laughed too. 'The mouths of babes,' said George to me, then turned to young Danny. 'I'll be your mummy's neighbour, and I'll try to be a good one. Now, young man, what's your favourite toy?'

'Fire engines,' he replied.

'Then next time I shall bring the biggest, reddest fire engine I can find in the whole of London. Agreed?'

'Agreed!' he yelled, then ran to hide behind my legs.

I began worrying that Danny didn't have many positive male role models; there was his granddad, and perhaps that was about it.

Bronte asked, bold as brass: 'So what's Surrey like, then?'

'Not so bad, if you don't mind southerners,' he replied. 'Too many Chelsea fans, but there are some good pubs and restaurants.'

I invited him to sit on the one settee, but he only sat down for a short while, and seemed keen to be up and help me in the kitchen. Whether this was a case of his feeling uneasy in the company of the others, or being keen to talk to me, or out of his desire to help, or a mix of all three, was hard to tell.

'So, do you ever watch a movie with your neighbours down south, or listen to music?' I asked.

'Uh, no.'

'What are they like?'

'I have absolutely no idea.'

'Well, are they a family with young kids, older couple, empty nest, or what?'

'I have absolutely no idea.'

'How long have they lived there?'

'I have absolutely no idea. Few months, I think. Or years. I think they're white, about my age, or younger. Or maybe a bit older.'

'That's so weird, that you don't know the folk on your street.'

'People really value their privacy.'

'Hmmph,' I said, for the first time wondering if living in a bigger house came with disadvantages. 'Do you live on your own?'

'Yes.'

'Do you ever feel lonely?' I asked.

'Um,' he hesitated. I felt bad, suddenly realising that I was asking too personal a question to someone I hardly knew. I meant it in a compassionate way, but maybe I was too direct. It was still just the two of us in the kitchen, and we had just put the garlic bread in the oven. It would have been worse if I'd asked him that in front of Bronte.

'Sorry,' I said. 'Didn't mean to be too nosy. I know I've got a gob on me.'

'No, it's a fair question,' he said. 'And do you know what? No one bothers to ask me. So, don't apologise. It's probably the kindest thing anyone's said to me for a long time. And yes, sometimes I feel very lonely.'

'Well, you won't be tonight. Welcome to Beeston, love.' Then I instinctively did a very bold thing: I leaned over and pecked him on the cheek. He smelled of cologne – an expensive one, Armani perhaps. He clearly had made a bit of an effort. I felt aroused, even though my little peck wasn't meant as a flirty thing, I really did feel kind of tender towards him. He

45

obviously was lonely, very assured but sad inside. He looked dead chuffed at the kiss on the cheek, anyway. It seemed to make him instantly more confident, almost radiant.

'Your daughter's a remarkable painter for someone so young…'

'Oh, I know. She's gifted. The teachers get all excited about her. Oh, before I forget, you mentioned something the first time we met about getting her work assessed by a professor friend of yours.'

'Thanks for reminding me. Yes, she's really a friend of my sister, Joy. She's called Alexandra and she's quite eminent, but of course very busy. I'll try during the next week.'

'I think that would mean a lot to her, though the teachers are thinking of her for art school already.'

'You said she paints your dreams. Do you talk about dreams over breakfast?'

'No, she just guesses them,' I replied. 'Same wavelength. My sad dreams become her beautiful pictures.'

'The one I saw didn't seem like a sad dream; more aspirational.'

'Well, about me wanting a bigger house, basically. I'm shallow!'

'Or maybe the rooms represent the spaces you're going to enter one day; spaces that you'll both inhabit. She painted them at the top of a tree. These visions are alive; they're part of you. Or they're new ways of thinking, new ways of living. Dreams are the memories we haven't yet created, the stories we're still composing. A dream is the way we begin to repair what's broken.'

'Really? Is that how it works?'

'No idea, to be honest. I only had those thoughts since seeing the painting. That's the kind of thing great art does.'

I was amazed by his little speech; he seemed transformed,

there was a fire in his eyes. I was suddenly desperate to spend hours just with him, listening to him talk and learning. I was nervous that I would say something stupid, or be too silent. I was also puzzled by what he meant by being 'broken'. Did he mean that *I* was broken? Yet he looked at me with keenness and desire. I knew that look well, of course, or part of it – but there was something else, with George, something of his soul, too. In the end, keen to avoid saying something silly while trying to be serious, I was desperate for the company of others. 'Shall we rejoin the others?' I asked.

'Of course,' he said, graciously.

The food was ready, so we picked it up, brought it in and placed it on the small dining table at the back of the main room. The TV was on but, as usual, I never paid much attention until the lottery programme. Danny had joined Bronte on the settee and was starting to look a little tired. George and I were on dining chairs near the table, at opposite ends. I asked him a few times if he wanted a place on the settee but he insisted he was fine. He surprised me by making observations on the reality show that was on the TV.

'This is boring!' said Bronte.

'I agree,' I replied. 'Let's have music hour.'

'Cool,' said Bronte.

I turned to George: 'Most evenings, we listen to an album, and we try to work out how they wrote the songs, what the lyrics mean. We take it in turns to choose, and once a week it has to be something completely new, that none of us has heard before. If we can't afford a new album, then maybe just a song or two, from download, or a radio channel. Gets us talking, instead of just sitting like zombies in front of t' telly. It were Bronte's idea.'

'That's wonderfully creative. I love that idea.'

'You really going all the way back to Surrey tonight?' I was

47

trying to sound politely curious, not begging him to stay, but I wanted to meet him again, and soon.

'Well, I don't actually have a bed next door yet, so no choice really! But I like driving, and the roads'll be quiet.'

'Right. Fair enough. And a nice, lazy Sunday tomorrow, I guess.'

'Yea, I'll probably do some work, stop me getting bored.'

'I love Sundays – when I have the weekend off, that is.'

'I don't like Sundays; never have. I find them a bit gloomy. Can't wait for Monday.'

'*What?!* You actually look forward to going to work?'

'Yea. Always have done. The best day of my life was turning eighteen. The next best day was the first day of my first job after graduating: trainee consultant at a big firm. I had a salary, a suit, a sense of purpose, business travel and interesting work. OK, the novelty wears off a little, but you can always find new challenges. I've never completely lost that feeling of exhilaration of the first few weeks of work. It remotivates me, even now, when I think back on it. Yes, work is good, leisure is dull.'

'Each to his own, I guess,' I said, still nonplussed.

'I think what it gives me is a sense of purpose; you know, direction, whereas idling away doing stuff feels a bit meaningless. You see, I was never much good at anything else: sport, music, socialising, any of that. With work I had a role, and I could use my brain and I knew what to do, and I could make an impact.'

'I hate work.'

'What do you do?'

'Cleaning. In shifts, for a big company with lots of clients. So, it's all offices and stuff. I hate the day before a shift. Once I'm there it's not too bad, and sometimes I have a laugh with the other ladies, though not all of them speak English. But no, I don't like it, just look forward to being home, here.'

'Why don't you go for promotion? You're obviously smart.'

I hated that question, in part because of my disastrous interview, yet I wasn't entirely sure why it was with such intensity. 'Change the subject!'

'Think I might take a comfort break,' he said.

'If you happen to be passing by the fridge on the way back, top-up would be nice.'

While he was gone, I reflected on the ambitions I used to have as a girl: to be a singer, or perhaps work in the theatre. I had loved putting on school plays. It always seemed that creative jobs were for people other than me, and most careers in the grown-up world seemed dull and grey. I had been good at essays at school; my vivid imagination running away with me, but you can't earn a living from that. It had to be something dull, like accountancy or sales, if you wanted a salary.

George returned with the bottle and refreshed my glass. I wasn't used to a man fetching stuff for himself from the kitchen, much less something for me. But maybe he really was just escaping the telly for an extra minute or two. As he returned, the lottery was on. It seemed clear he had never watched that before, and he tried to persuade me it was a bad idea to take part. But without hope, what are we?

8

A little drop of heaven

She appeared just as I was turning the key in the lock for the very first time, and talked to me, all friendly. I had to remind myself that she wasn't taking a shine to me; that such friendly neighbourliness was just how things were around here. It's funny, I had been on cultural-awareness programmes for Singapore, China, Brazil, Argentina and Mexico, but never one for Yorkshire. It's where I was born, and where I went to school, so it would not be obviously necessary. Although neighbourliness was a local trait, my own family had been rather withdrawn, and I lost my mother at a young age. So, I was quite astounded, and unduly excited, when Karen invited me to join her and her family, that very evening, for pizza and wine.

Dad didn't invite neighbours round very often. He was quirky and eccentric, but not unkind. He didn't have much of a sense of humour, though he enjoyed Morecambe and Wise. At least he liked his sport. On the living room wall were hung framed photographs of Herbert Sutcliffe and Hedley Verity, which he would polish with reverence, saying: 'Best batsman and best bowler ever to play for England', a view built upon legend, given that even he was too young to have seen them play. On a Saturday afternoon he would don a flat cap and tweed jacket and go to watch Roundhay Rugby Union Club at its home fixture, sometimes taking me along. This was the closest he came to passionate expression, when he opined that this or that passage of play was or wasn't 'good rugby football', always using the phrase in full, with the confidence that his judgement served as infallible arbiter. We would go to see Yorkshire or the test match at Headingley sometimes too. But he loathed Association Football, with its overpaid 'girly' long-haired pampered players, always feigning injury or 'crying to matron' as he called it, playing to the gallery and never applauding their opponents. So my one rebellion in teenage years was to sneak off to the rough side of the city on buses, to Elland Road to watch John Sheridan and Ian Baird and the other boys in white kicking a spherical ball that would roll along the ground and hit the back of the net. I also loved the neat symmetry of the circular and straight lines of the soccer pitch, like a geometry question at O-Level. On my first visit, I mentally calculated the surface area of the part-circle on the edge of the penalty area, to calm my nerves before the home side's penalty kick, wondering if I was the only one of the 30,000 spectators to be doing so. If I had known that pipe-smoking and Roundhay Rugby Union Club would become extinct before I even turned forty I might have paid more respect to Dad's interests but growing up I felt mildly embarrassed at his conservatism.

We missed Mum every day, my sister, Joy, and I. She was never there to see our achievements. Dad, who mellowed in his old age, was immensely proud. He was a curious mixture. He had an austere manner most of the time, and various prejudices, but he wasn't harsh. He never smacked us, for example, and he could be quite kind, often when you least expected it; a small, soft centre that was very small but very soft. While he never seemed to take much interest in our studies when we were young, at the respective graduation days he was bursting with pride. Perhaps he had struggled himself, at school, and had had to work hard to reach what used to be termed a white-collar job with a salary. I know that his parents had been very poor.

I had picked up the keys to property number three that morning, having exchanged contracts a couple of weeks earlier and completed earlier that week. With my lawyers, nothing ever takes long. The neighbourhood would be considered rough, to most of my friends and colleagues down south. Penelope, my ex-wife, of course, would have been horrified. She regarded Epsom as downmarket, for heaven's sake. Yet that was precisely the appeal for me, in many ways. There are few consolations to being lonely and living on your own; perhaps just the one – which is the freedom to make choices without consultation, to indulge personal passions and preferences. I loved the idea of escaping from the world of money at weekends. Going to the football again more regularly in recent years formed part of that desire. Living somewhere very different, without social-climbing moneyed people, was now to be another.

It's not that it's more 'real' than the lives of more privileged folk. Everything's real. And I certainly didn't have a romanticised idea of life in Holbeck and Beeston. It was just a change. Away from pretence and exaggerated formality, the judging and the attention to detail, the jockeying and positioning, the boasting over value of property, the £100,000 themed kiddies' birthday parties with entertainers, or the prized internships for adult children, or expressions of anxiety over this or that tax rate that might affect Jeremy and Jocasta's nest egg, that one can encounter at the dinner parties of Surrey and the Upper East Side. I exaggerate; it's possible to stereotype the rich as well as the poor, and, from time to time, in the world of private equity and chief executives, one comes across an urbane, relaxed and quite admirable individual who admires the philosophy of Søren Kierkegaard or the art of Pablo Picasso for their intrinsic value, and possesses a curiosity and understanding of their worth, or who really does invest more time and hard cash in charitable ventures than into a high-gain/high-risk investment opportunity.

I had no illusions about south-central Leeds. I did not doubt there would be poverty and other social problems, here and there, just as there are in all towns and cities. But the smile that Karen possessed, the way she lit up the whole atmosphere around her, possessed an uncalculating honesty and vigour that was absent from my moneyed social and work life. It seemed to say to me that life could be fun again: insecure but fun. She had an air of kindly wisdom, simultaneously knowing and ingenuous, in which much pain and much hope were intermingled.

The entire floorspace of the new house probably added up to no more than two rooms of my Surrey home which, I reflected, I should probably get around to selling unless, of course, in the back of my mind and taking into account the fact that I still hadn't been snipped, there may be a future nubile Mrs Mowatt, keen to oversee all of the nappy-and-toddler phase and selection of schools. This was unlikely but perhaps, subconsciously at least, I was holding out for the possibility. I had had one appointment for a vasectomy, at Penelope's encouragement, but I cancelled it. I had not booked another, and I had not sold the four-bedroomed home. Until then, I rattled around in the overly spacious house, or an apartment that I owned, when it wasn't rented out. There were rooms in the Surrey gaff that I had not entered for months, though I guessed the cleaners had, to keep the piano and furniture free of dust. An entire wing (I exaggerate slightly; it's two linked rooms) included a music and study room, replete with baby grand piano and portable recording studio, and a large, luxurious bedroom, with original abstract art (no posters) and a walk-in wardrobe.

I felt embarrassed that such a huge area should be taken up by just myself, as this friendly family welcomed me into their small home. I was introduced to young Danny, only three or thereabouts, who embarrassed his mum by asking if I were moving in. We both saw the funny side...

Bronte was there also, looking particularly composed.

Karen gestured me to sit down on the pea-green sofa, at the other end from Bronte; the space in the middle was clearly for Karen. There was a musty smell, but also a friendly, welcoming aroma: homely. The television was transmitting some garish game show which no one seemed to be paying attention to. The young lad played with his toy and Bronte was texting away on her phone. The biggest surprise, as I scanned the walls and the shelves around me, was the amount of artwork on the walls, and books on the shelves. Most of the framed paintings, perhaps all, seemed to be by Bronte herself, and one could perceive the beginnings of a style. One featured a realistic vase and a cubist portrait; it didn't quite work, but the audacity was inspiring. The books were of all manner of genres, shapes and styles, from pop music biographies to historical romances to seriously credible works. I noted Brontë, Joseph O'Connor and even a Louis de Bernières and some Iris Murdoch.

When Karen got up to fix some things in the kitchen, which was directly behind the only sitting room, I volunteered to help. I had found the nearest Morrisons and bought a bottle of Sancerre and some garlic bread, which she appreciated greatly.

It was increasingly clear, from the conversations and the manner of everyone, that there was no dad, no Mr Karen, rugby-playing or otherwise, on the scene, and inwardly an irrational excitement began to grow.

It was only when she asked me if I ever watched TV with my neighbours down south that I began to comprehend the scale of the cultural gulf between us. When I confessed that I scarcely knew who my neighbours were she seemed almost scandalised. She was so earnest and kind, looking at me with those gorgeous eyes, that I felt like an abandoned puppy she had taken in. Quite astonishingly, she then leaned forward to kiss me on the cheek. Her kiss was like a little drop of heaven on the side of my face. I could still pinpoint the exact spot, even afterwards, generating the same uplifting sensation throughout my whole body and spirit, ignited by the gentlest, briefest alighting of her moist lips upon me.

9

I'm different now

The House Dreams probably wouldn't be so intense if Darren and I hadn't gotten so close; at least I had thought we were close. We'd identified a two-bed terraced house with a garden, saved up the deposit, had the necessary joint earnings, only to be torpedoed by his credit rating, the silly, daft, naïve, selfish, stupid male cretin that he was. Is. Not ready to be a parent and a proper grown-up, my mum and friends told me. No, but I was. I've only got this one life, and no one to share it with.

It came to me again, only even more vivid this time, so I felt like I really was in this heavenly house, nearly a mansion, with its sunlit upper rooms, one after the other, even more than I was expecting; several bedrooms, secret bathrooms. I was drifting through them all, almost floating, entranced. The dream stayed with me, all day, like they sometimes do. It wasn't just The House that was other worldly, the nearby streets were too. I walked downstairs, into the hall, out of the front door, through a sunlit front garden and a continental-style courtyard with shady trees, into a beautiful maze of narrow streets full of cafes and arty boutiques. Then there was an interruption in the dream sequence, and suddenly I was back upstairs again, this time leaning over the dressing table, applying make-up. In the mirror I noticed a man watching me. He was handsome and sweaty, just in from the fields. I was wearing a short skirt, and suddenly pleased by the attention. My dreams only seem to turn erotic when there's a table, and I'm leaning over it. It was intensely arousing, and ever so slightly disturbing, as the situation probably wouldn't turn me on in real life, but in the dream, in the dream...

I woke up thinking it's funny how you can't control your desires; well, you can control what you do about them, but not what they are. They come from somewhere so deep you don't know where it is, and they catch you unawares, sometimes. Then the images of The House filled my head again, the sun pouring in through the large window, lighting up a four-poster bed and beautiful tapestries on the wall, and they stayed with me all morning. Like I had actually been there, or as if my eyes were like cameras and the pictures were printed in my head, always there for me to look up, like in a gallery. It came with emotion too; this vivid feeling of heaven or escape, that I tried to hold on to. It meant that I was a different person, ever so slightly different, compared with the day before.

I was the first up – only 6.30 a.m. Over breakfast, I read the property details from this week's bulletin, covering Harewood and Wetherby, mostly. There was a four-bed semi-detached house, garden laid mostly to lawn, two receptions, £375,000, close to local amenities and highly regarded primary and secondary schools. That looked nice: really nice. I could picture myself there, I thought, and I spent the rest of the morning doing little else. Terry used to tell me that Harewood House was built with slave money, and I was never sure if that were true. He was clever and good at school, was Terry, so it probably was. This information put me off the place, and I'd never toured round there. Wetherby, on the other hand, was nice. I had visited once or twice.

Darren saw the whole debt problem as a technical thing; a setback, and couldn't understand why I was so mad. The silly, charming, selfish and immature young man that I'd had the folly of setting up home, and having a son, with. I'd fallen in love with him, I really had. He was good-looking, good fun, and we had the same sense of humour. We weren't married as obviously we couldn't afford the wedding and the house; though one out of the two would've been nice. And he couldn't cope with the nappy phase; just couldn't or wouldn't cope. He liked the romantic idea of being a dad but not the practical reality of the crying and the lack of sleep and the lack of sex. So, he went back to his mum; well, I kicked him out, really, so hoping that Danny wouldn't turn out like that by the time he was in his twenties.

I walked outside. Passing next door, I felt slightly wistful that George had gone. It felt strange to acknowledge that I fancied him because he was so unlike my previous boyfriends; maybe it was a weird crush, I told myself. It was like we seemed to connect directly, before even speaking. And he brought a bit of confidence and class to the street and I thought how lucky I was to have great neighbours on both sides, not some crack den or anything. It was the Sunday morning after George's visit and I had an evening shift, the prospect of which filled me with mild depression and a vague, uneasy anxiety. That's one of the worst things about work: the very prospect of it ruins your time off, too. It hangs over you, like money worries and debts; all the anxiety that's tied up with your big and little choices to do with money, so that your time off is not really your own, because you've got these two monsters, the Next Shift and Money Worries, one on each shoulder, always there, gnawing away, chipping away at any sense of personal freedom you might want to have. To try to cheer myself up, and ward off the feelings on that Sunday, I had decided to follow up on the advice from Mum and go buy a plant pot for the front yard. I had always thought that it was frivolous to spend real cash on something that wasn't food or clothes or entertainment, but maybe it would cheer up our part of the street. I'd have to tend to them, obviously, but I'd get Mum to advise on that. She was going to take me to the garden centre, then come back with me to help. Dad might come too. We would visit Kevin's grave too, put fresh flowers on. Mum went every week.

Bronte was watching Danny for a few hours, while she did her homework. She was such a good girl, my Bronte. I walked to their house in Beeston, about a mile. Their door was never locked – I had warned them about that – so I just opened it. Ziggy the black-and-white Staffie-cross, with her huge Staffie smile, was first to greet me, wagging her tail and slurping my face as I crouched down to say hello, and give her a hug. 'I know, you haven't seen me for, like, three days! I know, it's been too long. It won't happen again, I promise, Zigs!' I pledged to the dog, then called out to the rest of the household: 'Helloo!' In the meantime, Zigs trotted over to pick up her favourite toy to present to me, then paraded around in circles, whinnying with joy, wagging her tail furiously.

'Oh, hello, Karen,' said Dad, arriving in the narrow hall from the TV room after a few moments. 'Your mum's in the back garden. I'll fetch her in and we'll get ready. Or do you want a brew first?'

'No, we'll head on our way. I don't want to leave Bronte and Danny too long.'

'Right y'are.'

'Geraniums are nice,' said Mum in the garden centre. 'They flower for a long time.' She traced her fingers over the petals.

'They don't like cold temperatures,' said Dad. 'Take them indoors in winter.'

Mum didn't reply, just wandered over to the pansies, brightly multicoloured, hundreds in tiny polystyrene pots, loving the sunshine. I gathered up a couple of both species and put them in the trolley. Mum looked at me with kindness, but then her eyes went sad again, almost vacant. After buying the plants, we called by to see Kevin. Holbeck Cemetery is midway between Mum and Dad's house and ours, so it was convenient. Kevin's headstone was grand; they'd given up holidays two years in a row to afford it. It was highly polished, dark bluish stone, with golden lettering; a bit too severe for my liking but a suitable memorial, all the same. Usually I cried, at least a little, more so than Mum, though she went every week and I wasn't always able to, what with the kids and work and everything. This visit was quite peaceful. The sun caught the golden lettering, and the reflection glinted in my eye, but it didn't feel spiritual. I didn't feel that Kevin was there at all; I just felt, as usual, this dreadful absence, this loss.

'Always in our hearts, love,' said Mum, kneeling by the grave, caressing the stone at the end of the visit, with the same gesture she had used on the flowers. Dad said nothing. She struggled to get up, so Dad helped her, clasping her hand with his, placing his other arm under her shoulder, lifting her up. There was a green patch on the front of her bright patterned frock from where she had been kneeling. Her brow was moist with sweat but she didn't wipe it. 'Right,' she said. 'Best get going.'

I often felt that I didn't tell them enough how much I owed them, and loved them, maybe because they seemed to get embarrassed by praise. Without their support, especially the child-minding, I fear I'd have sunk into despair years earlier. They were so close to each other, and lived their lives through me and their grandchildren, all the more since our loss. Dad, whose hair had turned white within weeks of losing Kevin, was quieter than the rest of us, never taking the lead in conversations. Mum had reacted differently; she had lost a load of weight, then put on a lot. She had periods where she talked about Kevin all the time – 'He would have loved this, he used to say that' – then other periods when she hardly mentioned him at all. The only time her mood sparked upwards was when playing or chatting with Bronte and Danny.

They dropped me off home, and stayed to help pot the plants. And it did cheer the place up; more than I'd expected. The smell of fresh, wet compost mingled with the fragrance of the flowers.

'Don't forget to water them if it hasn't rained,' Mum reminded me. She had bought me a watering can – far too big and bright orange. The four of us were stood in the front yard – Bronte had come out to watch – there was just enough room.

'But don't water them too much,' said Dad. 'They shouldn't be standing in water – that'll drown them.'

'Won't I hear the screaming, if they're starting to drown?' I quipped. Bronte giggled, but they didn't.

'Well, I'd best be on my way. You take care, my little princess,' said Dad to me, giving me a peck on the forehead. Mum was staying, to make tea for the children. Bronte was old enough by now but I didn't like just the two of them at home for more than an hour or so, and certainly not on an evening.

'Goodbye, love,' said Mum to Dad as he prepared to leave. 'Ooh, who's moved in next door?' She had noted that the 'Sold' sign had been taken down and that the place looked smartened up a little.

'Some rich chap that Mum fancies,' said Bronte, quick as a flash.

'Well, he's not rich, and I don't fancy him, but, actually,

61

he does seem quite nice. Came round ours yesterday evening; right friendly.'

'Well you didn't waste time inviting him round, I must say,' said Mum.

'It's a friendly neighbourhood,' I said, defensively.

'What did I tell you?' said Bronte, with a knowing air, in a manner that was both enchanting and slightly irritating.

'Well, don't get your hopes up, love. Doubt anyone with brass would live around here,' said Mum.

'I think he has another house or summat; just going to stay here for the Leeds games,' I said.

'Sucker for punishment then,' said Dad, with a weary air. He was even more gloomy and pessimistic about the football team than most fans. As I said, I never understood why anyone bothered. He began walking to the car.

'Bye then,' I said, suddenly keen to move the conversation away from George.

'Yes, bye, love,' said Dad to me. 'I'll pick you up around ten,' he said to Mum.

They let me wear headphones at work, at least, so I could have some playlists running in my head, and hum or sing along while I vacuumed and dusted. So as soon as Dad left I rushed upstairs to check my phone was fully charged, and to get ready for work. The hour or so before the shift was, in some ways, the worst, but, once it started, it wasn't too bad and I could count down the hours until I got home and could read Danny a story – though it would probably be too late – and have a quick chat with Bronte, check she had packed her bag for school, before she went to sleep. Another Sunday over; another weekend. Very much the same, yet also rather different.

10

The joy of family

I felt bad about going all the way to Yorkshire and paying such a short visit to Dad – less than an hour squeezed into the Saturday afternoon. But I was able to tell him that I had bought property in the region and could visit him more often, working from home in the Leeds residence, driving back to Surrey late on the Sunday evening. He seemed pleased; less so than I expected, but pleased.

The drive home that Saturday night was uneventful. My mood faded the further I headed south. By the time I stopped for a comfort break at Watford Gap the prospect of the large, empty house began to loom. Driving round the M25, a horrible chore at the best of times, I began to feel seriously low: almost unprecedented. I had always treated melancholy as a temporary condition, to be overcome by effort and achievement; the trick was to acknowledge it, but not to yield. Since the divorce, however, the feeling kept creeping in more often, when it was least expected. Solitude felt empowering when it was a choice, but could be a rather desolate experience when forced upon you. Perhaps I was just tired, I reflected. I felt slightly sleepy at the wheel, so I turned up the cold on the air conditioning, and the volume on Radio 3, to keep myself awake. The music was some jarring organ concerto by a composer I had never heard of. I tried Radio 2, which was so-so. I was bored with my CDs. With relief at having avoided a middle-lane collision, at around 1.30 a.m., I parked the Golf alongside the Mercedes Benz – I only have the two cars. I clicked it shut; then clicked the door open – most things are remote, digital and automated in my world. I poured myself a tumbler of water for by the bed, got changed and slept deeply.

The next morning my mood had scarcely improved. I had always hated the gloomy air of a Sunday and, once I had begun my professional career, all the more so as I was impatient to be back at work on the Monday morning – the best time of the week for me. The only way to mitigate the dullness of the seventh day was, of course, to work. So, I replied to a stack of emails, drew up an agenda for the next day's management meeting and phoned the caretaker of my London flat, checking that everything was OK, and did they need anything purchased. The only thing that lifted my mood was the thought of Karen, and the brush of her lips against my cheek. I lightly touched the area with my fingers, trying to restore the feeling of the moment of impact.

I went for a long cycle ride, in a bid for fresh air to lighten my mood. After my shower, and fresh orange juice and water, I decided to tour round the property, as though I were a visitor. I entered Amelie's rooms. The cleaners had kept them spotless, and free of dust; I could see my reflection in the sombre, highly polished wood of the piano, see the freshly lifted tufts on the Axminster rugs and smell the aroma of the scents I asked them to put in the vacuum cleaner bags. I lifted up the lid of the baby grand and tinkled a handful of notes that echoed discordantly in the cool, neglected room. I couldn't play. I wondered wistfully if any young fingers would ever practise the scales on this sadly neglected instrument.

I wondered what Karen was doing. I kept thinking, all that afternoon and much of the next night, even while I was cycling through the pretty Abinger Hammer village, with its cricket green and cute cottages. I was also thinking about her when I was checking the emails on my tablet computer as I sat at the huge granite island in the hi-tech kitchen. Would young Bronte like to have a piano? I wondered, after watching the depressing news headlines at 10 p.m. Silly thought, silly thought. Go to bed.

In my dream, I was to give a keynote address at a management conference in a hotel. It resembled the start of a recurring anxiety dream, in which the podium starts to fall apart, the microphone doesn't work and so on. On this occasion, the venue was beachside, and I was early, so I left the conference hall for a walk. In the dream, the hotel was surreal; all different levels and unusual angles, and I had to clamber through some narrow gaps in order to find the exit; but the beach was perfectly normal, with sand and rolling surf, seagulls and crabs. I walked a moderate distance, then turned back, but could not find the hotel. I kept walking, and walking. Then I recognised a part of the beach I had seen before, indicating I had completed an entire circle. I was on an island: a rather small island. The hotel was no longer there, and I was completely alone.

11

Your future husband just moved in

It was two or three weeks later when I next saw him, in early July. It was on a Sunday, one without a shift. I had already noticed his arrival the evening before; it must have been quite late because it was beginning to get dark. I had had to dash out to the convenience store before it closed as we had run out of milk for the breakfast. I saw that the lights were on in his front room, just winking here and there through the tiny gaps in the smart blinds that he had had fitted. He had probably visited midweek at times; certainly, plenty of suppliers had. All manner of furniture and gadgets had been delivered; he must have had some caretaker coordinate it all. The outside had been cleaned and smartened up. The whole street seemed a touch smarter, more self-confident. I felt a warm tingle of reassurance and hope at the thought of him settled in, a sensation that took me by surprise. As I walked by, I couldn't hear a TV, just the faint hum of some music, probably orchestral music. It was kind of eerie but also soothing, in the late evening light.

'You're looking cheerful,' said Bronte, as I walked in. Danny had gone to bed and she was watching TV, a chat show with Hollywood types being interviewed. 'Bump into anyone?'

'No, love, just pleased to get to the store in time,' I replied, wondering why she had asked, and whether I did look cheerful. 'I've got all Sunday off. Shall we go to the park tomorrow? I think it's going to be a nice day, and Danny's spending the afternoon at Sharon's to play with Jayden.'

'Mmm, I'm getting a bit old for the park, Mum. I was going to see Kirsty.'

'Oh, OK. All day? Is it not cool to hang out with your mum any more?' I asked, trying not to sound desperate. She just looked up at me, with a mixture of curiosity and affection, then back at the telly.

'Afternoon to myself, then,' I said. 'I shall read a book and play some classic Take That albums.'

'That'll not get me home in a hurry.'

'Back Street Boys as well!' I said, winding her up.

'I think your future husband has just moved in next door, you could spend time with him,' she said, cheeky as you like. I could feel myself blushing. Maybe it was an option, though, unless he was dashing off back down south.

'OK, well I'm going to have a bath and then go to bed, love, don't stay up late, and don't watch anything violent or horrible on TV.' That was another landmark I was passing: to bed before my daughter, unless it was a school night.

''Night, Mum.'

The next morning was sunny, but not too warm; there was a strong breeze. I just happened to be looking out through the window when I noticed George getting out of his hatchback car in front of next door and going around to the back of the vehicle to fetch something from the boot. He was wearing a tee-shirt and tracksuit bottoms, but still retained an aura of authority and calmness. I wandered out into the front yard.

Strong shoulders, I noticed. A face that was not eye-catching all the time, but rather gorgeous when he smiled, and he smiled when he saw me.

'They look nice,' I said. He had also bought some pots and plants to brighten up the yard.

'Oh hi. Yes, well I could see that you guys had made the effort too.'

'I'll water them, if you like, while you're down south.'

'That would be nice, thanks.'

He looked up at me, and we made eye contact. His look was searching, appreciative.

'You settling in?' I asked.

'Yup. Ready for the next season.'

'What, footie season?'

'Yes. Start going to games again.'

'"Sucker for punishment," Dad says. Leeds fans generally, I mean.'

'Yea, well, he's got a point. Anyway, what do you think of the yard?'

'Lovely.'

'Um, do you want to come in for a cuppa? Or have you got little ones to look after? Seems only fair, as you've invited me round yours already.'

'Oh, OK,' I said, brightly, I think. 'My little one is at a friend's and Bronte's gone out for the day anyway.' I hadn't been expecting his invitation, and hadn't expected how pleased I would feel.

The place was very smartly done, with polished wood floors, some framed maps on the wall and a globe. There was a fairly small TV but a smart-looking music system. He went to the kitchen to put the kettle on.

'I see you're Sagittarius,' I said, as he emerged from the back with two hot mugs.

'What?' he asked, looking bemused.

'All these maps,' I explained.

'Oh, I don't believe in astrology,' he said, quite dismissively.

'All I'm saying is that you were born between twenty-second of November and twenty-first of December.'

'Mmmph,' he replied.

'Well, go on then. When's your birthday?'

'Third of December.'

'Told you!' I said, trying not to sound too triumphant.

'You could have just got lucky,' he replied, a little put out. 'I've never been one for astrology, I have to say. I'm more inclined to believe that life can be explained in terms of flesh and blood, cells and electrical impulses in the brain. Tea all right?' he asked.

'Lovely,' I replied. 'What are you doing today?'

'Couple of things to do about the house, then I'm going out for lunch before heading back down the M1. I couldn't face going to the supermarket yesterday evening so there's nothing in except tea and coffee and milk and biscuits.'

'Oh, who are you going out with?' I asked.

'No one, just me.'

'Oh. Are you comfortable with that?'

'Used to it. I've travelled a lot, usually on my own.'

'Oh.'

'Unless, Karen…' He began.

'Yes?'

'Well, if your little ones are otherwise occupied, maybe you could join me? Just a simple lunch at a brasserie in town that I know. Pasta meal or salad or something.'

'Um, yea, sure,' I said, pleased and nervous and excited. 'I've got nothing on.' Mmm, not the best choice of expression. 'So to speak,' I added. Oh, God, that only made it worse, I thought, but he didn't seem to notice.

'Lovely. Shall I knock on your door around twelve? Here's my mobile number for good measure. Just text me if something comes up with the kids and you can't make it. You wouldn't have to call round.'

So thoughtful, I thought. I felt quite unnaturally excited as we exchanged numbers. I also felt embarrassed. 'Um George…' I began.

'What?'

'Is it expensive?'

'Oh, don't worry. My treat!' he said. 'I had your pizza last time so it's my turn.'

'Thank you, George, only it's been an expensive week, Danny growing out of clothes already.'

'Don't worry about it!' He really did sound proud at the thought of treating me.

'See you then.'

'See you!'

I texted both Sharon and Bronte to let them know I was having a light, informal, friendly lunch with George. Each texted me back a two-word reply, followed by the winking face symbol:

Sharon: *Hot date ;)*
Bronte: *Told you ;)*

I replied to both of them that it was nothing of the sort, just a neighbour, friend, he would have been on his own otherwise and so on. This time each of their two-word replies was identical: *Yea right.*

I spent some time getting ready. It wasn't often that I had a date – not that it was a date, obviously, but it was an outing into town. I spent twenty minutes on make-up and put on a designer frock from a charity shop in Headingley: fawn colour, mid-length, sort of sexy-but-still-respectable. One of my two pairs of heels – they nearly matched the dress. Hair had been washed and dried the day before. It's naturally curly and wavy so didn't look too bad even when I couldn't afford to have it done, which was most of the time. I checked myself in the mirror: not bad at all. George knocked on my door at twelve. Very punctual, I thought. But he's a businessman – or seems to be.

He drove to the city centre in his hatchback car – I didn't dare ask if he had had to sell the Mercedes Benz – and found a parking space easily as it was Sunday. We walked a short way to the brasserie, my heels click-clacking on the slabs and cobbles, hair blowing over my face in the breeze; him all quiet and executive-like. We just made small talk while we walked, about the weather and that part of town; it had been dodgy back when he was a kid, he said, but the riverside area was all smartened up now.

The food was lovely; a nice choice of wine, but I made the mistake of drinking three glasses, which is too much for me, especially in the middle of the day, and I became overindulgent with my emotions.

It had begun so well. One of the things that I instinctively liked about George's company was a feeling that I could discuss any subject, including difficult ones, and that he would take me seriously and say something smart. I knew better than to try astrology, and I wasn't really convinced by it anyway, beyond a few personality quirks. There was a bigger idea that was bugging me, from our earlier conversation, and I was suddenly impatient to hear his views.

'So,' I began. 'I've been puzzling over the thing you said about people being just flesh and cells and nerves and stuff.'

'Yes?'

'Well it's not true, is it?'

'It's what medical evidence shows us.'

'But what's the difference between life, and not-life? What makes something living?'

'So much is known now about how the human body functions,' he explained. 'Including even the human brain: which areas are responsible for emotion, for cognition, the role the nerve cells play. Certain parts of the brain light up with electricity when you're feeling certain emotions...'

I interrupted him, finishing a glug of wine, not really listening: 'Yes, but where does it *come* from? Does the electricity cause the emotion, or does the emotion cause the electricity?'

He hesitated. 'Good question,' was all he said.

I was intrigued that he didn't have a straightforward answer immediately, and I should have just tried to coax one out. Instead, I explained what lay behind my thoughts; how what I really wanted to know was why the doctors couldn't save Kevin, make his heart and lungs start working again, after the accident, if his parts were all in such good order, and I became teary. It was understandable I should become upset, but not really appropriate in the company of someone I hardly knew. Typical me, I told myself, launching into stuff without an exit plan. Obviously George was understanding; in fact, he said some kind things. But it was obviously too-much-too-soon, in terms of intimacy and conversational subjects, and so the lunch was both lovely and a disaster all at the same time. In the end, I was itching to be home. As he dropped me off, I thanked him for the lunch, and planted a large, wet, drunken kiss on his cheek, quite close to his mouth. He seemed both pleased and taken aback. Though I didn't suppose, as he gave me a wistful look as I closed the passenger door, that he'd ever want to take me out again.

12

_____

What is life?

She looked quite stunning; quite breathtakingly stunning. Hair long and wavy, pretty face with a nervous smile, a beautifully curved bust (I noticed, I'm only human) matching the equally graceful figure to which her pale fawn-coloured dress clung with a protective envy. I could essay in my mind the formula that would produce such elegant parabolic curves on an x-y axis, but that would rather destroy the moment. The poetry or the maths: which would best describe her?

And she had made this effort for *me*, little me. I had booked a table overlooking the river at a city-centre brasserie and felt rather proud when I called them back to change the booking from one person to two. I rather surprised myself in finding the confidence to ask her to join me, then she rather surprised me by accepting, and quite gladly. Not that it was a date, of course, she probably just had sympathy for me at the prospect of my dining alone. Then again, there was that dress, and the effort she had made...

After her second glass of wine, slightly drunk and a little

hasty in manner, she surprised me by asking a question whose depth I underestimated, initially. What is life? She wanted to know.

Where to begin? Was my immediate thought. I was a little thrown, not sure how to respond. Then she explained the events that underpinned her interrogation. She placed her glass down to tell the story: 'When our Kevin was killed in a car crash, he were only like nineteen. He only had a blow on the head and on the chest. His lungs were fine, his heart was fine, his kidneys were fine, his liver was fine, his eyeballs were fine, his other bits and pieces with names I can't remember were all fine. We know this 'cos we signed the papers to let them be used for transplants, so now they're in other people helping them live.'

Her lipstick was slightly out of place, a red smudge had escaped the lip area and slid out a little towards the cheek. She kept smoothing down the napkin on her lap in a repeated movement with her left hand, while her right hand held the glass. She continued: 'So all his parts, individually, were fine. My, they swooped on him, did the doctors, like a group of mechanical vultures. Couldn't believe their luck, a healthy nineteen-year-old. But dead. Healthy, but dead. Could they explain that to me? No. They couldn't put him back together again. Or rather, they could, but they couldn't make him live again. So, if what you said were true about a body being like just bits and pieces and nerves and electricity, the doctors could've fixed him, like mechanics fixing a car.'

I could see her eyes moistening as she said this. 'I don't know,' I replied. I looked down at my sea bass and mashed potato, a strand of spinach draped over the mash, the dead fish's skin curled up slightly, wondering briefly what the poor creature had felt as the net plucked him out of the ocean. I looked out of the window, at the swirling River Aire. It was quite narrow and unspectacular in central Leeds; not really a river, compared with the Paraguay or the Paraná. About as wide as an Olympic-sized swimming pool, thereabouts. 'I'm not a doctor,' was all I said.

'But maybe doctors don't know either,' she continued. 'What *is* life? What *is* it? And how can it just go? If it can be ended so easily, it should be re-startable easily. Like, he was so funny and smart and full of life and ambition just a couple of hours before and then. Pff!' She knocked her wine glass accidentally with her fork and it wobbled, but fortunately stayed upright.

'That reminds me of my favourite bit of poetry,' I said.

'Oh yes, what's that?'

'By Calderón de la Barca, "Life is a Dream".'

'What's it about?' she asked.

'Pretty much what you just said; the yearning to achieve, yet we all meet the same fate. Doesn't rhyme if you translate into English.'

She fell silent for a while and I did too, not overawed by her emotion, but mentally distracted by the disturbing clarity of her intelligent-naïve question. It reminded me of Albert Einstein's insistence that his big breakthroughs stemmed from thinking like a child. What *was* life? The question nagged; it puzzled. Science is too shy to address the matter directly, so we delve ever more deeply into the mechanics, like trying to understand music by studying the grains of wood in the violin. What was life? What was my life? How was I different from the water of the river outside, falling with unconscious gravity towards the River Ouse and the Humber? Human behaviour does not follow laws, I had learned in recent years. It cannot be modelled, or even really codified; we're too extreme, too shallow, too unpredictable, alternately too suggestible and too stubborn.

So I simply observed how touching it was that she remembered him so, and that she must have loved him.

'Yes, of course. Every day I miss him. He was my big brother, my hero; looked out for me. He appears to me in dreams. I was only seventeen then, Bronte was a baby. When you lose someone close it's a physical pain, right here in the chest and in the soul.' She pointed to the middle of her stomach. 'Then people say "Oh it'll get better." But you don't like them saying that, because you don't want to get better, or feel better, because that would be like forgetting.'

She paused again, and this time a whole tear ran down her left cheek. It struck me that I had never seen Penelope cry, nor openly admit weakness. I had admired such coolness and apparent resilience, with a young man's instinctive wariness of emotional candour. Karen's display of grief, which might have embarrassed my younger self, touched me directly. Her authenticity, her sense of loss, but also the yearning for her brother's missed life, was the opposite of self-indulgence. I resolved to say something coherent and supportive, rather than just 'There, there'. I composed my thoughts for a couple of seconds, then said: 'Except that Kevin would want you to feel better. He looked out for you. He would want you to have a good life, and to be happy.'

'Thanks,' she said. 'That's kind.'

I offered her a tissue, which she accepted.

'I'm sorry,' she said. 'I'm sorry. You hardly know me. I didn't mean to blurt out so much personal stuff. I don't know what you must think.'

'Please don't apologise for saying how you feel,' I replied. 'It's one of the most maddening things about living in Britain. There's little enough passion and emotion in my life, I can tell you! I'm honoured that you can share stuff with me.'

'I know, but even so.'

'And what you said about life was thought provoking. I shall think on,' I said after a pause. 'It's a recognised aspect of metaphysics; much debated; first cause and all that. Though actually, maybe not discussed enough.'

'Metaphysics, huh?'

'Yup.'

'OK. I shall think on too. Though maybe you're just being polite; I've been a nuisance, challenging your views when I don't really know what I'm talking about.'

'Until a few years ago I would have contradicted what you said and told you arrogantly that science has the matter all sorted. I was a slave to data, and evidence, and facts; believed in a scientific theory for everything, with laws. There were even mathematical models that the banks built for market behaviour, and I helped design the incentive schemes for them. It was very rational and evidence based, or so we thought.'

'Did it work?'

'No, it failed disastrously. Entire institutions went bust and we had a global recession. You see, people aren't rational or predictable, even when you incentivise them logically; and then there are the unexpected events. If only people could be persuaded to behave more rationally.'

'Yea, well, good luck with that,' she said, with pragmatic Yorkshire sarcasm, but in a good-natured way. 'So where does that leave you with your belief in evidence and facts and all that?'

'Well, I was disillusioned for a short while, but then I came across the research base for cognitive psychology. It's absolutely fascinating; people, especially in groups, tend to overestimate their abilities, see patterns where there are none, fail to challenge established stories when new evidence comes to light and so on. So, I've learned there's a lot of research about how people behave. And, yes, people are weird and unpredictable.'

'Yea, we've got a saying for that in Yorkshire: nowt so queer as folk.'

I just gave a rueful smile, I think... before saying: 'What would you like for dessert?'

She asked me about my work, and I said I ran my own business. She said her ex Darren did too, and that it must be difficult. I felt the gulf between us begin to grow again. Should I tell her that I'm worth a couple of million? That one of the Big Four consultancies approached me and the other partners about selling up, but that we didn't want to, because I cherished my independence more than money, and I wanted to look out for my staff (except for the treacherous couple who were after my job, of course)? It was so uplifting to be taken for who I was, and not what I represented, that I wanted to maintain the illusion at least a little longer. It was like being a teenager again, except that I wasn't much of a teenager when I was a teenager, and no one with Karen's looks would have sat down with me for a conversation back then.

I was utterly captivated by her tender heart, but did not know how to say this, and did not make a serious effort, so the short drive back from the city centre was subdued. More than once in these few minutes, I opened my mouth to say something, but admitting to my real feelings of yearning and desire would have sounded hopelessly premature, and I feared scaring her away forever. I was utterly lost: I had no points of reference for this new, emotional world. I had previously thought that songwriters and novelists had overdone the whole 'falling in love' business, not realising that their difficulty was the opposite: a full expression would be always just out of reach. The description is not the event. The map is not the territory. As I dropped her off at her home, I felt an intense pang of loss at the prospect of saying goodbye, her finding a new boyfriend and the more immediate prospect of a long, lonely drive down the motorway. She kissed me affectionately on the cheek, the other cheek to the one a few weeks earlier, so the sensation balanced nicely. I fought a powerful impulse to take her in my arms, and an even stronger one to invite her to my home, my kitchen, my bedroom. When would I see her again?

13

I wish I could turn down the volume on my heart

Maybe it had been the flowers in the yard. Flowers make me think of Kevin. Cars make me think of Kevin, so do football, fish 'n' chips, Beeston and Bridlington. So do rock gigs. He took me to see the Manic Street Preachers. Best big brother ever. I felt a bit low, that afternoon, thinking of how I'd lost it in the conversation at lunch, as I sat on the settee slowly sobering up, watching soap operas – at least there were some folk more miserable than me, I reflected. For all George's politeness and consideration towards me, I worried that my outpouring of emotion had put him off a second date – OK, I was finally starting to admit that it had been a date; otherwise, I wouldn't have felt so upset over it going so badly wrong. Why had he been so quiet on the drive home? He must have been itching to drop me off and get back to his grown-up life down south.

Sharon came round with Danny. She, of course, was all 'How did it go?' – excited for me, at least to begin with.

'Well, I think I do like him,' I replied. 'You spotted it before me, but, well, I think I messed it all up anyway.' I gave her a brief summary of our chat and the drive home.

'Sounds like you were just being emotional and honest. If he doesn't respect that, he's not worth bothering with,' she said. 'You look hot, he'll have noticed that. Give it time.'

'Thanks. There'll be lots of time, I think,' I replied. 'How was Danny?'

'Fine. They played nicely together, the two of them.'

'That's good.'

'When will the man bring me his fire engine?' asked Danny.

'Oh, I'll ask him next time,' I replied. 'He has to go to London specially for it.'

'OK, Mum,' he said, and dashed off to find his truck.

I was astounded to receive a text around eight in the evening – well, not to receive one, because there's often one going off, setting the phone to ping or bleep, depending on the sound I have. I assumed it would be Sharon or Mum. The surprise was that it was from George. It was all very proper: correct spelling, full stops and capital letters and all that. It went something like:

I really enjoyed our lunch, and it was a most fascinating discussion. I hope that we're able to meet again before long. I have to be back in Holbeck next weekend, so maybe we could meet again?

It was hardly flirtatious, and he was still only a friend, but my heart started thumping so hard I could hear it, and I wished I could turn down the volume, like you can on your phone. I wanted to reply straight away; but then I thought that I shouldn't, so as not to appear too desperate. Wait at least ten minutes, I told myself. I waited nine. Or maybe around seven.

Yes, it was lovely thanks. Sorry I went on so! Yes would like to meet again this weekend that would be nice Karen xx

Two kisses. Too much? I clicked 'send' anyway, and he replied straight back. Bronte, of course, was trying to read over my shoulder.

'Got a second date then?' she asked.

'None of your business,' I replied smartly.

'I'll take that as a "yes".'

'Cheeky.' She just grinned. So I added: 'How did you know it was George?'

'Body language,' she explained. 'You're all different when you're thinking about him.'

'Mmph,' I said. 'Lucky guess.'

'OK, we'll see how often I'm lucky, then.'

We texted each other several more times during the week; he said he was busy with work. Rebuilding his business, or dealing with bankruptcy, I wondered; not that it mattered. I was worrying about money myself that week, more than usual. The newspapers had been writing stuff about cutting tax credits, which sent a shiver of fear down my spine and created a horrible sinking feeling in my stomach, so maybe that was why the subject was in my head. I heard it on the news too.

His texts were the perfect distraction. They gave me hope. All were very friendly, passing the time of day or asking about my life. He didn't invite me for a meal out or anything, and so I was anxious that perhaps he thought I wasn't mature enough to be out with him in public again; worried that I would get merry and go off on some emotional subject, but he still seemed keen to call round all the same; said he had lots to do in the house but we'd be sure to have time for a cup of tea or sandwiches. I loved it most when we were exchanging texts in real time and I waited excitedly for his reply. I would feel real disappointment when he wrote that he had to go. On one occasion, that was me, because Danny had somehow gotten hold of the bread knife and was wandering around, pretending it was a sword. In the interactions with George, there was a sense that, if one of us tiptoed towards being openly flirtatious, we would tiptoe back again, but ever so gently, leaving me feeling reassured but slightly disappointed. For example:

Me: *I've stayed off the white wine since the weekend, you'll be pleased to hear. No more lipstick smudges on my cheek or the glass.*

Him: *Shame. The look suits you.*

Me: *What, messy and not making sense?*

Him: *Passionate, honest.*

Me: *Hair all over the place… splash of wine on my frock.*

Him: *It was an interesting discussion. I mean that. Looking forward to chatting more.*

See what I mean? Gentlemanly. Bit too much, if anything.

We met just for late Saturday morning coffee and biscuits as he had things to do for the house, and he wanted to visit his dad in Harrogate. I guessed that was all true, though I was a little miffed not to be invited out, but also relieved not to have the pressure of a date. I had counted off the days until he were to come; counted off the shifts, and the hours within each one, which was an established habit, but an even more anxious one that week, almost feverish like an illness. I had another Sunday shift, late afternoon and early evening, which was horrid as it kind of ruined the weekend, though perhaps not this one.

'You shivered as he walked past the window,' Bronte noted. She was very observant.

'No, I didn't,' I replied, blushing furiously, because I had. He knocked on the door. I must stop lying to my daughter, I thought to myself, as I rose to answer the door.

'Hello!' he said brightly, smiling with his dark brown eyes. He was only really handsome when he smiled; but he was very handsome as he did so. His hair was very dark and receding. He had a slightly heavy air about him, not athletic but with strong shoulders. His manner was so polite, it was quite exotic: he would say a full 'Hello' and 'Goodbye', never 'Hiya' or 'Seeya'. I found this strangely arousing, like meeting James Bond.

I had spent longer getting dressed than I would have done for going out, because I had to look cute without appearing to have made any effort at all. This can take far more effort than wearing a cocktail dress and maximising the slap. I had put just a bit of eye shadow on, and deep-cleansed my face. I had washed my hair, straightened it, then slightly un-straightened it, all with the attempt to give the impression that: 'This is how I look all casual-like, on a Saturday; I get up looking like this, honest,' but hopefully looking right sexy too. I was wearing a firmly padded bra, tight-fitting red top and high-waisted jeans, that were branded, secured for £2.50 from a charity shop in Otley.

Bronte had been looking after Danny as I was in the bathroom. 'Is that it?' she had said, as I appeared after forty-five minutes. 'I thought you were going to be looking like Jennifer Lawrence at the Oscars or summat.'

'It takes effort to look this casual,' I commented. 'Anyway, Jennifer Lawrence is blonde. I'm more like Gemma Arterton.'

'Folk have said that, I s'pose,' she said.

'Hello,' I replied, and invited him in. Bronte, mischievous as ever, suggested we could go to his place, and she could mind Danny for an hour. George raised an eyebrow, hopeful. 'More than welcome,' he said. 'If that's all right with you guys?'

'Sure,' I said.

As we walked the few steps to his place, I noticed it was the hatchback again, and there was a scratch and a bit of a dent near the back. The edge of the bare metal surrounded by flaky claret-coloured paint caught the sun, glinting in my eye.

We sat opposite each other at his circular kitchen table, which was a little too large for the room, so you had to push the chair in and wriggle round a little at certain junctures, such as where the fridge jutted out from the units. We were drinking delicious cappuccino from his gleaming new black and chrome machine that stood on the kitchen top and gurgled and hissed as it made the brew. There were some yummy Italian biscuits, and I ate rather too many of them, nervous like. The smell of coffee and cinnamon and fresh paint brought new life into our little street, I thought. It felt very continental – not that I'd been to the continent; just Tenerife once, with Darren and Bronte, before Danny arrived. Bronte was only eight then, and loved the warm sea.

'So, what's life like around here, then?' he asked. 'I've only seen it on match days before.'

'Well, you get a mix of folk,' I replied. 'Glad you've moved in, 'cos the tenants before were a bit funny; no problem to me but I never got to know them. Rita's next door and she's the best neighbour in the world. Her son Gary is twenty-seven, drives a van. Main dope dealer round here but Rita, bless her, thinks he does building and odd jobs. I don't want to tell her. S'pose he does help folk move furniture, now and then, and does a bit of gardening. And he's pretty laid back. That's about it.'

'So, you're happy here?'

'What?' I asked, slightly taken aback. 'Well, it's quite friendly, but no, I want a back garden. We were close to moving into a bigger place, me and Darren, but…'

'But?'

'Well, he'd run up debts that he hadn't told me about. Online betting: boxing matches, the footie, you name it. Five thousand pounds. I mean, thousands, not just a couple of hundred!'

'Well, I'm with you on that issue. It's an absolute scandal. You watch Sky Sports, a big live game, and just about every advert at half-time is some sports betting firm. I got my friend who's an MP to put down an EDM on the subject.'

'A what?'

'An Early Day Motion, in the Commons.'

'Hmm. Sounds like having a poo after breakfast,' I said. He giggled a little when I said that. He thought I was funny.

'It's a form of registering an issue. He got over a hundred signatures.'

'Doesn't get me my house, with a fifty-foot garden, mostly laid to lawn with a shed and flower borders, and room for a swing, which Bronte is too old for now anyway.'

'No.'

'Darren thought I was overreacting, but he couldn't see that it wasn't just about the money. I saw it as betrayal, not just of me but of Bronte and Danny as well; robbing them of stuff and opportunities. He was spending money, wasting money, on stupid sports bets that he never told me about; even owed money to payday lenders, though thankfully not loan sharks. And it wasn't just the money, it was the credit rating, I tried to explain to him, but he didn't really have a grasp of what that was; how it affected me, and Bronte, and Danny, and their prospects – not just him. So, I actually own the house, but the debts got put on the mortgage. So it's tight.'

'That is the best place for the debt,' he said. 'Lower interest and set against property.'

'If you know about politics and finances and that...' I began. I hesitated a little. Was I repeating the mistake of the week before, getting into deep stuff? I continued. 'Can you tell me if the government is serious about removing our tax credits?'

'Ah, well, you're talking to the right person. My company has advised employers on living wage strategies. So, what the government's talking about is moving from a low-wage, high-benefits economy to a high-wage, low-benefits one.'

'What? Are they cutting the tax credits or not? Because my family can't get by without them.'

'Well, I'm trying to explain how it's going to work; how it ought to work. You see, it's not fair that the taxpayer should subsidise mean employers, plus employers actually get better services and lower costs if they have better management and higher pay for workers...'

He sounded ever so keen. His eyes even lit up a bit, and he rocked forward on his chair, resting his elbows on the table, cradling the coffee cup with both hands, looking at me. I had wanted a straight yes-or-no answer, but he seemed to be getting into policy, or rather the thinking behind the policy. I only cared about the effects. But he did sound intelligent, and connected, and sexy. I wanted to be in that world of influence and culture and personal confidence.

'But what if they don't?' I asked.

'Hmm?'

'What if employers *don't* increase wages?' He seemed to grasp the issue, but not the point.

'Well, it's a no-brainer,' he explained. 'You can prove it all with stats. Expense is not the same as operating cost. Living wage economics is not a zero-sum game. The value add from engagement far outweighs extra short-term cost of a raise, if the strategy's right and the management's good, providing a win–win for all stakeholders.'

'Oh lovely,' I said, sarcastically but hopefully not too much so. I gave a bit of a smile. 'Tell you what, can you give me that in writing? I'll text it to my boss next time I'm in Morrisons.'

He laughed at that point. Then he looked very serious, also a little uncomfortable. 'I'm sorry, too much jargon. I am an idiot sometimes, get lost on the details and forget the bigger picture. Listen, what's the name of your employer?' he asked.

87

'Swish FM. It sounds like a radio station, but it's not. Nothing so exciting.'

'FM stands for Facilities Management,' he explained.

'I never even knew that,' I replied. 'Is that just a fancy term for cleaning and tidying?'

'Can be a bit more, but yes, I guess so.'

'They can be mean,' I said. 'If someone's off sick and you do more work to help out, they don't pay for the extra time you put in. So, we're not even getting minimum wage, some weeks.'

'That's outrageous!' he said. 'It's also against the law.' He seemed genuinely shocked. I just shrugged my shoulders, with a 'what can you do?' gesture.

'I shall look them up,' he said. He sounded determined.

'What, and have a word with the owners?'

'Sure. If I can get an intro.'

It was impossible to know if he were serious or not.

'I'd rather folk put pressure on the government to keep tax credits,' I said. 'Keeps me awake at night, worrying about that.'

'Well, I can't do much about that, I'm afraid. Not directly.'

'Sorry to get all serious, with politics and that. This coffee is delicious.'

'Not at all. I'm interested in policy stuff. Care for another cup?'

'Yes please!'

We chatted a bit more. Then he took me by surprise again. He had a tendency to do that. 'Um, Karen,' he began, sounding ever so serious. 'You're a great neighbour, and I'm down south a lot. I've had an extra front door key made. Would you mind popping in once or twice a week, just to tidy the post, maybe open the blinds? Please don't do any cleaning or anything. I'll return the favour.'

'Sure,' I replied. 'No bother to me. I work shifts so I could often call in middle of the day, for example.'

'Thanks. I appreciate that.'

'No problem.'

Secretly, I was elated. Apart from the trust placed in me, which made me feel drawn more closely to him and his world, I was always curious about other people's houses, and especially one belonging to George. I wondered if I would ever get invited to the one down south; the big semi-detached in Surrey, or whatever it was, assuming he was still able to afford it. I wondered how many rooms it had, and what sort of garden. As I walked the few steps back home I turned the key – a large Yale variety, pale gold in colour, with a square-ish shaped head – over and over in my hand, and for quite a few minutes afterwards, before finding a safe place for it in a kitchen drawer.

14

Money changes everything

On the Wednesday after I'd had lunch with Karen, I met my sister, Joy, for a midweek early evening meal, at a very exclusive place in the City that was her favourite, and where she knew the staff. When we received the bill, I reflected that the cost could have fed Karen's family for a month, thereabouts. For the first time in my adult life I began to feel uncomfortable about luxuries that I had always felt that I had earned, and thoroughly deserved. The wine was Puligny-Montrachet, from the vineyard of Millot Rougeot, 1986, a hot, dry October, subtler and more complex than some vintages, and a personal favourite of mine.

Mum had died in childbirth – not as rare in the modern developed world as you may think – but the baby survived. She was named Joy, and was six years younger than me. Her name was given despite the family being engulfed by grief, and this seemed to imbue her from birth with a keen awareness of the multiple paradoxes and counter-intuitive truths of human existence. It was she who warned me about the risks the bankers were taking. I ignored her, on the basis that I 'knew more' about the industry. She is the only person I have ever come across who's smarter than me. I read mathematics at King's College London, she read nano-quantum micro advanced theoretical physics and biology, or something like that, at Cambridge. She invented some things that she attempted to explain to me once or twice, to do with medical devices, and gained business experience by helping hi-tech start-ups in the Cambridge cluster. So being quite wealthy at a young age, with a little time to spare, I persuaded her to be Chair of the Board of my company; someone both to look out for me and hold me to account. Rather to my surprise, she accepted, and the role worked, which surprised some of my colleagues and advisers, though I tend to have a hunch about these things. So, we had a family business, for a while. She resigned when she took up another chairmanship of a life sciences firm, and when I opened up ownership of the business to new partners whose motives she felt were suspect. She seemed genuinely baffled that I was upset. 'It's a business decision, George. I'm still your sister. You should have kept yourself as sole shareholder.' If anything, she was kinder and more generous to me after that. Joy was still in her thirties, but always seemed slightly more mature than me. She was usually single, very ambitious and kept her sexuality and her relationships utterly secret. I thought better than to ask.

Joy had that air of absolute confidence, that only intellectual superiority combined with commercial acumen can produce. She didn't dress well, wasn't a good public speaker and swore on occasion. It didn't matter. Everyone was in awe. Everyone respected her choices and paid attention to what she said.

When I told her about Karen, I took myself by surprise. I didn't always find it easy to confide personal, romantic feelings with my sister, though she was the only person on the planet

91

with whom I could; and I was, after all, not in a relationship with Karen, so it still felt vaguely hypothetical. Yet Karen filled my thoughts to an extraordinary and persistent degree: while I was driving, while I was at the gym, while I was pretending to listen to a sales update at the Monday morning management meeting. I had texted her on the evening after our lunch – all polite, formal, unconfident of a reply. She wrote straight back. We exchanged further texts through the week, distracting me from work meetings, on occasion. They were chatty and mildly flirtatious at times. I had to maintain discipline not to be overly forward. The mere event of receiving a message from her thrilled me, but I did not wish to scare her away.

Joy was flatly unimpressed by the news. 'What, are you nuts? Things didn't work out with you and Clara, remember? You were worried an HR manager on fifty grand a year was a gold-digger, but now you want to date a single mum whose kids are on free school meals?'

'Well, I don't know if we'll have a relationship, she might reject me, but I can't get her out of my head. She's so strong and vulnerable, naïve and wise all at the same time. Intelligent but not highly educated, as far as I can tell; or maybe she is self-taught. Interesting titles on her book shelf.'

'So you're planning a Pygmalion act. Version ninety-three of the midlife crisis. Power trip disguised as charity, disguised as love.'

'No!!' I protested. 'I'm not planning a rescue. I'm not planning anything. And as for the gold-digging thing, well, I've kind of disguised the fact that I'm well off. I've bought a terraced house. I only take the hatchback up there – well, since the first time.'

'Ah, the fake crisis move. Weeds them out.'

'Yes, I mean no! There's nothing manipulative about it...' I began.

'There's nothing manipulative about deceit as a means to begin a relationship?' asked Joy, a genuinely quizzical look on her face.

Her directness was generally welcome, but could be a nuisance at times. I replied: 'Well, it's more honest in its way; we have the breathing space to get to know one another as people before the money thing gets in the way.'

'Money changes everything, as the great Cyndi Lauper put it,' she replied. 'So how are you going to handle it when she discovers that you have enough assets to buy her entire street and the one next to it?'

'That's an exaggeration,' I began. There was a stilted pause. I looked down at the cold squid rings on my plate. 'Well, actually, maybe it's not. One bridge at a time, I suppose. You worried I'm going to get hurt?'

'No! I'm worried she is, the poor lass. She needs to find a nice plumber or a supermarket manager with enough earnings for a little semi.'

'Bit snobbish, isn't it? You and I come from a similar background to her.'

'It's just being pragmatic. We built our way up slowly, with education. It's one thing when two worlds collide, but you're talking about different universes. Beeston is a different planet. No. Let's change the metaphor. It's like an aqualung diver. If she's down too deep and comes up too quickly, the blood pressure explodes and she gets paralysed. It's called the bends. Or...' she hesitated. 'It's like the three laws of thermodynamics.'

'No, it's not.'

'The first law is: you can never win; you can only break

even. The second law is: you can only break even at absolute zero. The third law is: you can never reach absolute zero.'

'*What?!*' I asked, dumbfounded.

'It's not the most apt metaphor for social status and romantic connection,' she conceded.

'For the most intelligent woman on the planet, you do talk some bollocks sometimes.' I said.

'Yea well, it's the wine. What I'm trying to say is,' she recommenced. She was quite uncharacteristically drunk, her longish mid-brown wavy hair had fallen into the wine glass, and she did not remove it immediately. She must have had a cocktail or three before we met; I had arrived a little late. 'Absolute zero,' she continued. 'The true, pure meeting of two souls isn't really possible.'

'Well, there's as much chance with Karen as with anyone, then,' I said.

'OK. The aqualung imagery was more accurate.'

'Too late,' I said, mildly triumphant. I hadn't won an argument with her since she was six; even so, she wasn't all wrong. 'Shall we get the bill?'

On Saturday morning I drove back up, starting very early, and had a large cooked breakfast at Leicester Forest East motorway services. At some point between Leicester and Nottingham the miles left fell below a hundred. Just seventy miles from Karen now, I mean Leeds, I was thinking... Then a bit later: just fifty. Then I could see Sheffield's Meadowhall Shopping Centre from an elevated section of the M1; its drab greenish spires like a mockery of a cathedral. Only thirty miles. My spirits were lifted up higher in my breast with each passing mile. It would be customary at this point to observe that it was like being a teenager again, but the truth was that I had never felt like this: not ever. I had no precedent, no reference point, no plan, no idea. I was just a huge impulse with a human being in tow.

Her blue-grey eyes did blaze as she said hello when she answered the door, and I felt warmed and reassured that I had not been completely imagining the attraction she felt for me. Though she was dressed casually, I could see she had made some effort. It was her canny daughter Bronte, playing Cupid perhaps, who offered to look after the little one while Karen came round to mine. We drank cappuccino and ate Italian biscuits at the kitchen table. She surprised me again, asking about the government's pay and benefits policy. I was ready with what I thought was the decisive argument, about the commercial good sense of employers paying the living wage, a subject on which I knew the evidence, but she was only anxious about losing tax credits. I got carried away with a little speech and deployed a bit of management jargon – a recurring weakness. She made a sharp satirical quip by way of reply. It hadn't fully occurred to me that the margin between coping and not-quite-coping in any interim phase in a transition to a living-wage economy could mean devastation for some families.

The little speech I gave had gone down perfectly well in management conferences and briefings to think tanks, but I quickly learned that discussing low-wage policies was very much tougher with someone who actually was on a low wage. With good grace, she changed the subject, and even apologised, still somewhat abashed at her emotions the week before over lunch. I could have tried to explain to her that she needn't have bothered; that it was precisely during her tender effusion that I had begun to fall in love with her.

I had had a duplicate front door key cut and asked if she would mind gathering the post and just checking on the place from time to time. I had worried that it might seem impertinent, or something of an imposition, but she appeared quite delighted.

As I reached Toddington Services on the way home, checking the time via a wristwatch rather than the car display or radio, I noticed I was wearing the cheap slimline option, purchased for high-crime areas – I once had a watch cut from my wrist by a laughing teenage mugger on a main street in Lima, who rapidly disappeared into the ghetto – which meant that I had left the Hublot in Leeds, probably on the bedside table. It was probably valuable enough for Karen to sell via eBay and raise enough to clear her mortgage, take the family to Florida for a month and buy some new outfits. I hated myself for letting that thought run through my head, but, once it had done so, I couldn't undo it. In any case, it wasn't so much that I did not trust her; my concern was rather the opposite. I was worried that she would think that I had left it as a test. Karen was someone I trusted instinctively, and I had a good track record. I never relied entirely on instinct, but sometimes let it influence me. Your most rapid, instinctive feelings tend to lead to your very best decisions – or your very worst. But there was something more, I realised: her good opinion of me was worth far more than any watch, or property, or, well, anything.

Would it be worth returning to retrieve it? I decided not. The round trip would add 300 miles to the journey, and make me exhausted for the early part of the week. I had some big meetings and potential contracts coming up. Poor decisions would cost me more than the value of the watch. I carried on home.

15

Home alone. Just not my home...

Bronte had drawn my dream again. Just a pencil sketch this time, of a woman opening a large double door with a 'No entry' sign clearly visible, and with a cheeky, knowing look on her face as she glanced over her shoulder. It was a clever, funny drawing, and her teachers loved it. In my dream, I had entered a house I knew I wasn't supposed to be in, and I tiptoed about, thrilled and scared at the same time. There were hidden passages, and secret gardens. Again, there was an erotic theme that took me unawares. I couldn't recall exactly who caused this or why, but it was all linked to being in forbidden territory. As I awoke, I was intensely aroused. What was the matter with me? I asked myself.

The only thing more spooky than Bronte guessing my dream, was that both the dream and the drawing seemed to predict what I was about to do. I had left it a couple of days before entering next door, despite itching with curiosity. By the Wednesday morning I reckoned it would be appropriate. He had had the door replaced with a solid, shiny wooden one, coated with layers and layers of varnish, smooth and luscious beneath my fingers as I slid the large key in and turned. It opened effortlessly. There was not much post; just a couple of official-looking ones that I picked up. I went to the kitchen first, and placed the envelopes on the circular table with its patterned chrome surface, like in a continental café. Would it be OK to make myself a cappuccino? I made an effort, but put the capsule in the wrong way, or something, and it didn't really work. I became nervous, unduly so, worrying that I had broken it. I checked the fridge, which was nearly empty, but contained a bottle of white wine and some milk. I had best take the milk with me, I reckoned, as it would be off by the weekend. I placed it on the table.

Next, I checked the front room. Everything was immaculate. The settee and chair were matching; they had a cast-iron frame but very comfortable cushions. I sat in one, and watched the sunlight glinting off the glass-topped coffee table that stood on a classy-looking ancient rug. The floor was highly polished wood, also basking in the warm sun. The TV screen was on the wall – not too big. There was an expensive-looking music system, and rows and rows of CDs, nearly all classical. I ran my fingers over them, just to feel more in contact with George. Then I did the same with the spines of the books on the bookshelf. At school, I felt intimidated by literature, but I had begun reading a few years earlier, and found some authors I liked. It all started when I saw the Bridget Jones movie and I overheard a couple of people say the book was better, so I gave it a try and it was – she was much less pathetic in the book, much more smart, so I liked her and started to read more books. Not only romances but the occasional serious book too, though there were a few I had bought that I hadn't got round to reading. I found it was a great way to pass time when on the bus and I was lucky in that I didn't get travel sick. I decided to try *Jane Eyre* once and I liked her.

I didn't recognise many of George's authors. There were many in French and Spanish, and there were some properly serious English ones, such as Dickens and Shakespeare and the Brontës but loads of others whose names I didn't know. I ran my fingers along the spines and some of the covers. My fingertips were tingling with a kind of magic. I wanted his confidence and learning to seep up into my soul through my fingertips as I caressed his books. They even smelled nice. Reluctantly I let my hands drift away from the shelf and I walked into the hall. There was nothing left to be done, and there was no need to go upstairs, but I wanted to, all the same. Softly, as if trying to evade detection, I tiptoed up the soft, newly carpeted stairs. There was, I told myself, a theoretical possibility that a burglar had let himself in by the first-floor window, so I had best check.

This would be George's bedroom, I guessed. This was one room I definitely must not enter, I told myself. His private space. I went in.

There was a large double bed that filled a good part of the room, a wardrobe, a mirror fixed to the wall and a tiny bedside table with nothing on but a rather bulky, old-fashioned looking watch. There was no bedside lamp; he had had lights fitted into the wall above the headboard. The floor, like downstairs, was this beautiful polished dark wood, and he had put another lovely old rug down. I walked around the side of the bed quietly, almost with reverence like in a church. I then noticed that there was a very small shelf underneath the mirror with nothing but a bottle of cologne: just aftershave, but it was George's aftershave. I got up and lifted the bottle carefully, nervous lest I should knock it to the hard floor and it would shatter. I leaned over and inhaled deeply. It smelled of him, of course, and I was suddenly intoxicated. I sat back on the bed and then, quite instinctively, undid my sandals and lifted up my feet onto the bed, and then half turned to prop up a pillow and laid back on it. I imagined him entering the room at that moment. He would be pleased to find me, I was sure, delighted even. I felt excited, as I was certain he would be.

I felt warm. I wasn't sure if it actually was warm in the room, but I felt warm, almost hot, and quite giddy. I removed my top, impulsively and because it was daring; exactly because I shouldn't, removing it slowly and ceremoniously, as if for show. I shocked myself for doing so. I almost felt compelled by the giddy atmosphere of just being in his space. I had been such an obedient, dutiful mother for so long, with little fun apart from drinks out with Sharon from time to time, and no sensual experience at all. I hadn't even cheated on Darren, despite his unreliable behaviour, and quite a few guys coming on to me from time to time, one or two of whom were hot. Nearly all the time, given my situation, I was in role completely as a mum, as a shopper and as a worker, and I hadn't felt sexy for a long time (except in my dreams); but everyone is going to, from time to time; no matter how deprived in monetary terms, and especially if you're completely deprived of any physical touch, because that's human nature; and of course the more you've missed out, the more intense the feelings can be, especially when they creep up on you. You can go for days, or even weeks, without a conscious sexy thought, but the feelings are going to ambush you eventually, when you're least expecting it, when you're just doing some regular everyday thing – you know, for example, sneaking into your hot crush's bedroom, smelling his Armani cologne and stretching out on his expensive duvet, taking your top off, writhing around, picturing in your head everything you want him to do to you, one day. We've all been there.

Everyone likes to fantasise when they're home alone – as I was. It just wasn't *my* home. I traced my fingers over the outline of my lacy bra, imagining that it was George's fingers. It seemed so wrong that this body was only ever appreciated by myself, or from afar. Was I tempting fate? Perhaps you shouldn't indulge your fantasies, I told myself, as it raises expectations. Then again, I could just enjoy the moment, which was intensely thrilling, as I let my imagination pleasure me.

I ran my fingers of one hand down over my belly button, until they reached the top of my jeans. I caressed the button with my fingertips. If George were here, this is what he would do to me, I was thinking. I slid my head down the pillow a little so that I was lying flat on my back, and began to relax more, feel less abashed and less ashamed. It really was an immensely comfortable bed – even and smooth, soft but at no point sagging. The plain cream-coloured duvet was clean and deep. I liked the smell of the cologne, still lingering faintly in the air after I had lifted the large glass stopper in the bottle and replaced it. If only he were here. Maybe next time, he will be, I thought as my fingers danced over my zip. Maybe this is what *he'll* be doing before long…

Suddenly I felt colder, self-conscious and a little ashamed. Maybe there had been a noise, or a cool draught. I sat up, replacing my top, and looked about. Everything looked the same, but it felt suddenly different, like someone had been watching me, though there was obviously no one around. I shivered a little and then bent down to find my sandals, placing them on my feet and buckling them up. I felt guilty, but only ever so slightly. I touched the cologne bottle very lightly once more, and then left the room. I walked down the stairs and paused, for no particular reason, on the bottom step. At this moment I noticed a small cream-coloured oblong bit of

101

apparatus, screwed into the wall, near the ceiling. There wasn't much doubt as to what it was. George had sensibly placed a security camera directed at the front door. It seemed natural, and perfectly in its place, but, as I crossed the threshold back home, I froze with anxiety, my body going all cold and then suddenly hot again as my cheeks burned.

What if there had been a camera in the bedroom?

Oh. My. God.

I could let myself back in to look, of course, but I decided not to, for fear of what I might find and also, given how tiny cameras could be made these days, and how they could be disguised (or maybe that was only in James Bond films), I was very aware that if I appeared to find nothing it would give me false comfort.

I had an afternoon shift, so Danny was with grandparents until after Bronte was home and could babysit. I would be back mid-evening. So, I had an hour or two before going to work. I placed George's key safely back in the kitchen drawer. What if he had been watching me, live or in a recording? I would be mortified. Then again, turning the possibility over and over in my mind, maybe he'd just be turned on. I awarded myself a little smile. I began to feel turned on by the thought of him watching me, and the thought of him being aroused in turn. Oh, how deliciously naughty you can be in your most private thoughts.

At least I alternated between this little fantasy and a vague feeling of panic. I decided to text him, all normal, and hoped to receive a normal reply. I waited and waited and waited for, ooh, nearly ninety agonising seconds, before I received a cheery message from him. I just wrote that all was in order in the house, he'd left his watch by the bed, nothing untoward. He replied to say simply that that was good to hear, have a good week and so on. I was on the settee at the time, and just sank a bit deeper into it, with relief. Of course, he could have been watching me but was too gentlemanly to say anything. But that would also be good, wouldn't it?

16

Keeping watch

Monday morning, and I noticed a little dent in the nearside back panel of the hatchback, courtesy of having bashed into a large plant pot on the gravel drive at the Surrey abode a week or so back. It was uncharacteristic of me both to have a silly accident and to wait so long before organising a repair, but I'd never been in love before. I was teaching myself to become accustomed to the licence I decided it could give me: to become a little more spontaneous and disorganised in my daily life. It was exhilarating to experience the first crush of a teenager again – or, rather, for the first time, as I was an emotional and sexual virgin all through my actual teens and a short way into my third decade. I did not know if it was regression or rebirth; if I were becoming emotionally stunted or if I were only fully awakening for the first time. Much less did I care. What happens is what happens.

During the Monday morning management meeting I entertained myself by doodling a giant 'K' in my notebook, and then another one, and another one. I gazed briefly out at the River Thames. The moorhens were back, and I was briefly fascinated by how such a delicate-looking water bird could withstand the ferocious current, swimming and swimming to get to the ingeniously crafted nest aboard the floating rubbish-collector. The struggle, the yearning: stronger than any tide. The conversation in the room was about the details of a contract that I had delegated to others, and I let my thoughts drift; or rather, they pulled me away. My feelings were all upside down. Before, I had associated joy and exhilaration with control and autonomy: turning eighteen, living away from home for the first time, getting my first salaried job, first promotion, setting up my own company, buying a fast car, driving it. Now, I was letting go, down the diamond ski run, speeding away to where it may take me, to ecstasy or ruin or both.

I became dimly aware that someone was trying to attract my attention.

'George, I think that call is for you? Are you with us?'

'Mmm?' I said. There were a few murmurs of laughter.

'I was asking,' said Tony. 'Do we have the in-house resource if the Britco contract is signed and we're starting next month? Or are you just worrying about Leeds United's inevitable descent into tier three?'

'Which contract again?'

'Britco.'

'Yes, well no. Maybe just get the one freelancer in. Helena's free, she called me the other day.'

'Good. Next item?'

Susannah, an established and highly competent consultant, spoke: 'George, we need to talk about the Technik contract…'

Uncharacteristically, I interrupted her. I knew that I hadn't been on the top of my game with that client, and I felt defensive: 'No worries, Susannah. They're my contact. I'm meeting with them this week.'

'But…' she began.

'I've got it in hand,' I said. 'But email me your concerns beforehand. I want to talk about a potential client. Swish FM… I think we should look into them.'

'Who do we know there?' asked Luke, the one I didn't trust.

'No one.'

'Then why? Who? Where's our in?'

'I'll make the initial contact. They're seriously sub-optimal,' I replied. I was actually waffling, as I had carried out very little research on the company, but managed to sound assured.

'Based on what data?' he asked.

'They're typical low-pay, low-productivity, mid-cap clients. That's where the biggest gains are, the happiest clients. You can return them a few mill in the first six months, if they employ thousands. Facilities management and hospitality; we need to focus on those sectors, especially mid-sized firms. Some of the bigger companies are getting their act together. Bad management is not nearly as fashionable as it used to be, sadly. Some people can actually get by without us. They read *The Management Shift* by Vlatka Hlupic, and they're away.'

'So,' asked Tony, checking a few company details on his tablet computer. 'Nothing to do with the fact that their head office is in LS1, the home county? You just want to arrange meetings for a Friday before match day?' He wore a mischievous-friendly grin.

'Sara,' I turned to our human resources director. 'Can you remind me, is it really against anti-discrimination legislation to sack someone for being a Chelsea supporter?'

'Probably not if he's white, straight, male, etc., George,' she replied, deadpan as you like. 'But there's this other legal concept called "unfair dismissal". Do we have to go through that again?'

She added this question in her best faux-patronising voice, and there was laughter around the table. Tony joined in. He knew that I liked him, and that it was the ones I didn't trust that I didn't engage with in banter. At the end of the meeting, I sought out Susannah, to apologise for cutting her short, and repeated the invitation to email me any concerns. She agreed but gave me the most icy look.

I returned to my desk and, stubborn and defiant, ignored the polite warnings of my colleagues. I looked up the chief executive of Swish FM, finding his LinkedIn profile quite easily: Derek Cooper, a moderately overweight business manager with a Bruce Willis hairdo, probably overconfident, judging by the smile in his photo, with a finance background. I recalled also that there was a business reporter on the *Yorkshire Post* who owed me a favour, so if Swish rejected my overtures, I wondered if a bit of publicity on their working practices, their breaches of minimum wage law, might nudge the business our way, and prompt them to improve pay for Karen and her colleagues.

It was on the Wednesday that I had a little bleep on the mobile phone that I carried with me – the one linked to the security systems in my house. A motion sensor had been triggered, indicating that someone had entered the Leeds place. I assumed it was Karen, and switched to the tablet computer, with its larger screen, to pick up the live feed, taking it into my private office and closing the door. Sure enough, she was entering the front door, stooping to pick up the few items of mail. I only had three cameras: hall, sitting room and bedroom. There being no back windows, it didn't seem necessary for the kitchen. I felt rather touched to see her diligently checking the place, even tidying things and brushing a little dust away as she did so, with her delicate fingers. Then she went upstairs; not strictly necessary, I thought, but I smiled at the conscientiousness – or perhaps audacity – of the gesture. I switched the stream to the master bedroom. I could see the Hublot on the bedside table. As Karen entered, she ignored it completely, but instead seemed curious about my bottle of cologne on a shelf. She even opened it, and bent over to test the fragrance. Then she sat on the bed, on the far side, with her back to me. She leaned over to one side, her right-hand side, and was clearly fiddling with something with her right hand, presumably removing her footwear; indeed, she then repeated the movement on the other side, lifted up her bare feet and lay back on the bed, half sat-up, with shoulders and part of her back on the pillow.

I felt slightly taken aback that she would enter all parts of the house, not just check the post and give a quick look over the ground floor. Her presence in my bedroom, and her interest in my personal possessions, might have caused me to feel mild affront at her invasion of my personal space, but instead I felt something closer to exhilaration. Maybe she's just tired, I reflected, enjoying a rare moment of solitude away from work, chores and children. If she slept a while, that would be fine; I would feel proud to have created a quiet space for her to rest. I felt touched that she should be so relaxed in the environment, reassured that she had treated all the items with respect and moderately excited that she should be in my bedroom. I took my eyes away from the live feed for a moment, and returned to a work document, but struggled to concentrate. When I switched my attention once more to the link, my pulse quickened. Karen had removed her top. Removed it. Completely. Did I really see that? I closed down the window, then opened it again. There she was, reclining fully, wearing nothing but a bra and jeans (and presumably knickers). Her delicate fingers, having found their way along the smooth wooden polished shelf in the hall and the cold glass stopper of my cologne bottle, were now running along the edge of her bra, and down to her belly button. She had closed her eyes. She was lying on my bed, smelling my aftershave. Might she, was she, could she be, actually, thinking of me?

Oh my word. Should I continue watching? Was I intruding on her privacy, or she upon mine? I closed the screen, embarrassed but also, I had to reflect, more aroused than I had ever been, or even considered possible. There was a knock on the door, to which I responded with alacrity and relief, keen to return to corporate ordinariness, trying desperately to banish erotic thoughts by concentrating fiercely on themes designed to quell arousal: the possibility of a Greek exit from the Eurozone; Leeds United's erratic away form; Leeds United's erratic home form; exchange rate risks over doing business in Argentina; the appalling design of automated customer service systems and how they needed redesigning from top to bottom. Almost there, I thought. The caller was Vicky, to remind me of my 3.30 p.m. meeting. I called her in, staying seated and behind my desk, just to be on the safe side.

'Thanks, Vicky,' I said. 'Helena likes strong coffee, without milk or sugar.'

'Right you are, George. You OK?'

'Yes, fine.'

'Good, I'll show her in when she comes.'

'She's always punctual.'

Vicky gave me a mildly puzzled look before turning on her heels and departing. I almost blurted out that I hadn't been looking at porn, in case she had noted an agitated and mildly guilty air; and, of course, I hadn't – just something a thousand times sexier. There was a ping denoting an incoming text message. It was from Karen, and my already-racing heart accelerated:

Hi George, just calling in to say I checked over the whole house, all in order, picked up your mail. BTW u left your watch by the bed, in case you were looking for it. See you at the weekend? Karen xx

I replied:

Hi Karen – good to hear, and thank you! Quick message as I'm just going into a meeting. Yes, would love to see you at the weekend. George x

Only one kiss – from me that's a big gesture; though would she know that? An hour later, after the meeting, I turned on the live feed for the bedroom. Karen, of course, had long gone, but I wanted to catch a trace, a ghost of her presence – to glimpse a few of her molecules on the sheet or the bottle of cologne. She had taken the trouble to smooth the surface of the duvet cover and pillows. Everything was unblemished though not, I reflected with excitement, untouched.

17

What will the señora have?

'What'll you have?' George asked, all confident and authoritative, like he were the owner of the place. I loved that.

'Mmm, I don't know where to begin!' I replied, scanning my eye down the menu. I was almost dizzy at the choice: seafood, aubergine dishes, Iberian ham – surely, I reckoned, tastier than mere 'ham'. In the end I just said: 'Maybe a little veggie starter, the aubergine thingy, and prawns for the main course.'

'Good selection,' he said, approvingly.

He then spoke some fluent Spanish to the waiter, which I loved; not just about the menu but probably some other stuff too. So clever, so sexy. I picked up that he called me *señora*, which was cool, and made me feel sophisticated, in a strange, shallow sort of way.

'So, I guess you wouldn't want to take me back to the place we went to before, after my performance,' I said, sipping the wine, slowly this time.

He looked puzzled. 'Performance?'

'Well, you know, me getting tipsy and emotional, before you hardly knew me.'

'As I said, please don't apologise. You were charming, heartfelt, genuine.' He was looking down at his glass as he began saying this, which unsettled me slightly, thinking he was 'just saying it', but then he lifted his head and looked directly at me, and into me, in a warm and intimate way that thrilled me all the way to my bones. I felt relaxed and excited at that moment, all at the same time.

'I just thought we'd try somewhere different,' he explained.

It was the Saturday evening immediately after the Wednesday when I had been in his bedroom. Any nervousness over the possibility that he may have seen me, or otherwise had 'known' that I had been there on his bed, had disappeared from my mind, or almost disappeared.

Leeds city centre was always simmering on a Saturday evening, sometimes boiling over. This restaurant was in an area between the river and the Corn Exchange. It had an edgy feel, where you had both the smart set and the stag dos. There'd be middle-aged couples on the way to the theatre, and lads just back from the footie. Everyone had an opinion and a drink. Normally I would just be walking by, gazing in with longing at the diners, or the choices on the menu pinned up on the outside. Now, I had a paper one in my hands, browsing at leisure. The place was full, and at times we had to raise our voices slightly to be heard. I had put on a posh frock, plenty of make-up and my best high heels. It felt tremendously good, after all the years of scrimping and saving and bus rides and inexpensive treats, to feel all middle class for a change, an equal with the smart set; to have finally arrived, if only for a few hours. You learn to seize and treasure your moments, and keep them alive in memories. I looked around at the large bar and restaurant area, which was open-

112

plan and modern, but in a rustic, authentic sort of way with lots of wooden features. I tried to memorise lots of details about the décor, about the dishes I chose, about what George was wearing and what he said, mentally placing them all in my head, preparing for my future memory, like recording a TV programme you can watch again and again. There was a handsome young couple – younger than me. He was white with lots of product in his blond hair, but in a stylish way; she was black with beautiful long cornrow locks and a chic outfit. They were chatting quietly, intimately. Footballer and pop star, I reckoned, fantasising. Maybe *she* was the footballer and *he* was the rock star! That's possible, these days, I reflected. I committed the image to memory, in any case, completing the scene for my future recall.

'I like the way you've done your house,' I said, immediately wondering if I should have introduced a potentially awkward subject. 'I take it your watch was still by the bed, I just left it where it was.'

'Yes, thanks,' he replied. 'I have another one, but thanks for letting me know. And for checking on everything, and tidying things. I do have a security camera, just on the front door, but it helps that you tidy the mail, open and close the shutters now and then, that sort of thing. Like I said, please don't do any cleaning or chores, and I owe you a favour!'

At the mention of the words 'security camera' my pulse rate leaped up briefly, but then I relaxed as he mentioned that it was only the one for the front door. But then I began to panic again, thinking: was he just saying that to spare me embarrassment? Had he brought the subject too obviously into the conversation, this 'There's only the front door camera' thing? Then again, if he *had* seen me, sniffing his cologne, lying half naked on his bed, touching myself, and was cool with it, that was good, wasn't it? So, if there was no camera there, it was good. And if there had been, maybe that was even better. I began to feel this strange, giddy feeling in his presence both of being secure and also going on an adventure. As well as collecting images of that night to store in my memory, I was starting to imagine scenes from the near future: a late-night kiss, and embrace, running my fingers down his chest... Another glass of wine and I was positively hoping he had seen me that afternoon and was turned on by the sight.

Sharon had brought Jayden over to mine for a sleepover, and was watching the kids. She had been in the bathroom with me as I got ready. 'I can always stay over here with Bronte and the boys, sleep in your bed in case you get lucky,' she had said with a wink, that I saw in the mirror, as I was putting on the lipstick. I gave a little start, causing a bright scarlet smudge on my cheek. I gave her a look, and said: 'Look what you've made me do, with your filthy one-track mind' – but with a grin, and she just giggled. I wiped the stray lipstick off my cheek and started again.

'Well,' I said to him. 'Maybe that's the one good thing about living in a back-to-back. No back door or window for the burglars to get in.'

'You are amazing, you know,' he said to me, looking directly into my eyes with even more intensity. I began to shiver with pleasure inside.

I held the gaze for a while, then looked away, over towards the window. I had been expecting him to say something about security at home: locks and windows and so on. 'What do you mean?' I asked.

He hesitated, obviously deciding to choose his words with care. 'You have this vibrancy, this spirit, despite...' He paused.

Ah, that was it, he was trying to refer to living in a small terraced house as a single mum without sounding patronising. I decided to help him out: 'It is a struggle at times,' I said. 'I

114

make no bones about it, being a single mum, limited income, but you have to have hope, don't you? You seize moments. And I have Bronte. And Danny, obviously, though he's too little to help out in a practical way.'

'The three of you are astounding. You have more joy than most people I know. You'd be amazed at how miserable some rich folk are.'

'Singing helps.'

'Hmm?'

'Bronte and I sing. Together. On the bus, in the park, when we're doing the washing-up. We sing harmonies, make up our own lines for some of our favourite songs. Sometimes, when we're in the mood and on form and in tune, it's like you're floating. It's wonderful. Then we giggle afterwards and have a hug. That's how she gets to interpret my dreams, I think. Maybe rich people don't have to sing to keep their spirits up, because their spirits are already up. Or they just hum a tune when they're looking at all their savings in their accounts. So, yeah, we sing a lot. Maybe it's joy, maybe it's desperation. But I love it because I feel close to Bronte that way.'

'You must sing for me, sometime. Both of you. I'd like that.'

I think I just smiled at that point. He seemed so genuine and caring. I wasn't sure that I would want to sing for him, if it were a performance, because to me it was always a private thing, just me and Bronte, our private language. Could I let George into our world? I was starting to think of it the other way around: could I begin to think of leaving him out? Too soon, I told myself, too soon; yet still it felt right.

He picked up the bill. I had made a gesture, but he waved me away. By way of compromise, I left a fiver as a tip. We shared a taxi home, both of us on the back seat. I left my hand quite close to his; they were both rested on the space between us. I lifted mine up, and rummaged with both hands in my handbag, pretending to search for something. This gave me an opportunity to place my hand back down, a bit closer to his. He fidgeted ever so slightly with his hand, such that his little finger lightly brushed mine, the tiniest touch giving me a wave of pleasure inside. He had made a couple of observations about the traffic, or the weather, or both, but we also shared a few moments of silence.

As we got out of the taxi in our street the air felt suddenly cooler and I shivered a little, my bare shoulders exposed to the gentle breeze. He leaned over to kiss me, and there was an awkward moment when it was unclear whether he was aiming for the mouth or cheek. That's a very, very big difference at that sort of stage in the relationship. Sometimes, even, I felt for the man in that situation, as it's all down to him. I just held my face steady, so he kissed me on the lips, briefly, tenderly, and it was intoxicating, uplifting; there was more communication between us in that instant than in the conversations.

He took a slight step back and held my gaze. 'What a lovely evening.'

'For me too,' I replied.

'Well goodnight,' he said.

I was disappointed, but too nervous to make a move myself. 'Goodnight,' I replied, and turned slowly to let myself in.

I gave Sharon a rapid description of the evening, talking non-stop for a few minutes, leaving nothing important out. She just rolled her eyes and said: 'He's obviously a bit shy and a bit proper but absolutely crazy about you. Go on,' she said. 'Send him a message.'

'He might be asleep.'

She let out a cry of exasperation. 'Oh, Karen, you really know nothing about men, do you? Or, indeed, other humans. He kissed you not fifteen minutes ago. Send him a message. Quick, while he's still up!'

'OK!' I laughed, with nerves, I think. I texted him. He texted right back.

18

The waiting room

How much of one's life is spent waiting? For a train, for a date, for a telephone call, for an email, for a meeting. After my interview with Helena – she was available for hire, we hired her; what a refreshingly intelligent, pleasant, uncomplicated person to do business with! – I was waiting for the end of the working day, unusually for me. Then I was impatient to get home. The central London flat was rented out, so I was on the slow, crawling commuter train out of Waterloo. The first-class carriage is just as slow. Once home I went for a short cycle ride, exercised in my personal gym, tried to concentrate on a book, then a movie.

These were all just different compartments of the one large waiting room that I inhabited, consisting of a narrow corridor of London and Surrey plus a slice of the motorway network, in the days that stretched before me, longing for my next meeting with Karen. The wait went on. Most of our thoughts are about the past and the future and we forget that life is lived in the present, and that the past and the future don't really exist. Or is it the other way around? Is life nothing more than fond memories, painful regrets, wild optimism, fear and dread? Is it 'the present' that is the illusion? How long does it take to make a decision? Less than a second, some say, but the consequences last for the rest of your days.

Sometimes, you choose the waiting room you're in; but sometimes the room chooses you. By late Wednesday evening there were approximately sixty-two hours until I would meet Karen again, depending on the traffic that coming Saturday. This was 3,720 minutes, or 223,200 seconds. In two hours' time, it would be 3,600 minutes, sixty times sixty. This was one of my favourite numbers, though my favourite of all was 2,520, which is 360 times seven, and 420 times six, and is the smallest number divisible by every integer from one to ten. It would always puzzle me as a young man that most people didn't think like this. A preoccupation of my life had been: What are numbers? Karen's had been: What is life? I so needed her in mine.

Performing such mental calculations was a good way of passing time spent on the running machine. I was knowledgeable of the Mesopotamian origins of our sexagesimal system for measuring time, contrasting with the decimal numeral system of Arabic origin, and was capable of delivering an informed summary of the subject should anyone care to listen (I discovered that few did, at dinner parties and the like; it certainly wasn't the high point of the most recent date I had had, some six months before, with an earnest art dealer from Kensington who loved cats). Then I calculated my average speed in kilometres per hour, based on distance and time elapsed; of course, the running machine would have done that for me, at the pressing of a button, but I preferred to work it out myself, keep myself mentally sharp.

I returned to the question of the remaining sixty-two hours

and how I ought to regard them. It was surely a significant amount of wasted time if I categorised them as simply waiting? Would it not be healthier to regard those hours and minutes as representing opportunities for recreation, and for advancement of the business? But if the latter, was I minimising the intensity, the momentous impact, of seeing Karen again? What purpose was served by seeking to dull those ecstatic moments that seemed to me at the time, and since, to be not merely a high point of one's life, but its whole purpose? The waiting is not futile, perhaps; it may serve a purpose; its very tedium accentuates the intensity of *those* moments, and of your life. Waiting is part of the architecture of high human emotion. On the other hand, perhaps she had no interest in a relationship with me, and is much despair not caused by unrealistic expectations?

In any case, to what extent could I minimise, temper or control my feelings for her? It turned out, not at all. The desire was just *there*. I could only control my behaviour, my decisions. My mind performed these circular rhythms as consistently as the little wheels in the running machine. At four kilometres, I slowed the machine down, picked up a towel to wipe my brow, and stepped off. The room was stuffy and smelled of my own sweat. I had forgotten to open the window. I fumbled with the cool metallic window catch and pushed open the white-framed pane, letting in a rush of fresh air and the twittering of robins and cooing of woodpigeons from outside. Shower, then bed; then if I sleep well I would be quite rapidly down to just fifty-something hours' waiting time, then less than two days by the afternoon.

The second date was better than the first, and was more unambiguously a date. We met briefly as I arrived in Leeds early afternoon, then she knocked on my door at around seven (another few hours of waiting, as she had chores to complete), and we caught a cab into town. She was beautifully dressed and made up, and I felt flattered and exhilarated by the effort she had made. She was so keenly appreciative of everything that the whole evening was a joy. I could see her scanning the room, almost with wonder. She loved the wine, the menu, and asked me to help her choose. The waiter came over. His accent was high Castilian.

'*Quiero preguntarle. El pulpo, está fresco?*' I asked him.

'*Claro, señor. Son congelados inmediatemente, y hay vuelos directos. Llegó ayer.*'

Reassured that the octopus was fresh, I ordered some. I didn't think I was showing off – I hated that British attitude that speaking another language was somehow 'pretentious' – in any case Karen seemed charmed and at ease, which was all I cared about. She asked about the house, and naturally I did not confess to my accidental voyeurism. I made casual reference to a single camera in the hall, which was a lie, but one designed to put her at ease, in respect of her privacy. The whole incident had caused me to feel distinctly uncomfortable about a camera in the bedroom, given the theoretical possibility of a security breach to my online system. I had disabled it in the afternoon and planned to have it removed, so I could tell myself that my lie was only partial.

She charmed me again, effortlessly, with her artless appreciation of life despite her adversity; when I attempted to express my admiration for her without condescension, she intervened with sensitivity. The evening passed as a delight; there was just an uncertain moment after the taxi dropped us off back in our street. I naturally leaned in to kiss her, unsure whether cheek or lips was appropriate. I was highly attuned to the risk of being too forward, and repelling her from me forever. She did appear to lean in a little herself, and our lips met, tenderly, for a few seconds, a fragile but hungry bridge

121

between two souls. I stepped back a little, and she took this as a cue to bid me goodnight and turn in. I watched her go with an aching sadness and impatience mingled with hope.

I entered my own front door, closed it behind me, then leaned my back against it for a good while, closing my eyes and breathing deeply. My spirits were far too turbulent to permit sleep for an hour or more, so I paced around, made myself a cup of weak tea; turned the TV on, then off again, picked up my copy of *GQ* magazine and flicked through the clothing advertorials. Then I heard the distinct ping of a received text message from my phone, lying on the coffee table. I picked it up. It was from Karen, and my spirits and heart rate soared.

Hi George, just saying thank you for a lovely night really lovely. Thanks so much. U still awake? Karen xx

I replied immediately, of course.

Yes, still awake. Lovely to hear from you. Likewise, I had a great evening; wonderful. Didn't want the evening to end. George xx

Some moments passed without reply, that were agonising. Had I been too forward? I immediately thought. Should I send another text, with an apology? I reread my text. No, I hadn't invited her round, merely expressed regret at parting. That's allowed, surely. Finally, I heard the ping as she replied. I checked my watch. It had been a full three minutes.

Maybe it doesnt have to just yet. Wot u doing? Xx
Drinking a tea. Reading a magazine. It's a bit boring xxx
Want company? xxx
Of course!! xxx
C u soon xxxxxxxx

Within a minute I had opened the door to her. A second

later we were kissing; hungrily and passionately this time, not hesitantly, and were wrapping our arms around each other. A few minutes later, we were in the camera-free bedroom, ripping off clothes, searching and yearning with our hands and tongues. I gasped, close to overexcitement at the sight and feel of her naked body, but we settled down between us, found our rhythm, alternately giggling, whispering little murmurs of guidance and appreciation, sighing with pleasure. One imagines the pleasure of lovemaking in anticipation, yet the physicality of the act can come as a shock; the reality of a different smell; the sheer, rude splendour of the proximity; the wordless interaction between different parts of two different bodies unfamiliar with each other as they negotiate their mutual pleasures. I sought to be at once strong and tender, to focus more on her pleasure than mine and the more I did so the more she relaxed, arching her back, crying out with joy, and then subsiding, collapsing, wriggling with contentment; me ecstatic and enraptured, watching her.

Then she lay on her side, head propped on her hand, elbow pressing into the pillow, eyes blazing, burning into mine, saying nothing. Then she leaned forward, kissed me tenderly on the lips again, and said: 'Sharon's got the kids. OK if I sleep here? I'll just text her.' After a couple of minutes and a few bleeps on the phone, she announced: 'My best friend just called me a dirty stop-out. But in a nice way.'

19

If your bird is broken

'What time is it, George?'

'About four.'

'I'm thirsty.'

'I think there's a bottle of water in the lower shelf of the bedside cabinet.'

'Hmm, lovely. Do you want some?'

'Yes, please.'

'I love these sheets.'

'Egyptian cotton.'

'And this bed. Is the one down south bigger?'

'About the same.'

'So do I get to visit your place?'

'Sure. Next weekend, maybe.'

'It'd mean a babysitter again. And switching a shift. But, George...'

'Yes?'

'How would I get there?'

'I'll come pick you up.'

'Really? It's hardly just round the corner.'

'I don't mind, I really don't mind. And I need to visit a business contact in York, so I'll arrange that for the Monday morning after I take you back.'

'Don't you mind all the driving you do?'

'Not at all.'

'No chance of you moving back to Yorkshire then?'

'Interesting thought. I could move myself, but relocating the business would be tricky... plus it's a partnership nowadays. Then again, it would annoy the guy who's angling for my job, so there's that to be said for it...'

'Men! Why can you only be happy when you're putting a rival down! Drives me nuts! Everything's got to be a competition!'

'Life is a competition. Love's a competition. Everything's a competition. I run a business because it's the only arena where I win. I can't do sport. When I was at school and we played football at the lunch break, there'd be two captains to pick the sides, taking it in turns. I was always the last to be picked. Always. Then a partially sighted lad called Ralph came to the school when his family moved into the neighbourhood. He was quite a confident character, considering, and positive. He would stare out at us through the one eye that had a little bit of vision, like this... He had this look of curiosity and fascination in his face. Anyway, he lined up to play that day he arrived, so I thought: "Finally, I'll not be last."'

'What happened then?'

'Well, he was last to be picked – for a few days. Then it was me again. Ralph was quite a handy midfield player, as it turned out.'

'Really?'

'Yes.'

'For real – that's a true story?'

'Yes. It's not funny.'

'Oh come on, it is a bit funny. You got picked for footie after the blind kid!'

'He wasn't blind, he was partially sighted, and with a tidy left foot.'

'Let me look at your left foot. Mmm, not bad. Good thigh muscles. Flat stomach. Fine chest. Strong shoulders. You work out?'

'Yes. Gym, cycling, all that. I can do power, just not so great on the coordination. The football bounces off my shin. The golf ball goes no more than forty yards.'

'They say you should try something difficult, something different. It expands your mind.'

'Who's "They"?'

'I dunno. Folk. Experts. I read it in a magazine.'

'I don't disagree. The brain is a muscle, like any part of your body. You have to exercise it.'

'We've sure exercised our bodies.'

'Yours is... Wow.'

'My teenage boyfriend Terry and me used to play this game. It's not really a game, it's a mental exercise. He called it "Perspectives". You had to try to think of something you'd never thought of before, while you were looking at the world from a completely different angle. So, we'd lie on the bed with our heads at the foot of the bed, and then look out at the sky and the rooftops, first through one eye, then through the other. If a bird appeared in view, we had to imagine what it was thinking, where it had been. You get in touch with your inner bird, your spirit. If your bird is broken, you fix its wing first. Also, you can think in sentences, or pictures, or words. You can choose which. Each word has a personality, so does each picture, each thought, each bird.'

'He's very smart, your Terry. What happened to him?'

'Life story another day. Tell me about your life. Your business. Your home down south. Is your bird broken?'

'That's not fair; I tell all and you tell nothing.'

'I told you summat. About my game called Perspectives. It's your turn. You haven't told me anything yet.'

'I have an ex-wife, Penelope. And her daughter, from a previous marriage, called Amelie.'

'Are they nice?'

'Amelie is.'

'So why marry Penelope then?'

'There was a certain allure; she was very sophisticated, attractive, interested in me. I thought it was love, only later I wasn't so sure. She seemed to become cooler towards me ever so gradually, over the years. I sometimes think that it had all been an illusion, but I do have a few photographs from the honeymoon and we did look happy. It's just strange that I can scarcely remember that; how it felt. You can forget emotions as well as events. I didn't know love could just corrode, without either of us wanting it to. Unless she did, of course.'

'You must have loved her. That's so sad.'

'I don't know. Love is so elusive and abstract, don't you think? Her mum was lovely – quite sweet. Dad was horrid. Rich and arrogant, looked down at me, I think. I suppose with hindsight it is a worry if you're getting on better with your mother-in-law than with your wife.'

'With Terry, we were too young. We were only teenagers, and I felt that it was, like, something sort of holy, spiritual, because he was so artistic. A blending of souls, but I guess it isn't. Does something become different just by thinking about it in a different way? I don't know. I don't know if that were love or not.'

'Maybe there are many different kinds; maybe everyone's experience is ever so slightly different from everyone else's.'

'So, what's your house in Surrey like? How many rooms?'

'You'll have to wait and see.'

'I'm imagining it now. If you're thinking about it too, I think I can pick up your images through brain waves. I'll have to place my head close to yours, like this. Right, now, I'm picking up a nice sitting room, wooden floor – no, maybe fitted carpet. Pictures on the walls.'

'This could be any front room! This isn't telepathy.'

'Shh, don't talk, that'll make it harder for me. Now, bedrooms. Mmmm I like the look of the master bedroom. I bet you've got maps on the wall.'

'Educated guesswork, no more.'

'Don't mock. You could be glad of my telepathic powers one day, when I pick up on my antennae that you're in trouble; you're cornered by supervillains with devilish powers somewhere in Beeston, surrounding you and determined to exterminate you and all your kind.'

'No. Millwall got relegated.'

'My telepathy may still come in handy, you know. You'll have to tell me your superpower one day.'

'I thought we'd established that your skill was intuition and guesswork.'

'They are all closely related skills. You'll learn, in time, my friend.'

'I look forward to the lessons.'

'Do you ever get lonely, living on your own? Why not take in a lodger?'

'I don't spend a lot of time there, and I like my own company.'

'Don't you ever do, you know, entertaining?'

'I'm not a very entertaining person.'

'Don't you like people?'

'Yeah sure! People are all right. Well, apart from extroverts.

I mean, they never shut up, do they? And always talking about themselves: their career, their ambitions, their love life, their car. Never ask about you. And you can't get away! They don't permit a break in the conversation, or a change of tone giving a cue to exit. They probably talk all night, some of them. So, yes, I do find those folk difficult. And introverts, also: don't you find that all the onus is on you to make the conversation? They never offer anything. You introduce a subject, invite a comment, and they just give a terse reply, sometimes just one syllable. So, you try another subject, then another. It's exhausting. So, yes, apart from extroverts. Well, and introverts, I like all kinds of people.'

'That's very broad-minded of you. I'd like some more water. Can you pass me the bottle?'

'Sure. Here you are, master of telepathy. So, what am I thinking now?'

'That you like my body but you really need to pee.'

'Hmmph. Lucky guess.'

20

<hr>

Life in the fast lane

When he arrived, this time, it was in the sports car. I had assumed he had had to sell it, but there it was, gleaming silver. It was shiny inside and out, with a scented air freshener dangling from the rear-view mirror, in the shape of a Leeds United badge. It felt like he had had it valeted for the weekend.

'You've still got the convertible, then,' I said, approvingly. 'Is it comfortable for a long ride?'

'Oh absolutely. Superb, provided there are only two of you.'

He was looking relaxed and cheerful, in a way I hadn't seen before. He was wearing a short-sleeved shirt with a collar, chinos and expensive-looking sunglasses. I didn't know many of the brands. I was thinking about his body, now that I'd known every inch of it, or most of it; thinking about it and about him in a different way. He was no longer just an idea or just a neighbour. And he was driving a total of about 500 miles that day, and another 250 miles the day after, for me. Just for me. Like, wow.

He took us out on the A1. 'Too many roadworks and speed

cameras on the M1,' he explained. He took it up to a bit of a speed, obviously knowing the gaps in the camera network; touched ninety or ninety-five here and there, but safely, smoothly, on the four-lane sections. I loved it. If we crashed, I could die happy – well, worried about Bronte and Danny, but you know what I mean. We stopped for a rest and snack at somewhere called Baldock Services, which I think was near Cambridge. After we got back to the car I just hung about it, putting on and removing my sunglasses a couple of times, sticking my hip out to one side in a sexy way, pretending to scan the horizon, but really just leaning against the vehicle.

'Are we ready?' he asked. 'What are you doing?'

I gave a little sigh. 'Nothing. Just hoping there'd be someone I was at school with in the car park who recognised me. No. Still, never mind.' He just smiled. I gave up and got back in, leaning the seat back a little further, closing my eyes.

'So now we're lovers, and we're also neighbours...' I began, once we were back in the car, heading south towards the M25.

'Right...' he replied. I thought he was going to say some more but he didn't.

'What happens if it doesn't work out? That could be awkward.'

'Let's make sure it works out then,' he replied, calmly, confidently, like he had a plan. 'That would work for me.'

'You might not like me the more you get to know.'

'Why? What you got planned? Any big reveals?'

'Everyone's got secrets.'

'Well, that's fine, I guess. As long as your secret does not involve a six-foot-three, semi-estranged, jealous husband, mad as hell with a baseball bat.'

'No, nothing like that,' I laughed a little, then stopped, realising he was serious and probably at least a little bit nervous.

'Darren and me split two years ago. He's not violent and I haven't seen him since. Last I heard he was with someone new.'

'OK,' he said, quite sensitively. 'You don't have to tell me the tale now.'

'Thanks. Not a dramatic story, just sad; the debt thing really was the whole story, though he didn't see it that way. I'd rather talk about us than about him. I mean, I'm not bitter about what happened, it's just not my favourite topic of conversation.'

'Fair enough. I'll put some music on. Car's got great speakers. What do you like?'

'Have you got any Take That, or Gary Barlow?'

'No.'

'Toni Braxton, All Saints, Destiny's Child, Beyoncé?'

'No.'

'J-Lo, Sugababes, Maroon 5, Arctic Monkeys?'

'No.'

'David Gray, Emma Bunton, Jamiroquai, Adele?'

'No.'

'What have you got, then?'

'Verdi, Mozart, Bruch, some Schubert. I could play you the whole of Beethoven's Ninth Symphony. That is awesome at full volume on these speakers on a long journey.'

'Anything non-classical?'

'Joni Mitchell, Bob Dylan. *Rumours* by Fleetwood Mac. Oh, Kaiser Chiefs, I think. Have a look in the compartment.'

'Kaiser Chiefs! Let's have that then! How come they're just about the only rock band you've got?'

'They support Leeds,' he explained.

'Oh yeah, of course.'

I rifled through the CD collection until I found *Yours Truly, Angry Mob* and put it on. He turned up the volume, and we sang along, and I thought back to our lovemaking the week before. It had been so much more powerful than I had dared to expect. You can think about something in advance and it's always different when you actually experience it; but sometimes, just sometimes, it's better. The exchange of texts before I went round to his place was so sexy – nothing explicit; not sexy in an obvious way, just the speed he replied with, the keenness he had to meet me, sent me dizzy with desire – and the way we just began kissing immediately, as though green lights had appeared above our heads, and his powerful arms wrapped themselves around me, so tight it felt as though they'd gone round twice. Upstairs, he almost became overexcited when he first saw and felt my naked body, running his hands a bit too quickly over everywhere, but then we settled down and I found I could just whisper things to him, or get him to change things with gestures, deepening the feeling and the pleasure. I had never before really thought of sex as an act of communication as well as lust.

In the car that afternoon, listening to the music, all the feelings from the lovemaking and the rest of that amazing night surged back through me again. I felt both relaxed and excited. When we came off the motorway, and drove through country lanes, he took the roof down and the wind rushed through my long, flowing hair. If it hadn't been for the prospect of more great sex that afternoon, I would have wanted that sensation to carry on forever.

Then we finally came to his apartment, or house. It had a gate and everything, that he opened with a remote button. The wide tyres scrunched loudly on the gravel, and it actually took a few moments to go down the drive to the parking spot. I tripped as I got out of the car, after congratulating myself for being a 'visual' person. I was wearing highish heels and the left one stuck in the gravel at an awkward angle so I half fell, my nose coming close to a large potted bush with a strong aroma, I think it was lavender. So, it was a while before I righted myself properly, trying to regain my dignity, and looked around. Then this wide, white, grand, huge building thing came fully into view.

Oh my God. What the actual fuck.

21

I'm not shallow. Well maybe a little bit...

Of course, Joy was right. Not about everything – I wouldn't credit her with that – but the extreme change to which I was subjecting Karen may just have been too great, and stretched the human spirit beyond the point of elasticity, even if it seemed to be in the right direction. I felt this as we arrived in Surrey together for the first time, and was witness to her reaction at the scale of my principal home. I had said nothing to prepare her. I even deliberately avoided a cue: when she expressed surprise that I still had the Mercedes convertible it suddenly occurred to me that I had disguised my net worth rather too well, and that she had perhaps been imagining that I had been struggling. Of course, I loved her all the more for that; that she could want me even as she thought I was worth nothing or even minus several thousand. But perhaps I had taken things too far. Karen was perhaps expecting to arrive at a three-bed semi in Sutton or Cheam, mortgaged to the hilt, the place stale with the bachelor odour of sporting sweat and take-away meals, unopened credit card bills and HMRC correspondence piling up on a dirty floor mat, and a sleazy lodger who didn't always pay his rent. Perhaps she had been prepared to roll her sleeves up as soon as she got there, don the rubber gloves and help me give the kitchen a good clean-up.

As she stepped out of the car, she announced: 'I want to get a good view of your place. I'm a very visual person. Whoops! Oh shit.'

One of her heels had become stuck in the gravel and she stumbled, falling onto all fours briefly, before quickly getting herself back up. Then I could see her eyes scanning the full width of the property like a camera lens whirring through its quarter circle for a panoramic spread. Her jaw actually dropped as her mouth opened; a gesture I had often read about but never, until that moment, witnessed.

'So, is this, like, a huge apartment or have you got the upstairs as well?'

'Yea, that's mine too. We'll get to that. Pretty soon, hopefully.'

'Oh my God,' she said, as we entered, and walked around the first of the two main reception rooms, about thirty feet by twenty, sequoia floor, hi-tech music system and TV. The art deco black and chrome sofa and chairs that Penelope had selected (after about three months' deliberation), and glass coffee table, with books about architecture and Picasso. A framed printed copy of Mappa Mundi hung on the wall opposite the music system. Karen was correct about the map in her telepathic venture.

It was when we reached the kitchen that the tears began. We walked around the central island, just a few years old with specialist vegetable-cleaning sinks and the like. As we did so she ran her finger along the pure granite top, turned half

136

around to look me squarely in the eye, and said: 'Kitchen's bigger than our ground floor! George, what the actual fuck!'

'So, you like it?' I asked, calmly.

'Oh, George, I love your house! I mean, your personality. I'm not shallow. Well, maybe a little bit. Fuck. I mean, what the actual fuck? Fuuuuuuuck!'

She uttered the expletive like an oration, holding her mouth open for a long while, round-eyed with wonder. Then she welled up, and began crying.

'What's up?' I asked, moving up beside her, placing my arm gently around her shoulders. I had not been expecting such a reaction; though I swiftly recalled that Joy had.

'I don't know. I don't know,' she said, now shaking, convulsing with tears. 'It's too much. Maybe we should go home. I don't know.' The tears just ran and ran, down her cheeks, onto her breasts, trickling and soaking into the cloth of her top like a river running into the desert. 'Oh, George. What am I going to do? What are we going to do?'

'Well, I was going to propose taking you upstairs to the large double bed and making tender love between the Egyptian cotton sheets.'

'Well yes, but after that.'

'After that I'm planning a nap. I've been up since four.'

'George! You know what I mean.'

'Actually, I have absolutely no idea what you mean. This is new territory for me too.'

'You mean, you've never had a poor girlfriend before.'

'No! I mean, I've never felt like this before, or even close. I feel like Captain Kirk stepping onto a different planet; but a good one. Paradise.'

'He always got the girl, didn't he?'

'*Is this what you humans call "kissing"*,' I said, mimicking a TV alien voice. She giggled, though was still crying; it was all very confusing. I took her by the hand, intending to take her upstairs. I expected resistance, but there was none. She was still crying as we ascended the broad, curved staircase that looked out over the spacious hall through the elegant wrought iron banister, and as we entered the master bedroom with a tiny click of the handle in the heavy-set door; and a little more after we made slow, tender love; but crying in a good way, I think. I slept for an hour and a half afterwards. I was not aware if she had slept. I awoke as she got herself up, and let herself out and down the stairs. I could detect her direction, despite the astonishing gentleness of her small bare feet upon the wooden flooring. Yet her spirit was still with me. I felt a kind of rapture: almost dizzy. I knew I didn't want to wake up without her again. It was insanely premature to think about this, but I wanted her in my life continually, and forever. It was in that period after waking, while she disappeared to my kitchen, which I immediately wanted her to regard as 'our' kitchen, that I made my resolve.

She was gone for fifteen minutes, and reappeared with two cups of tea.

'You were a long time,' I observed.

'I wasn't snooping. Well, just a little. I have to find my bearings. But I couldn't find a kettle.'

'There's a boiling water tap.'

'Yeah? Never come across one of those before. So, I made us some tea by boiling water in a pan.'

I just smiled, and looked at her, adoringly. She was wearing nothing but a long tee-shirt, an incredibly sexy look. Hair tousled, one leg stretched out on the bed, the other tucked under her. I was aroused again already.

'So, George Mowatt, you have some explaining to do.'

'I've owned and run my own business for ten years, Mowatt Consulting; it became a partnership last year, to spread the ownership, and we changed the name. We advise major companies, help them improve the way they manage and reward staff. We combine statistical analysis with team development. I build in a commission for us that gives us five per cent of resulting profits on top of a basic fee. Customers think it's a bargain but they make so much money from the changes that it's made us very successful too.'

'Yes, but who loses out?'

'No one.'

'Someone must. Like, the workers.'

'Big myth. I spend my working life dispelling that myth. My customers increase workers' pay and their profits at the same time. I'm trying to get an interview with the boss of your company.'

'I don't need rescuing. It's too much.'

'You don't have to feel guilty about enjoying a bit of luxury. Get used to it. Maybe your kids will like it too.'

'But… but,' she looked up at me, hopeful, nervous. 'What are you saying?'

'Marry me,' I said. I hadn't planned to; it had been prompted by her question and the way she looked at me. It was my turn to feel nervous, as she opened her eyes wider, with shock, then looked down. 'Sorry,' I said. 'Too soon, too weird, too inappropriate, too presumptuous, too forward.'

'Some of those things, yes,' she replied. 'I think. Whatever presumptuous means. Oh, George, I'm not saying no, I'm saying I love this and let's just keep talking about it. What if Bronte and Danny spent a weekend here and loved it, and then something came up and we broke up? It would be almost cruel to them.'

'Then, let's not break up. It's perfectly simple.'

'Oh, George!'

'Is there anything you have to tell me?' I asked. 'You're not still married to someone, are you?'

'No! Nothing important. There's no one else, if that's what you're worried about. Hasn't been for two years!'

'Let's take it step at a time, then,' I said, probably sounding more assured and confident than I felt. Inside, I was in turmoil.

'Yes, I want that. Let's make plans. I love this. I love being with you.' She took my hand, opened it, and traced her fingers over my outstretched palm with a faint delicacy. She sounded almost plaintive, and I wondered if she were regretting not just having said 'Yes!' to my utterly unexpected and dramatic, unplanned and absurdly premature, question. I had to make things easy for her, neither go cool nor commit the folly of repeating the proposal.

'Let's start with plans for next weekend,' I said. 'We could go to Knaresborough.'

'Why?'

'I like it. Fond memories of a school trip there. York, then?'

'Oh, I don't care, George. We can go to Cross Gates shopping centre if you like, or Doncaster airport. As long as I'm with you.'

'I'll surprise you, then,' I said, smiling and relieved.

There was a pause, then she gave a mischievous grin. She really was most pleasingly unpredictable. 'So, George. What's your superpower? I still want to know,' she asked this with emphasis, as though she had asked me several times already.

'I don't really have one, unless it's making money,' I replied. 'I seem to have a knack of spotting ideas others don't, and identifying the folk who can help me deliver. Once you've got one success, people keep coming to you. I set up a charity, trying to give my wealth away, but it just bolstered the brand image and even more business came my way. It would be rude to turn it away.'

'Must be a terrible burden,' she said, with heavy sarcasm. 'Oh, I would so hate to be weighed down like that, continuously; having all those embarrassing beachside villas with ocean views and an infinity pool, and a magic hot water tap for making your brew.'

'I can see which luxury is most valued in Yorkshire. Anyway, it's not all it's cracked up to be. Money can't buy you love.'

'Neither can poverty, love.'

'But it's true, and do you know what? It's the one, the only, exception. It can buy everything else. Money doesn't just buy physical things. It buys lots of abstract things. It can buy you dignity, respect, status, companionship, influence – lots of influence; far too much influence – good taste. You know the stately homes of England; lovingly curated by the National Trust? You know what paid for some of them? Slave money. Taking people from Africa by brute force, chaining, whipping them, dehumanising them, forcing them to work in the sugar fields. The owners recycled the money to buy a reputation, hiring the best landscape gardeners and architects. It's money laundering, and it goes on today. These days you buy a superyacht or a sports team. Rich folk all look the same from the outside, whether you've been involved in extortion and slavery or built up an honest company like me, built around helping people. If the crooks don't get caught, then we look the same; and for the biggest crooks there isn't a court system big enough. But there's one thing that money cannot, absolutely cannot, buy – it actually makes it more difficult – and that's real love: real, visceral, can't-take-a-breath, dizzying, ecstatic, walking-on-the-air, heavenly love.'

'But that's good, isn't it? That money can't buy you love?'

'Well, not for me, no. Money's all I've got.'

'Not now. You've got me.'

'That's what I wanted to hear.'

22

An all-too-decent proposal

'He asked me to marry him.' I told Sharon after George dropped me off the next evening, and after I provided some delicious details about his house.

'Seriously?'

'Of course! I wouldn't make that up.'

'No, I mean, did *he* mean it seriously?'

'I think so. He looked kind of downcast when I said I would have to think about it.'

'You said *what*??!' her eyes nearly flew out of her head, and she spilt tea on her jeans, causing her to rub at the damp patch with one hand while she set the cup down with the other. 'You're telling me, Karen Barnes, that this lovely, hunky, spectacularly solvent guy who's crazy about you pops the question and you say "maybe"?! Are you seriously out of your tiny, pretty mind?'

'Well, it's all too soon! I hardly know him. We've had, like, two dates. We've made love three times. Well, four actually,' I added, allowing myself a triumphant smile at the recollection of our most recent bonding, late on the Sunday morning. 'I thought he just said it by accident. What if Bronte and Danny get used to the good life then it all ends?'

'Well, as long as you get him down the aisle pronto before he's got time to research "prenup lawyers" on Google then you're set for life! Idiot.'

'Oh, Sharon, you don't understand. I don't want to see him like that; like a pot of money. I see him as vulnerable, funny, sexy. I really, really, really like him – probably even love him. The money thing makes it worse, or, at least, complicated. I wish he were just a bit better off; all this is too much, it's too confusing.'

Sharon just rolled her eyes at this point. 'Looks perfectly simple to me, love. You're the one who's confusing matters. You're saying you turned him down because you *do* love him? That makes no sense at all. You won't marry him for money, and you won't marry him for love either. Poor lad can't win!'

I said nothing for a little while. She tried again. 'How did he actually phrase it? What were his actual words?'

'Marry me.'

'Not exactly vague then. What happened next?'

'Well, I was speechless. I mean, literally, totally silent. That's never happened to me before.'

'I can believe that,' said Sharon, quick as a flash. I just gave her a look.

'It were, like, weird,' I continued. 'It was like something so totally unexpected that you feel perfectly entitled not to have a view, not to have to make a decision.'

'But you do have to make a decision. Or you did. You may have just made the wrong one, of course,' she reasoned.

'I don't know. Yes, probably.'

'What are you going to do?'

'Keep on seeing him. We've got plans for next weekend.'

143

She breathed a hefty sigh of relief. 'Well, that's something. But he may never ask you again. You do realise that, don't you?'

'I know. I know.' I looked down at the carpet, wincing at its patchy, worn features. I stood up. 'I'll get you a cloth for your jeans,' I said.

'Oh, don't worry. I'd best be off home. I can put them straight in the laundry.'

On the long drive back up to Yorkshire he had been lovely and in a good mood, as far as I could tell. If his nose was out of joint, he was gentlemanly enough not to let it show. He asked me a bit about my life, and how tough was it as a single mum. I explained how I'd never planned to be single, and in any case the first couple of years with Darren were really good. This was just after a phase where I nearly had gone off the rails like my former best friend Dawn. She was my partying best mate, but gradually got into drugs, and then into prostitution to pay for it all, and how I had broke with her, and it was like breaking up with a lover – almost worse, in some ways – but I had to, to save myself and try to be a good mum.

As I spoke to George in the car, I felt myself drifting into territory that I was beginning to regret, just like on our first date (OK, it was a date). I was worrying if I was boring him, or scaring him. Once I get going on a story, I don't seem to be able to stop. But he just listened, and, at the end, as we parked up in our street and he pulled up the handbrake with a smooth, classy subdued sound, not the loud rattle like in a cheap car, and turned off the engine, he just picked up my hand, turned towards me and gave a deep look straight into my eyes. Which I found reassuring unless, I worried immediately, it was a 'goodbye' look. But I didn't think so. All through the car ride I had been both ecstatic and anxious; determined to treasure each precious minute with him, while every nerve in my body was stretched like elastic as I began to feel the impending sense of dread that he was about to politely, considerately, explain that our relationship was going nowhere. Then, a few weeks later, I'd learn that he was dating some professional lady down south, or maybe even from Leeds, but someone very different from poor, confused me. I would have the rest of my life, which could turn out to be fifty years or more, to regret those tiny few seconds of hesitation and silence, sat half cross-legged on his beautiful double bed, the sheets still warm and crumpled from our lovemaking, after he had said 'Marry me'.

23

A not-so-wild youth

'So, how's Eliza Doolittle?' asked Joy, all droll and superior, but friendly, as soon as we met in the usual City bar.

'As lovely as ever,' I replied, deadpan.

'Dear me,' she replied. 'Dear, dear me. The poor lass.'

'It's a terrible, terrible thing, to fall in love with someone who actually cares for you,' I said, returning her sarcasm. 'And for her! Poor Karen! For a single mum to contemplate a relationship with someone who adores her, who runs a successful business and has a nice house. You should put her in touch with the Red Cross.'

'So, are you going to marry her? Have children with her? Where? Surrey? Yorkshire?'

'Oh, I dunno. We're going to be daring, and different; real outside-the-box thinking for two lovers embarking on a love affair. We're going to go out for evening meals and days out, maybe some walks by the sea. We're going to get to know one another, and see if our love deepens or whether it's not going to work out…'

She interrupted, shaking her head. She was wont to do that – both habits; interrupting me and shaking her head; sometimes either, sometimes both. 'Oh, George, that can't work in this situation! It's not a level playing field, it's not a real situation. You don't have that freedom. You're not like any other couple. You really haven't thought this through, have you? What if it didn't work out? You can't ignore the money question, neither of you, no matter how you try. You'd have raised the prospect of a life without poverty only to snatch it away again. I'm sorry, but you're going to have to marry her now. Otherwise it's a horribly cruel game you're playing. You have no other honourable choice, whether the relationship works out or not. And no prenups.'

'Well, I did kind of mention marriage, blurted it out, prematurely, as it happens.'

'You did *what*? Oh. Well, do I offer congratulations to you and your fiancée, in that case?'

'Well, she kind of didn't say yes, to be honest. Said it was too soon, which it was.'

'Mmm, that's intriguing. Maybe I've underestimated this young lady. George...'

'Yes?'

'You're not making this all up, are you? A sort of postmodernist joke?'

'No! You'll get to meet her, maybe soon.'

'I can't help worrying it'll end really badly, with both of you hurt.'

'That's true of any enterprise, anything new, ever. Especially a new relationship. You should...'

'I should what? I should try it sometime?'

I was appalled and briefly terrified, not answering for a short while. There was an unwritten rule between the two of us that I never, ever, asked her about her love life, a secret more resolutely guarded than the Bletchley code-breaking centre during the Second World War. How come the younger sister is the boss? I wondered. I had thought that, probably, she was lesbian, but worried also if I were cleaving to a stereotyped notion. She often wore suits, never make-up and though her hair was often long it was rather shapeless and never contaminated by hairspray. She never betrayed a maternal instinct, loving her career and her interests.

I sipped on my whisky. 'How's work?' I asked, and she was off. I wasn't really listening; something about a new round of funding for a cure for Multiple Sclerosis, or it might have been Parkinson's. I was struggling to pay attention. I was missing Karen, thinking about what she said to me on the long journey back from Surrey at the weekend, how I felt sadder the closer we got to Leeds. This time, the sight of Meadowhall Shopping Centre in Sheffield prompted in me a melancholic Sunday afternoon feeling that I had never experienced before, only heard about, as our brief, beautiful weekend together drew to its close. She was telling me a part of her story that quite captivated me, and I began to feel an even deeper love mingled with immense admiration for her moral courage. It took her from Meadowhall to home to relate her tale, which was sad though full of hope.

'So, I had this best friend Dawn, and we would go out together, city centre, on a Friday night. This would be, like, eight, nine year ago, when Bronte were little. My mum would babysit, and I think she really wanted me to have a good night out once a week, to compensate for missing out on fun earlier, given I had a baby as a teenager. So, I had licence to stay out as late as I wanted, though I think my dad always fretted about me. He'd always stay sober Friday nights, car keys in hand, waiting for a text or a call from me so he could come pick me up, bless him. "I'm only ever ten minutes away, love," he would say. "Call me if you need, and I'm there." And I would just shrug off his concerns, like you do, when you're young. I'd gotten to know Dawn through work – and for a year or so it was great fun. We had some massive nights, lots of laughs, playing tricks on men trying to chat us up. I love dance music, and there were times when you're dancing and you'd just get this surge through your body, and it goes through everyone else as well, and it's like you're being lifted away somewhere else, to some different, better place. You want that feeling to go on and on, but of course it can't; but it's still worth it. I even used to enjoy the Friday afternoon at work, contemplating the night out, what I'd wear, where we'd start out, who we'd meet, where we'd go on to. She was a bigger drinker than me. I liked getting merry, but I hated losing control, so I would often have one drink for her two, or even three. There were lots of tricks you could play to make sure you didn't get pissed, if you're a secret non-drinker. I'd pretend to take a sip of my Bacardi Breezer when I'd really just blown a few bubbles into it. Or, if I was ordering the drinks, I'd get a lime and tonic and pretend it had gin in it.

'I wasn't really dating at this time: wasn't ready for a relationship. I had a one-night stand with a guy who seemed nice, and it was fun, but I still felt a bit sleazy afterwards. Then Dawn started dating this slightly older guy called Greg, who wasn't that good-looking but he was really smart, and quite cool. He were a musician, I think, or claimed to be. He had a tiny apartment quite near the city centre so we took to meeting at his place before going out. That's when the coke started. He would chop up some lines of cocaine on a kitchen surface, ready for when we arrived. I'll admit that I would do a couple of lines, and usually it felt really good, better than booze in some ways, and I'd feel even more up, and enjoy the dancing. But for Dawn, she was just like hyper about it, got totally hooked. She was having loads of fun, but I was beginning to have less fun, and it was almost like she was zoning out at times. Once I phoned my dad real early, about half ten, pretending to be feeling a bit sick, but, really, I was just feeling left out, and ever so slightly scared. Dad was there in ten minutes flat, true to his word. I told Dad it was just an upset tummy and all I needed was a bit of meds and then a good sleep. It was a rainy night, I remember, and as soon as he parked the car, he got out and ran round to me, holding his jacket over my head, ushering me into the passenger's side, which was totally unnecessary, but really nice. I felt slightly embarrassed because I wasn't really ill although, in a way of course, it *was* an upset tummy, so maybe I wasn't lying, because this feeling of fear, you really kind of feel it in your guts, don't you?

'Shortly after that things got even worse. Greg dumped Dawn after he saw her all over this guy at a club. She never said she was upset about it; never talked to me about it, pretended everything was OK, but of course that's all a real danger sign, isn't it?

'And around about this time, I got really frightened one time. Dawn copped off with someone, and his mate thinks he's entitled to have a go at me, and I'm, like, fending him off, but he's drunk and all over me. I could smell the lager and cigarettes on his breath, it was horrible. I could have been raped; thinking about it, I probably very nearly was. But there was this security guy who noticed what was going on 'cos we were only fifty yards from the club. He just picked the bloke who was harassing me up by the scruff of his neck, both feet literally dangling in the air, sets him a few yards away like he were a toy he'd got bored playing with and just said some words in his ear that were enough to send him scarpering, quivering with fear. He stood by me 'til Dad showed up. We had quite a conversation. I asked if it was a difficult job, and if he minded having to stay sober at weekends. He said no, he never drank, he was a Christian, which surprised me. Funny, you think of bouncers as being dead hard, but he saw his job as being a moral mission, like a guardian angel. I wonder how many rapes he prevented. Anyway, my dad shows up quickly, looking all worried. I made light of what happened, otherwise Dad would have insisted on a description, found the lad and beaten him to a pulp. I already had a brother in the grave, I didn't want a dad in prison.'

At this point she paused in her narration, and reached into the passenger's door compartment for a bottle of water. 'Sorry,' she said, 'I'm thirsty. Do you want some?'

'No, I'm fine,' I replied.

'Am I going on too much? I know I sometimes don't know when to stop when I get going with a story.'

'It's fine,' I said. 'Please carry on. I'm listening. I'm by your side. I'm on your side.'

'OK,' she said, and briefly held my hand as it lay on the gear stick. 'Well, there were only a couple more Friday nights for me. Dawn's behaviour was getting extreme. Without free coke from Greg, she had started looking for other ways to get her hands on it. She turned up one night with a roll of banknotes at the bar, and had obviously already had a few lines. I thought she was dealing, or stealing from people, but the story, when it came out, was even worse. She had started to do blow jobs for money; she were pretty and could charge a lot. She couldn't see how it was such a big deal, saying it was an easy way to make good money, better than a day job, but I just wanted to, like, vomit on her behalf. I wasn't feeling all superior – well, maybe I was – but more, just, totally different. Her life was going in a very different direction from mine. For me, the Friday night out was just a part of life; the main thing was family. For her, those nights were the only thing, the thing she lived for. So, I just sat down with her and said that I wasn't going to be going out Friday evenings any more, and we couldn't be friends. She got all mad, said I was judgemental and a snob; I thought well, if I was, so be it. I'd rather be more sober and have a nice family, and not get raped or worse. Even before the incident, I had been starting to get a bit fed up with the club scene. There had been one evening I had a cold and didn't go out, and I watched cartoons with Bronte and we giggled together and I just drank cocoa, and I was thinking I had had more fun that night than the Friday before, out on the tiles with Dawn.

'So, when I said I wasn't going out any more she got mad with me, stormed out, then texted an apology. Then called or texted me a few times after that, but I didn't reply. It's probably the hardest thing I've ever done. Maybe I should have tried to save her? But the people I had to save were me and Bronte. That's who I had to look after. It was weird how breaking up with a best friend is just like breaking up with a lover, but I had to do it. I think she just sank further and further, she's probably on the game full time now. I don't know.

'For a while I went to the opposite extreme, joined a church and was completely sober. They were nice people, but a bit full-on, and I couldn't quite feel what they felt. Then I decided that I just didn't want to have an interest, outside of the home. My family was my interest, and my religion. Then I met Darren, and he was funny and kind, or seemed to be to begin with, I just didn't realise he was still immature. Anyway, that's it. I said, life story, one day. That's one chapter at any rate. Confessions, you've heard me warts and all. It'll be your turn next!'

We pulled into our street and after I parked up I just held her hand. She appeared to be under the impression that she ought to feel ashamed at relating tales from her wild youth, which wasn't even particularly wild, despite the temptations, but I was filled with awe at her courage and good judgement at such a young and vulnerable age. I should have said something like 'Best mum ever', but this thought occurred to me an hour or two later. Instead I just gave her what I hoped was a look of reassurance and love.

I was recalling much of this, that weekday early evening in the London cocktail bar, City types quaffing and chatting around me, until I became aware of another female voice, vying for my attention. 'What do you think I should do?' asked the voice.

'Hmmm?' I asked, looking up at Joy.

'You haven't been listening to a word of what I've been saying, have you?'

'Not really,' I replied, deadpan. 'Sorry, I was miles away.'

'This is why I don't get married. That's what it's like. That's what I've heard, anyway. Doing everything, taking responsibility for everything, while the man pays no attention.'

'You should meet her.'

'Who?'

'Elize… Karen, I mean,' I replied.

She smiled and said: 'You having another drink, Professor Higgins?'

24

The age of austerity

I counted off the days until I saw George again, worried during the hours that he didn't call or text, but equally anxious when he did, fearing some kind of 'we need to talk' serious thing going on, prelude to him dumping me. I was almost hoping he would just get on with it, then I'd begin the emotional recovery that much sooner, returning to my difficult life, a big bit of hope snuffed out. The fear was almost worse than the event would be. Almost. Hope is a precious, delicate baby and it's a big responsibility to keep hold of him carefully. But you can't always protect a baby from a deadly infection over which you have no control.

When there were only two and a half days left before seeing him, I thought back to exactly two and a half days earlier, and realised that those events seemed really recent, making it feel like not such a long time to wait. Then when there was only a day and a half left, I'd think back a day and a half, and so on. The beauty of this way of thinking being that each time you carry out the exercise there's less of a period of time to think back on, and to wait for. Well, it's either a clever way of thinking about a wait, or proof that I'm completely barking mad and neurotic; one thing or the other. The problem with it is that it can make the time pass even more slowly, if it's pretty much all you're thinking about; and it was all I had to think about, during the shifts, given that cleaning doesn't really require any brains at all.

Late on Saturday morning, when I only had one hour to wait, I thought back one hour. I still had the cup of tea that I had made an hour ago! Mind, it was stone cold. I'd forgotten about it while Sharon called to talk to me about Jayden, panicking he was really ill but didn't warrant going to casualty so I looked up the health centre's weekend number for her. But then I got a text from George reporting an accident in the roadworks in Nottinghamshire delaying him by about an hour. So, I had to wait another hour before I repeated the 'one-hour' wait technique, worrying that there would be a further delay. How long can this go on?

Finally, I saw his shadow pass across the front window, and the cheery ring on the doorbell. I leaped up. Bronte just glanced at me over the phone she was looking at, all calm and superior, headphones on, like she was the adult and I was the child.

'Hello,' said George, with a huge, warm smile as I opened the door.

'Hi,' I replied. 'Come in.'

I had tidied the front room, though Danny had done his best to untidy it again, putting out his toy train set that Gran and Grandad had got him for Christmas. George managed to guide his way through the mess and sit on the one armchair, while I was on the settee with Bronte, who was ignoring us and our conversation, or maybe pretending to – maybe her music was turned off. Sometimes, hours later, she'd quote something that I said and occasionally it was mildly embarrassing.

'Good journey?' I asked, all nervous.

'Er, well, not really, as there was this long hold-up,' he said, smiling at my forgetfulness.

'Oh, of course. Sorry. Memory like a sieve. Do you want a cup of tea?'

'Er, lovely, thanks.'

I leaped up, accidentally disturbing Danny's train set, just as the wooden locomotive was going round the corner.

'Hey!' he shouted.

'Oh, sorry, love, sorry. Here, I'll fix it.' I stooped down to reattach the wooden rail, fumbling and needing three goes at it.

George spoke up: 'That reminds me,' he said. 'I have a little gift for the young man of the house.'

He presented a large, wrapped gift. I thought it was a nice gesture to have gone to the trouble of wrapping it, given that it wasn't Danny's birthday. My boy grabbed it a bit too eagerly for my liking.

'Say thank you to the nice man,' I said.

'Thank you!' he said, clearly enough, as he ripped the paper to shreds. 'It's a fire engine! Look, Mum!' And he began playing with it, making it attend an imaginary accident on the train line.

We all looked down and admired its fiery redness. George then turned to Bronte and said: 'I've received an email from Alex, the art professor. The good news is she would be delighted to see your work, but I'm afraid she's in New York now, so it may be a little while.'

'OK,' said Bronte. There are maybe twenty ways of saying 'OK' that range from the sarcastic, to the indifferent, to the lukewarm, to the really enthusiastic. This one was keen enough, I reckoned. George seemed satisfied.

Then I went to the kitchen to make the teas. George asked Danny about his train, but I couldn't hear a reply. He was quiet, especially with new folk. I came back with the cups, trying to smother the rattling noise the two of them were making as my hands trembled. 'Shall I put on some music?' I said, impulsively. I hadn't planned to say it.

'Er, sure.'

'As we listened to your Beethoven and Kaiser Chiefs in the car, I thought I'd play some of my favourites.'

I saw Bronte rolling her eyes, as I stepped from the corner. She pulled her headphones down, said: 'Well, I'll have to go up to my room if I want to hear summat decent.' But she said this quite light- heartedly; it was a running joke between us.

'I love music,' I said, still chattering nervously, as I put the CD on and turned the volume up a bit; not too loud, but enough to fill the room. 'I love the way it can be happy and sad at the same time, and it brings out feelings you didn't even know you had... OK I'll play you my favourite song of all time. You're not to mock, even if you don't like it. There's so much feeling; well, for me anyway.'

To my amazement, he started singing along, quite in tune as well. 'Hah!' I said triumphantly. 'So, you do know some pop music after all. Guilty pleasure?'

'This is a Bob Dylan song,' he replied. 'I didn't recognise it to begin with, but now I do.'

'No, it's not! It's an Adele song. Her all-time classic! Bob Dylan is that old man with the croaky voice.'

'But he wrote it. I know it from the *Time Out of Mind* album in the nineties. Not his best album, but it has a couple of classics. This version's better, I'll give you that.'

'He didn't write it. He can't have. It's got so much feeling. It was written by a woman! It must have been.'

'OK, let's look it up,' he said, all smug.

'Oh, I *hate* smartphones!' I said. 'I used to be able to win arguments. Now they have to be settled with facts.'

'How tiresome,' he replied, all straight-faced for a short while, until he couldn't help himself and a bit of a smile crept up at the edges of his mouth. I realised the silliness of what I'd said; how I'd said the word 'facts' as though it were some sort of a nuisance. He was right, of course. The song had been written by Dylan. Who'd have thought it? One day, I'll be right about something and he'll be wrong. I've got a whole celebration planned: ticker tape, balloons, some bubbly wine and those little canapé things that you have at posh events – everything. I resolved to learn more about metaphysics than he would ever know, once I had got my head round it.

'OK, let's change the subject,' I announced, after the song had finished. I suggested we move to the table and leave Danny the floor space near the comfy chairs. 'I'll put on some Kaiser Chiefs. Cheer you up. Right, so, George Mowatt,' I said as I sat down facing him, looking up at that loving gaze he would give me with his warm brown eyes. 'Your turn.' He smiled, and I smiled back, like a mirror.

'My turn?'

'Summat about you. I've told you a bit about my life story, but you're still a big mystery to me.'

'Well, it's not a hard-luck story, but I don't come from privilege, in case you're wondering. Our house was a three-bed semi in north Leeds. Tidy but quite small. My mum died giving birth to my younger sister, Joy, so I can remember Mum but Joy can't. She was lovely, gentle and kind-tempered, unlike my dad, who was a bit more strict. So, it was a complete tragedy. His sister helped raise us; she lived nearby and had no children, so kind of adopted us, in effect. It worked out fine but of course I missed Mum.'

'Oh, my word, no!' I said. 'That's so sad. I'll never get to meet her.'

'Sometimes,' he said wistfully, looking away from me, as if something on the wall had caught his eye. 'I can remember her voice and face quite well; other times it seems like a dream. I don't know... I've lived with it for so long now, and of course I've now been gone from the parental home longer than I ever lived there.'

He paused a short while, and I wasn't sure whether to say anything. His voice had gone shaky for the only time since I had known him; he had always been so assured before. Then he resumed his story. 'At school I was the classic geek, although I don't recall the term being around then. I liked mathematics, and physics, and history. I studied hard and I liked to get good grades. It didn't make me popular but that made me all the more determined, because I thought it was so unfair that you should get picked on for working hard. I got that discipline instilled by my dad: that you should always try your best, and it was a good discipline. I wasn't going to give up on that. I remember being baffled that some lads in our year didn't want to study and thought it was cool to bunk off or skip homework. They gave me a hard time and made me miserable at times. It wasn't that I felt all intellectually superior, it was just that I couldn't get my head around the mindset of not wanting to do your best at something. To me, it was like sport – not that I was any good at sport, but I understood it. I mean, if you're playing a game of football, you concentrate on the ball, your position, making good passes and good decisions, running hard. You don't wander off the pitch after twenty minutes because you've spotted an attractive girl or want to go down the shops. To me, it was exactly the same with homework and exams. You tried your hardest, you did your best.

'So, when I started to become successful, I felt like I totally earned it. I even resented paying tax for a while. I figured, if those lazy, arrogant, bullying lads couldn't be bothered to study and are now on the dole, why should they be bailed out by folk like us who worked hard and got on? But now I realise that it's a bit more complicated than that. So yeah, I guess I may have been a bit obnoxious between the ages of twenty-five and thirty-five. There wasn't a car that was too fast, a watch that was too expensive, or an apartment that was too lavish, or a house that was too big, or a girlfriend who was too pretty. It was all about me; well, at least, it was in my private life. I like to think I was a good boss, after I set up on my own.'

'But,' I said, daring to interrupt. 'I don't know how to put this. You must have diddled some folk along the way, like, to get rich. Someone must have lost out.' I could see his hackles raised, and that he nearly lost his temper, but, to give him credit, he didn't. I could see the issue mattered that much to him, and it must have sounded like an accusation, the way I put it, so I felt a bit bad.

'That is such a myth,' he answered, all calm after taking a deep breath. 'Loads of folk think that, and it's just not true. If you treat your staff well, and your customers, and you don't mess up the environment, and you produce something socially useful, then you can make lots of profit, create lots of jobs, and you pay tax to help pay for the health service and whatnot. That's how it works.'

'So, you don't think that it's the rich to blame for all this austerity we're having?'

He gave a wistful smile. 'The rich aren't all one thing,' he replied. 'I mean, if I said "All single mums are this and that" you'd probably be offended. Every single mum's different. It's the same with the rich. There are some right sons of bitches, and some boring ones, and some surprisingly decent ones. It's all a mixture. Austerity is a by-product of the debt crisis. Here, though, I do have a confession, but it was an error of judgement, not an intention to rip people off...'

'Go on.' I loved it when he explained stuff to me; it turned me on, but also made me want to learn more myself.

'Well, between about 2004 and 2008 my company designed pay schemes for some of the investment banks. They were designed to incentivise the traders to be efficient, maximise returns, blah blah. I can honestly say that I raised a question with one of them about whether they should be using economic profit, rather than accounting profit...'

'Oh, economic profit, definitely,' I quipped immediately, all straight-faced, nodding in agreement. 'That's always better, I find.' He smiled again; another lovely, warm smile.

'Anyway, I got shut down in that meeting. After all, it was for them to manage risk, I was just designing their pay. Well, a lot of them were dealing in CDOs, or Collateralised Debt Obligations.'

'What the hell are they?'

'Well, if you don't know, you're in good company, because the bigger problem was, as it turned out, the traders didn't understand them either,' he explained. 'So it ended up as a massive debt bubble – essentially just a giant version of the problems your Darren got into, but without any collateral like a house to put behind it. And on top of that, Gordon Brown broke his own fiscal rules to borrow at the top of the cycle...'

'I bet Gordon Brown's not a good cyclist.'

'No,' he said, deadpan. 'So, this austerity we have, it's not really caused by the cuts. The cuts are a by-product of the debt crisis. A lot of it's inevitable, I'm afraid.'

'But can't the banks be made to pay it back?'

'Up to a point, some of them are, but it's complicated, because the money was never really there in the first place. There's more debt than there is money. It's a problem with the whole design of the money-supply system.'

'Can't the government just print a load of money?'

'They've done a lot of that too.'

'I still don't see why tax credits should go. This austerity's gone on quite long enough.'

'But, you see, it wasn't real growth, back then, it was debt!' he said, becoming animated again, but in a good-natured way. 'The anti-austerity protestors can't have it both ways. They can't simultaneously denounce debt-fuelled, banker-led, unsustainable growth and use it as a basis for their spending plans!'

'Well, now you put it like that, it's obvious our family has to go without its summer holiday.' I found him fascinating but frustrating when he was talking policy. He knew so much, but was vague when it came to practical answers. It occurred to me for the first time that intelligent, powerful people really had very little idea of what was going on, and less control over things than I thought they had. Maybe they had less control than *they* thought they had, too.

'Sorry,' he apologised. 'Jargon again. I know. It's not fair. Capitalism's not fair. Socialism's not fair. Life is not fair.'

'All I can say is, this austerity, this banking crash, all these problems. It had nowt to do with me.'

He sighed deeply at this point. 'I so wish I could say the same.'

25

You shouldn't marry out

'My, you're pretty. What are you doing with our lad?' This was Dad's greeting to Karen. She only blushed a little, accustomed to such a compliment and perhaps mildly offended that he should refer to such a superficial matter. At least he didn't mention money.

He had a lovely first-floor sheltered flat overlooking some quiet grounds, and a flat TV screen against the wall that seemed disproportionately large given that it was only ever turned on for the rugby and the cricket.

'He's nice. You should give him credit!' said Karen, bright as a spark.

'Oooh Yorkshire lass. I like that,' he said as he heard Karen's Beeston accent. 'I've told him he shouldn't marry out. Always a mistake to marry a foreigner.'

'Penelope was from Godalming,' I said.

'Well, not Lancashire at least,' he replied. 'So, what's your name?'

'Karen,' she replied.

'That's a nice name. But you know what, Karen. He can't play cricket.' She giggled at that. He continued: 'Treats the ball like it's a hand grenade. I would get a score of twenty or thirty on a good day. George here,' he pointed his gnarled thumb towards me, as though I were an errant schoolchild and he a strict sports coach. 'Struggles to get five.' He then held up five fingers, by way of emphasis.

'Well, I don't follow cricket anyroad,' said Karen.

'Well, you should. That lad Joe Root is good. I saw him on the telly over the summer. Better than Boycott. Reminds me of Len Hutton.' His eyes would mist over at the mention of the name Len Hutton, a player from before I was born. 'What did you say your name was again?'

'Karen.'

'Well, you've got lovely hair and dimples. I don't know what you're doing with our lad. But if you have a boy, you should name him George, same as me and same as the father.'

'Dad!' I said at this point. 'I think we're getting ahead of ourselves. This is a first meeting.'

'I think George is a lovely name,' said Karen, brightly and diplomatically. The hint that she may want my baby filled me with love and arousal, in equal measure.

'It is coming back into fashion,' I said. 'It wasn't cool when I was a teenager.'

'Thanks to Wills and Kate,' explained Karen. 'They named their first lad George. Our future king.'

'They did!' said Dad, brightening. He was the biggest royalist in the realm. 'And now they've got a daughter too.'

'Princess Charlotte!' cooed Karen. 'She's gorgeous, isn't she?'

So, the two of them could bond over the Royal family's golden couple. I scarcely followed such matters, but I was pleased. We had been dating a few weeks. Summer was fading and I was exhausted from all the driving, was missing work a few days and probably neglecting the business, but deliriously happy, even more than I had expected. Even though the football season had started again and I now had accommodation close to the stadium, I had only been to one game. The house bought for one purpose was serving another. We tried during this time to be normal. None of it was normal, but we tried. It was hard to avoid the 'M' word, because it underpinned so much; which restaurant to go to, her beginning to ask the question 'Are you sure you can afford…' while quickly realising she didn't have to complete it. She never asked for anything expensive, or even inexpensive; she just let me choose, which may sound deferent and paternalistic, but the atmosphere felt free and loving at the time. It helped that I enjoyed a pizza ate off our laps in her front room at Beeston, or a cappuccino and cake at Watford Gap services, as much as a fancy restaurant down south. I only cared that I was with her, that I could hear her saucy giggle, catch her eye and watch the gentle gesture with which she brushed a wisp of hair from her face.

'Where's Joy?' asked Dad suddenly. 'Is she coming?'

'Next week,' I replied.

'I haven't seen her in months.'

'Dad, she was here ten days ago.'

'Hmmph.'

Karen spoke: 'It's a lovely view you've got.'

'Yes, not bad. They won't let me smoke a pipe.'

'Just as well,' she said. 'It's bad for your health. We'll want you around a while yet!'

'She's lovely is this one,' said Dad, looking at me. 'Yorkshire lass, as well,' he repeated. He started coughing.

'Are you all right?' asked Karen, placing a hand gently on his forearm. 'See what I mean? Last thing you should be doing is smoking a pipe. Shall I make you another cup of tea?'

'That would be nice. Strong and two sugars,' he replied. 'And a jammie dodger.'

Karen seemed to have a more natural ease with him than I did, which may be rather common for a woman with a strong family ethic, when dealing with a grumpy and unpredictable father-in-law. It had certainly not been the case with Penelope. I recalled with a shudder of shame the last time she had visited Dad, and snobbishly mocked his taste in ties. She muttered something about the paisley pattern and the colour choice on our way back down south. I recall glancing at her superior air with what I hoped was a look of disgust, before returning my attention to the road, as I was driving. She did not appear to notice, still apparently congratulating herself at her good judgement. A respectful person would have appreciated his effort in dressing smartly for his daughter-in-law. In retrospect, that was the last straw for me, more than her affair, and by the next Monday I was in touch with the divorce lawyer. Karen was such a charming comparison.

'What do you think of this?' asked Dad, pointing at something in the *Sunday Telegraph* and directing his attention to me. My spirits sank. He did not notice, and continued: 'Do you think Cameron will fulfil his pledge to give us a referendum?'

I sighed. 'Sadly, yes, we just have to hope we stay in the EU.'

'Rubbish!' said Dad. 'Time we stopped being run by Brussels!'

'We're not run by Brussels. All the big decisions are made in Westminster. Brexit would be a complete disaster,' I replied. 'Bad for the economy, public finances, society, everything. Scotland would go,' I said, more resigned than angry.

'Nonsense!' he said. 'We'd get our country back, stop paying these millions to the EU bureaucrats.'

'I'm too tired to have this conversation, Dad. I don't even know where to start.'

'You should pay respect to your dad's opinions.'

'I do, actually. I just disagree.'

'It's what your mum would've wanted,' he said, and flashed me a look. I looked down, startled. He hadn't mentioned Mum in about ten years, and never before as a weapon in an argument. I felt like I'd been stabbed, and my hands started to tremble. It was like she had died again, in front of us, and I had to miss her all over again. 'I think we need to start heading back,' I said. 'I've just noticed the time.'

'You've only just got here!' he replied.

'I have a lot of work to do, and Karen has a babysitter who needs to go home,' I explained.

'Well, it's been great to see you. You need to keep hold of this one, Son,' he said, and turned to Karen, giving her a huge wink.

'See you soon, Dad.'

'I do try to avoid political arguments with Dad,' I explained to Karen, once back in the car.

'Was it just about politics?' she asked. I didn't reply. The silence went on.

'I thought you were both Tories,' she said, sensitively acknowledging that Mum was a subject for another day.

'We are, but there the similarity ends. We disagree about almost everything.'

She smiled. 'They do say you get more right-wing as you get older.'

'In the case of my dad, that was never possible, given his starting point. A shade to the right of the Klingon Empire. If anything, he's mellowed a bit.'

'Well, it was a nice first meeting, thank you. He's a bit of a character.'

'Oh, he is that all right. He liked you, anyway. Being both pretty and Yorkshire kind of melted his heart.'

'I won't 'fess up that I vote Labour,' she said.

'I think he'd forgive you that.'

'He's got a point on Europe, anyway – all our money going to those fat cats in Brussels.'

'Who run the single market that underpins our prosperity.'

'Precious little of which reaches our street. Well, until you came along I suppose.'

There was an awkward silence, which Karen broke, quite cheerfully. 'Well, yes, maybe avoid politics all the same, in future meetings.'

'Suits me,' I said. 'Politics is horrible. Unavoidable, but horrible. Can we change the subject?'

'Sure,' she said.

'I meant to tell you. I heard again from Alexandra, the art professor. She's hoping to be in London in a couple of months' time.'

'Oh, that's good news, I'll tell Bronte. It would be so good to get her work looked at and, well, to make contacts in the art world and all that.'

'Indeed.'

'Hopefully her career will go further than mine ever did.'

'Ever did?' I asked, amused. 'Why are you talking in the past tense? You're only young! Plenty of time yet, to train for something new.'

'What do you think I should train as?'

'You're very sharp and quick witted. Such strong verbal skills. That would seem to point to sales, marketing or PR.'

'They all sound terribly complicated.'

'They're not. They require knowledge and some training. But they're basically about communication.'

'Mmmph. I've always found... I don't know how to put this

168

without sounding sorry for myself, but I get irritated by the higher ups: you know, government agencies, managers. On the one hand, they tell you: "You've got to work, and get on! Don't rely on benefits! Provide for yourself and your family!" But then when you do go for a promotion they're all like: "Well, who do you think you are, going for a proper salary without a degree? What experience do you have? Get back in your box." OK, not exactly those words, but, well, it's mixed messages, that's all I'm saying.'

'I've never thought of it like that,' I said. 'But I know, from my own day job, that some managers are terrible, but also that some are much, much better than others. So, maybe you've just been unlucky. And they do love someone who shows ambition, even if they're tough in a job interview. And you're smart. Let me put it another way. Suppose you had a marketing job, where you had to learn about a product, and come up with slogans and ideas for promotion, and it was in France, and you had to do it all in French. How is your French?'

'Um, not good. Not even basic, really.'

'OK, but then someone comes along and says: "Hey, Karen, there's been a change of plan: same job, but you can do it in English from an office in the centre of Leeds." Imagine the wave of relief you'd experience.'

'Yea, OK. I see where you're going with this.'

'Well, millions of marketing jobs, maybe even the majority,' I continued, 'right across the world, are in English, and most of them are filled by people who had to learn English as a second language. So, think of the head start you have on them.'

'So, what you're saying is, basically, I've got a lot of opportunities, just by having the language I have and living where I do.'

'Exactly. Millions of people cross the world to try to get into this country.'

169

'Hmmph. Never thought of it like that. Keke at work came from Nigeria, only has a cleaning job but it's good money for her family. She's smart, too.'

'It's always possible to think of things in a completely different way.'

'Terry always used to say that.'

I fell silent, trying to hide my selfish disappointment. I did wonder if it was once too often that I had heard that name, but I let it pass.

26

I just knew

Terry appeared in my dream, for the first time ever, as far as I could recall. Until he showed up, it was the usual House Dream, with a slight variation on layout and number and style of rooms. I ascended the stairs to the unexplored bedrooms. The rooms were even larger and more wonderful than usual; there was a heavenly sunshine falling in through some skylights. There were several bathrooms, I had forgotten how many, and I was just wondering which one to use for my shower when Terry walked in. I walked over towards him. He looked the same as sixteen years earlier, with his dreamy smile and high cheekbones. He leaned in to kiss me, and I was immensely turned on. I wanted to kiss back, but I felt guilty, being vaguely aware that I was committed to someone else. Strangely, in the dream, the figure wasn't really apparent as George – it was just 'someone'. I pulled away, but Terry still smiled. 'I gotta go,' he said. 'But I'll call on you soon.' At that point I woke up. My first thought was that it was odd that the large house fantasy would continue even after I had gained a

171

wealthy boyfriend. If I had felt secure about the relationship, it shouldn't have occurred; if I had not, surely it would be a dream about the house falling apart, or something. I had read about dreams just being an outlet for your fears and hopes and anxieties. Then again, dreams are not logical. They may mean something, they may be sending you a message, or they may just be a bit random. I dream in colour. I don't have smells or music, just images and voices; sometimes the images are fuzzy and the voices are loud. In this one, Terry's voice had been deep and clear; enough to wake me.

I could hear that Bronte was downstairs, so I got up to rouse and dress Danny and get him to the toilet before going down.

She was at the breakfast table, eating her cereal, not listening to music on her headphones, which was unusual.

'You're up early,' I said.

'Yea.'

'Everything all right?' I asked.

'Yes.' A pause. 'Mum…'

'Yes?'

'Why do you never talk to me about my dad?'

'Um,' I felt uneasy, alarmed at the coincidence of her question and my dream, and too wrong-footed for a convincing answer. 'Well, he has his own life now. We were ever so young, just schoolchildren…'

'Was he a bad guy?'

'No, no, no! He was lovely, quite gentle. A little bit in his own world at times, you know, not listening, but kind mannered. Very intelligent and artistic, just like you.'

'Then why don't you get in touch with him?'

'Well, there are lots of reasons. I mean, maybe I should, though I'm not sure how…'

'Oh, come on. It's the age of Google and Facebook. It'd be easy.'

'OK, well, I'll think about it, honey. If you're sure that's what you want. We can never know what his reaction will be. But I guess I could try. Anyway, love, is there any reason you're thinking of this now?'

'Well, it's just that he appeared to me in a dream.'

'*Really??!!*' I asked, startled. 'When?'

'Just last night,' she said, her head recoiling a little from the force of my answer. 'I knew it was him; all black and handsome, same cheekbones as me, looking at me with his deep, piercing eyes.'

'Well, it is just a dream, love. What did he say?'

'Nothing, really.'

'How did you know it was your dad?'

'I just – *knew*.'

'So, he didn't say anything, just looked at you.'

'Almost nothing. But he felt ever so close. He just said: "See you soon, love, gotta go."'

'Well, Bronte, I'll tell you what. There's this one person I'm in touch with from school. She's called Jade. She's a friend of someone called Dave, who used to follow music, and probably still does. Anyway, Dave was mates with this guy Steve, who knew this much older guy Craig who apparently is, or was, bass guitar player in a band where Terry is the singer. Or was, last I heard.'

'Oh, well, we've got him cornered, then. How long ago was this Steve, or was it Craig, in a band with my dad?'

'Oh, two years ago. Or maybe five. But I became friends on Facebook with Jade just a month or two ago.'

'Yes, well. Well done, Sherlock. Your work here is done. Is George coming today?' she asked.

'Yes. Well, he's going to the Leeds game, for a change, then he's coming here for his tea. Is that OK?'

'Yea, sure, he's cool. I hope he's got some news about the professor.'

'Oh, he has actually! She's hoping to visit England soon,' I said.

'OK,' said Bronte, sounding more disappointed than I expected. I suppose it was a bit vague.

Then she stood up a little hurriedly, pausing to retrieve her headphones that dangled from the phone and got caught on the edge of the breakfast table. 'Just going to get a shower, Mum.'

She spent the morning in her room, and I did some laundry and cleaning, while keeping an eye on Danny and his toys. I was watching the clock run down, again. George had said he would call in for a cuppa before the game. But at around 1.30 p.m. the phone bleeped. It was a text telling me he had an emergency work thing that morning that he had to deal with, plus there was another hold-up, so he would have to dash to the game and I wouldn't see him until after. This made me feel gloomy, but he put seventeen kisses at the end of the message, which turned me on. I just wanted him to be there, right then. Sometimes, I got fed up of waiting.

I heard loud conversations outside, shortly before the match, and a few Leeds supporters were walking and chatting animatedly as they came down the street, while others were parking their cars outside. Then I waited and waited for the final whistle. I did check the score online from time to time, relieved to note that they were winning, for a change. That should put him in a good mood. I went out into the tiny front yard at just after five o'clock, pretending to do a bit of gardening in the plant pots. I spotted George as soon as he turned the corner, caught his eye and we smiled at each other. We were chatting just outside the house for a few minutes; he planned to go into his place, shower and change before coming round. As we did so, another few fans came walking down the street. There were three lads, two white, one black, all kitted out in Leeds United shirts and scarves, and I sensed they were slowing to a halt as they approached our house. Just at that moment, Bronte stepped outside. The shortest and slimmest of the three, the black lad, caught her eye, then looked directly at me. 'Hello, Karen,' he said, as though we had met last week.

'Hello, Terry,' I replied, even more startled than I would have been normally, given the dream. 'Um, this is my eldest, Bronte, she's fifteen.'

'Sixteen, actually,' she corrected promptly. In any case, it was hopeless to maintain any further pretence, as the two of them looked again at each other with their identical eyes and matching cheekbones, Bronte's skin colour exactly at the midpoint between his and mine. Then she said to him, daring as you like: 'We've been expecting you.'

Terry looked at me again and announced: 'Well, Karen. Looks like you've got some explaining to do.' He said this with a smile of curiosity and delight.

Bronte then finally looked at me. It was hard to maintain eye contact. 'Looks like we won't be needing the help of Facebook then, Mum.' She also had this smile, the identical one to her dad.

27

Everything I'm not

One afternoon, after a match, I exchanged a few words with some fans walking over the pedestrian bridge that crossed the motorway on my way to Karen's street. On occasion I liked to invite myself into some fan talk, lonely soul that I was. I slowed down a little, owing to a half-stumble on a step, allowing them to catch up. They were discussing the team and the game, which was a 2–1 win, with a nervy final few minutes as Leeds had been 2–0 ahead with twenty minutes to go. Given the erratic form, we home supporters were hugely relieved, especially as the opponents were one of the high-placed teams.

'Woodsy's not exactly Mark Viduka, is he?' said one of them.

'Oh, come one, he's good. Only goal scorer we've got, anyway,' came the reply.

It was at this point that I dared to butt in: 'When he's leading the attack, the rest of the team has a better shape and more confidence, so it's not just the goals he scores.'

'Yeah maybe,' said one of them.

'Look, he got one today,' said another, who was black and

looked vaguely familiar. 'We won against a top side. Let's just drive home, go to the pub and have some beers.'

I did not feel sufficiently invited into the group to continue the conversation; also, as I hadn't been able to call in briefly at Karen's before the game, owing to traffic problems, I was almost in agony with desire to see her face again. Accordingly, I quickened my step, ahead of the three lads lamenting the loss of goal scorers on the transfer market in recent years. The names 'Becchio' and 'Beckford' peppered the conversation.

It was when the lad who spoke up on behalf of Chris Wood spotted Bronte in the front yard, that I made the connection. His eyes, and his cheekbones, were the same as hers. They made their greetings as though they had been waiting for that moment, and half expecting it to be that day. They were utterly, supernaturally prepared. Karen looked at me: helpless, bewildered, beseeching, totally *un*-prepared; saying nothing, intuitively sensing that a look could convey the complexity and conflict of her feelings, while saying something would involve a selection of words, and therefore be limited – a distortion. Her dilemma was obvious, so I said in as kindly a manner as I could: 'I think you three need to go in. I'll be in my place.'

'OK!' she replied. 'I'll call on you a bit later.'

'That would be nice,' I replied.

There had been no doubting his identity, just from his appearance and the way in which he and Bronte looked at each other; each pair of eyes matching the other's. So this is Terry, I thought. There was something in his reaction that showed surprise, and an expression close to delight. My first thought should not have been a selfish one, to worry about me and Karen, but it was. During every second that Karen was looking at him, with a mixture of astonishment and nostalgia, I felt like a character on the edge of a cartoon being rubbed out by the illustrator as a mistake.

Terry called to his friends: 'You two go to the pub. I'll see you in an hour or two. I'll get the bus.'

The friend with the longer hair asked: 'What's going on?'

The other said: 'Oh, don't be a muppet, Craig. Isn't it obvious?' The lad called Craig still looked baffled, but his friend just urged him along. They got in their car and drove off.

It was about an hour later that she knocked quite timidly on my door. I let her in and made some tea. We sat at the slightly too-large circular kitchen table. 'It doesn't make any difference to us,' said Karen, rather unconvincingly.

'No, it doesn't make any difference to us,' I replied, unconvinced. 'Why did you never tell him? Did he think you were getting an abortion?'

'He didn't even know I were pregnant.'

'Oh. Did he just end the relationship?'

'No. I did.'

'Why? Was he mean to you? Did he cheat?'

'No. He was lovely. He didn't do owt wrong; I just didn't want to land him with the responsibility. Look, we were ever so young. We only had sex three times, and once without a condom.'

'Why?'

'Oh, same as anyone! Spur of the moment. Just being young and stupid. I said I were on the pill. It's difficult to explain; well, you know how carried away you can get, making love. I wanted to really feel him, without rubber. At the time, I dunno, it felt... this is going to sound silly... almost kind of spiritual. Like a union of the two of us, completely bonded together. But of course being pregnant isn't spiritual, it's very physical. Although, of course, Bronte is an angel, and she is kind of spiritual too, although too damn smart and quick witted at times for my liking... So, anyway, when I found out I were pregnant, I ended the relationship, without telling him

178

about the baby. He were very upset; thought maybe my dad was racist or summat, which he really isn't. I just said we were so young, and we weren't going to end up married. I think I really broke his heart. We weren't at the same school, you see, we'd met at a big gathering 'cos both our mums worked at the same place. So, I never saw him from that day to this. I think he went away to university, and maybe lived outside of Leeds for a while. He's from Chapeltown, not round here. Only my mum knew until I were showing, then my dad knew, and he were OK about it, just about. Kevin was still around then. He was great. The doctor had offered me a really early abortion, but I just kept delaying and delaying, sort of half deliberately, until it were too late.'

'So, what now?' I asked, trying desperately not to sound jealous, and probably trying too hard.

'Well, I guess he'll have to be in Bronte's life.'

'Of course. That could be good for her.'

'Yes. It doesn't make any difference to you and me,' she added, seemingly forgetting that she had said this before.

'No, of course not. Does he have children? Is he married?'

'No children, he said he has a steady girlfriend. An artist. Terry's a photographer. I always thought he would be.'

'Listen,' I said. 'Thanks so much for coming round, but I'm really concerned about Bronte. You should get back to her. It was good of her to be OK for us to have this chat.'

'So, are you coming round later?' she asked.

I hesitated. 'I don't think that's a good idea. I think you need to have a long talk with Bronte, and be with her this evening. You maybe don't have to tell her much about your past, but I think you have to spend the evening with her.'

'Of course, of course. But this doesn't change us, does it?' she said, oblivious to the fact that it already had.

179

'No, of course not,' I replied. 'Let's have a coffee in the morning, before I head back south.'

'*Why* do you have to keep going back there?'

'For work,' I replied. 'If it's any consolation to you, I've probably been neglecting work a little. Everything's getting tangled, isn't it?'

It was a subdued morning chat, and a gloomy drive back down the motorway for me, in the grim, pale autumn light. We exchanged many texts that evening, yet I still felt the pain of loneliness before sleeping; in turn I was filled with guilt that I should be feeling so much more about myself than about Karen and Bronte and her dad. That last thing I did before bed was contact Joy, to arrange an evening meal on the Monday, the next day. Fortunately she was free, and she turned up punctually, eager for the news.

'One of the fathers has turned up; he of the daughter, the sixteen-year-old,' I explained.

I could see the effort she made to hide her thrill at such an exciting twist. 'And was he delighted at how his offspring had turned out?'

'Rather startled to discover she existed at all, as it happened.'

She just smiled, then started humming the *EastEnders'* theme tune, before quipping: 'Ah. Funny old world. Of all the lives that could have ended up like a soap opera, I had always thought that yours was the least likely. So, what are you going to do?'

'There isn't much for me to do. He seems like an interesting character, not a lad from the estate. He's been to uni, is a photographer. Has a steady girlfriend, apparently, no kids of his own.'

'Well, it's not really a problem, then, is it? The daughter has a dad in her life, you and your Karen can keep seeing each other.'

I stayed silent, looked down into my malt whisky, swirled it around a little, watching the liquid cling to the side of the glass as it subsided, slowly, with desire, lighter but more viscous than water.

'What is it?' she asked.

'It was the electricity, between them.'

'Karen and the dad.'

'Yes.'

'Mmm, must have been powerful for you to have picked it up.' She gave me a studied look.

'I got a shock, worse than static.'

'Wow. Sounds like it's still powerful. It is electricity that runs our head and hearts.'

'Or, as Karen put it once, does life cause the electricity, or electricity cause life?'

'Quite a deep thinker, your single-mum lover. It so happens I've been asked to give a peer review on an academic paper on this very metaphysical point. It's a valid critique; the forensic attention in the scientific world to process, and comparative neglect of origins. You find this bias more in the life sciences than in physics, which is arbitrary. What began as a healthy rejection of religion has arguably become a limiting belief. I shall give the paper a positive review, but I may be in a minority. Your Karen is ahead of the intellectual curve.'

'You should meet her.'

'About bloody time. Why haven't you arranged that before?'

'You seemed to disapprove.'

She laughed out loud. 'Why do you need my approval?'

'I don't, but I'd want a first meeting to go well. And I wasn't sure you'd be interested.'

'Well, I want to meet my future sister-in-law. She's going to be part of the family. She's met Dad. He couldn't stop talking about her. A beauty from Leeds, he said. Thinks she's a famous actress and has been looking for her on the TV.'

'OK, I'll set it up. Assuming, of course, that our relationship continues.'

'Well, if it can't cope with this disruption, it would be sure to get knocked off course by something bigger before long. Why are you so nervous?'

'Just a feeling.'

'Normally, you're evidence based.'

'Feelings are important; they're everything. This is a love affair, not a laboratory experiment with a control group.'

'Then why are you looking so miserable?'

'I'm not. Just insecure and anxious. Terry is everything I'm not: handsome, young, artistic. All I've got is money.'

'Well, if that's your worry, you might have dated someone from your own income bracket, as I advised you. But given where you are, that anxiety is never going to go away completely. That's your world. That's how it is. If things were different, they'd be different. But if your only problems in life are that you think you're too rich and your girlfriend is too pretty, you need to take a step back and give yourself a lesson in perspective.'

'Aye, I guess so.' She didn't seem to see that my problem was insecurity, not arrogance; that I wasn't thinking I was close to having everything, but rather that I was on the point of losing everything, or everything that mattered.

'Fight for her. Women love that.'

'Oh come on. This is not the Middle Ages.'

'I don't mean literally; just show her you care.'

I couldn't admit to Joy the deepest reason for my unease, given the natural prudishness between siblings. It was Karen's description of how she wanted to feel Terry physically, and the visceral jealousy that this provoked. This comment, made casually in passing, combined with her rejection of my proposal, though admittedly premature, left me feeling second best to the first love, who seemed destined to become the Great Dad. It was certainly novel, as an average-looking wealthy guy, to be treated as the hot lover, not the steady husband, and perhaps I ought to have felt flattered. Yet, I didn't. Fight for her? That was a ridiculous idea. But a crazy, spontaneous, momentous gesture; yes, I could do that. That evening, as I started to fall asleep, a plan began to form. I was interrupted by a couple of texts from my colleague Tony, keen to talk, which I ignored, reckoning I could catch up with him later in the week. Love came first.

28

Things are going so well it's impossible to be optimistic

Terry called again a couple of days later. We had a long chat, then he took Bronte out for a coffee. I was looking forward to him coming round, far more than I should have. It wasn't that I was in love with him still, even below-the-surface – well, not really. It was just that when we made eye contact, it was like time travel; I was completely taken back to the teenage days when we would lie on my single bed back home and we would look at each other, and then at the sparrows on the roof across the street, wondering about their back stories and their plans for life. He had such a deep, penetrating, loving gaze; and maybe I did, to him. It certainly felt like it. So, when he turned up, all punctual, to take Bronte out, and he looked at me, I did feel, not desire exactly, but the memory of desire, deep down. And maybe that's the same thing.

Bronte had been remarkably good with me; I had been worried about a big backlash: why didn't you tell me more about him? Why did you never let him know? Why didn't you contact him years ago, as he's so nice? That sort of stuff. But she didn't. Maybe it was the fact that I had only been the same age then as she was now, and she was thinking about how she would cope, and was being sympathetic to me. Or, more likely, she was simply curious about Terry, and excited that he was wanting to be part of her life. Of course, the backlash could still come, only later.

Missing George was horrible, much worse than usual, as it was also combined with anxiety. Terry and I had done nothing but exchange looks and chat a little, but George picked up straight away that there was something still there. First love is life changing, and maybe that feeling never leaves you completely; it's always there, like a ghost inside your body. They weren't rivals, of course, but there are many other ways in which feelings can get complicated, and wires can get crossed, and jealousies rise to the surface. Late Tuesday evening, after my shift, was the worst. He couldn't chat, he said, as he was about to start a really important business call. It could have been true, of course, but I felt a sickening feeling of dread. An hour later, he sent me a sweet text, but a bit lacking in tenderness or intimacy, I thought, unless I was being paranoid. It took the edge off, but I felt a lurking sense of despair.

Me: *Goodnight babe. Catch up soon. Love you xxxx*
Him: Nothing for an hour.
Him: *Hope you're still awake. Yes, the day went well; tired now. Looking forward to seeing you next time. Love to family. G x*
Me: *Yes, still awake, waiting for your text! Xxxxx*
Him: No reply.

Bronte came back after meeting with Terry. It was the Wednesday, a week later. George had not visited over the weekend, saying he was working. Terry and Bronte had been gone around an hour and a half. She was smiling, eyes lit up completely. 'Oh, it's brilliant, Mum. Today I learned how to develop photographs the old-fashioned way, in a dark room. Terry says there's stuff you can do on print that you can't do on digital. So, I'm going to do photography too. And they're going to create my own section in the studio! I will just be able to paint there for hours.'

'That's wonderful, love,' I said, sounding positive but feeling it was all too swift and that something was surely going to go wrong, though I wasn't at all sure why or how. She seemed to detect my worries.

'Is all this OK for you too, Mum?' she asked, and I welled up with pride at her maturity and her concern.

'Yes, of course, love,' I said. 'I'm just so proud.' I was resting my bum against the kitchen top, holding the teacup with one hand, the other arm resting across my tummy. She was stood opposite, hair all neat, clothes all smart, smiling. I just sighed. 'And I guess it's good for me too. I was just thinking, it's a funny old world. You wait ages for a decent bloke, then two show up at once.'

'No pleasing some people,' said Bronte, quick as a flash. I just smiled and she went up to her room, to listen to music and do her homework. She's so smart, I reflected, with pride and concern.

Terry had promised he would call round with his girlfriend, and he did, the next day. Terry's girlfriend was totally different to what I expected; except that I wasn't sure what to expect with Terry, so any expectations I may have had were unclear. He was always so unpredictable, so determined to break any routine or pattern. Her name was Astrid. She was white, very pale, with long, straight blonde hair and arty clothes which seemed to be second hand, and they didn't 'match' colour-by-colour, except that they did match overall; so garish and uncoordinated and unstylish that it was stylish, in a way, if you wore it with confidence like she did. Or maybe you could just wear anything with cheekbones like hers. She wore huge glasses with a circular design and thick black frame. She had a low-hung tapestry bag that stayed on her shoulder all the time, like it was an item of clothing.

They stayed for about an hour, talking about exhibitions and stuff. We looked at Bronte's drawings and they complimented them, saying she could study; they could teach her. I told them I had no artistic ability, and Bronte had just picked up crayons and started drawing from the age of three, so it was obviously inherited. I felt excited and uneasy, keen that we should all get on, but worried about the pace of events. It was great for her dad to be involved in her life, but the more I felt that, the more I feared losing it. I also felt intense guilt that I had not tracked him down earlier, and brought him into our lives. I kept looking over at Bronte, concerned for her, but she kept giving me a look that said: 'Oh, don't fret, Mum! Everything's fine except for you fretting!'

But I did fret. Mums do. It's part of what we're for. What if she bonded tightly with Terry and Astrid, I wondered suddenly, only for them to go off to California for a month or three years or something like that, doing painting exhibitions on the beach or learning yoga. What then? Have they thought about that? There were other scenarios that went through my head, most of them much worse. Things were going so well it was impossible to be optimistic. Astrid kept saying she loved my eyes, my hair, and she would like to paint me. That ought to have given me a lift but it actually felt only slightly flattering; also, a little bit, not intrusive exactly, but too familiar.

When they got up to go I was relieved; I was hoping Bronte would go to her room too, as I needed to be alone for a while, or maybe call George; if there was anyone I was going to talk to, it would be him. Bronte said goodbye brightly and did go to her room. I followed the two of them out into the front yard, chatting about trivial stuff like which bus to get. Astrid had gone on ahead and then Terry turned round and said goodbye and thanks to me, all effusively and friendly. Then he leaned in, I assumed to peck me on the cheek, but he kissed me full on the lips and I was excited, like we were back in my room again sixteen years earlier. I kissed back, a little, instinctively, then remembered myself and pulled away. My God, what was that? Just a few seconds, but oh so wrong. I would hate to admit that I enjoyed it; although I wasn't even sure that I did. It was just… strange. More like a memory than an event.

'Oh, sorry,' said Terry to me first, smiling nervously, then turning around to Astrid. 'Force of habit – old habit. You jealous?'

'Oh, I love jealousy, babe. I can work with that,' said Astrid, totally unperturbed and, by all appearances, enjoying the scene. 'Jealousy is fuel.'

I was impressed with her coolness, but then worried that I might get invited to join them in a threesome. Then I heard a car revving as it turned the corner, leaving the street rapidly with a tiny squeal of tyres on tarmac as it did so. I seemed to be the only one of us who heard it.

29

Your destination is ahead

An unplanned visit: that would be romantic. In the sports car, of course. There would be no practicalities necessary on this visit – no trips to the furniture store or the tip. I planned it for the Thursday, twelve days after Bronte meeting her dad for the first time. I hadn't visited at the weekend, claiming too much work, which wasn't really true; partly I was giving space to Karen, Terry and Bronte to let them adjust to their momentous change. And partly I was sulking.

An unexpected visit in the following week, a romantic gesture, should put me back in the centre of Karen's world, I hoped. I set off from work early in the afternoon, informing Vicky that I would be on the move and wouldn't be back until midday the next day, asking her to reschedule an appointment. She looked a little startled at my choice, but immediately set about rearranging my meeting and informing the partners. Just before doing so she opened her mouth, as though about to announce something, but seemed to think better of it, and looked back at her PC.

'Will you be in the office at all tomorrow?' she asked, with a mildly disapproving air, as though she were the boss.

'Yes, around lunchtime.'

'OK. Safe journey!'

'See you tomorrow,' I said, crisply and in a businesslike fashion as I left, though feeling mildly ill at ease as I awaited the lift and then left the building. I checked the situation on the motorways on my road traffic app. There was a short red line heading northwards near Luton, and a much longer one in Nottinghamshire. I could switch to the A1 on the Milton Keynes to Cambridge road, recently improved with a dual carriageway, and hopefully be there for around seven, with a red rose and a box of chocolates quickly purchased in central London before setting off. I had gotten way beyond Cambridge before it occurred to me that she may have had an evening shift, or other plans, but decided it was too late to check or to change. I could leave the gift with a card on the doorstep. She ought to appreciate the gesture, and I had my own place anyway. We had last exchanged texts on the Tuesday evening. I had had to apologise for a very short message, owing to an impending conference call with a potential Silicon Valley client, but then compensated with a longer message later. She replied, sweetly, and I assumed all was good between us. The A1 was long, so long that evening. Sometimes it seems a swift journey, and the distance is not far compared with the USA or Argentina, but not that night. The traffic flowed freely but it still seemed so long. It was dark nearly all of the way, and I felt tired as I saw the sign for the M62 as I entered Yorkshire, crossed the Humber, and began counting down the miles to home, which is how I had started to regard the tiny Leeds house.

I had turned on Maggie's voice, despite the familiarity of the route, as I was so tired and thought she would help me stay awake and avoid missing a turning. 'Your destination is ahead,' she said in her calm, reassuring voice as I turned the corner. Immediately as I did so I could see Karen just outside her front door, saying goodbye, it seemed, to a slim young man who resembled Terry, although I could not be certain as his back was towards me. He leaned in and kissed her, and stayed in for the kiss.

It was like a movie, in slow motion. She closed her eyes and stayed there for a few seconds, before pulling away, a little flustered. I almost felt touched by the tenderness of the scene, amid my humiliation and despair. There was another young woman, with straight blonde hair, standing nearby; it was unclear if she was Terry's friend. I immediately performed a U-turn and drove sharply around the corner; I did not know where.

Had I really seen that? Just a few gestures, seen from a hundred yards or so, and my world, my prospects, were blown away. It was as though a bomb had destroyed the bridge that promised to lead me over my river of troubles to my future. I was furious, too. I had brought Danny a toy police car, to go with his fire engine. It was on the passenger's seat beside me. Also, I had received a further email from Alex, the art professor, who had given me some dates she was due to be in London when she could have met Bronte and seen her work. I had gone to the trouble for her, and her family, only to learn she was cheating.

Maggie, needlessly to say, was absolutely livid, having just guided me safely and correctly to my destination over 250 miles. 'At the first available opportunity, perform a U-turn!' she instructed, angrily. I pulled over to the curb and turned the satnav off. I did not know where to go. There were streets in all manner of direction, but no choices. I was far too tired to contemplate driving back to Surrey, and far too ashamed to

191

consider sneaking into my Leeds home. After a few minutes' contemplation, I drove the mile or two into the city centre, making a couple of circuits of a one-way section close to the river, near to our first lunch date. On the third time around, a car left a parking spot, and I manoeuvred the Mercedes into the metered space. I switched the engine off. I was hungry, so I began unravelling the cellophane off the box of chocolates that lay on the passenger seat, the thin clear plastic making its light wrinkly sound as it clung to my hands with static. Irritated, I scrunched it into a ball, and picked up the unopened card that had been ready to deliver should Karen not have been home. I gathered the detritus together, opened the door, got out of the car and pushed them into a nearby bin. The weather was drizzly, breezy and bleak; the atmosphere workaday with just a hint of fervour. It was a Thursday, and there were a few knots of people chatting animatedly as they headed to restaurants and pubs, but not the frenzy of a Friday night. I checked the parking information – no coins needed in the evening.

I sat back in the driver's seat and began eating the chocolates; all of them, even the strawberry and the coffee ones; first the top layer, then the second. They made me feel worse – physically sick as well as emotionally wretched. I felt desperately sad and mildly nauseous. I had never cried, man or boy, but I could feel myself welling up. The phone bleeped that I had a message. I wondered if it was Karen, but it was not. Rather unusually, for a mid-evening, it was my fellow consultant Tony Sheridan:

George, I think I should give you the heads-up. Luke's getting all agitated; wants a partners meeting. Rumours are that legal have got an issue that might get ugly. Call me first thing. Tone

Oh great. Internal politics erupting at the precise moment

I was almost unable to handle it. One of the key attributes of being a CEO is to stay calm even when you do not feel it. Sometimes the gulf between what your emotions are and what you say is so immense it feels like lying. This was one of those times. I texted straight back:

Luke is a stirrer. Will have to sort him (STRICTLY between you and me). Legal would've told me if it were serious. I'll call you at 7. I'm back in the office midday. G

There was a boutique hotel nearby and I asked at reception if there was a room. With it being a midweek, autumnal night there were plenty. Normally, I would go for the most expensive suite, but not that night. I felt vaguely undeserving of luxury. When I went out for a meal, I skipped a couple of trendy eateries, and ate a pizza and drank a large Peroni in a popular Italian franchise place. The beer fizzed in my mouth and anaesthetised my feelings a little. I finished all of the pizza, crust edges and everything, despite feeling mildly sick. As I got back to my room, I finally received a text from Karen.

Hi babe going to bed early as Im knackered. Terry came round to see Bronte which was nice. Facetime me if your still up otherwise sleep well babe talk tomorrow K xxxxxxxx

I did not reply.

I didn't sleep well – from midnight until 2 a.m., and then again from 3.30 a.m. until 6 a.m. I skipped the hotel breakfast and got on the motorway early. By 9 a.m. I was more than halfway back to Surrey but feeling tired and the traffic was building. There were two more texts, both of them filled with angst, from Tony and Karen. The former desperate to meet me as soon as I arrived at the office, the latter asking me if I was busy, saying that she was missing me and could we talk in the evening or at the weekend. I felt guilty because I had completely forgotten about the promise to phone Tony at breakfast time; as regards Karen, the feelings were more compromised.

The traffic became worse. There had been a bad accident ahead, and I was stuck for around an hour, the radio DJs irritating me with their fake cheeriness, even on Radio 3. I tried a couple of CDs, but they were all too sombre. Everything was too cheerful or too sad. I tried calling Tony, but had to leave an apologetic voicemail; then Vicky, via the hands-free and I apologised to her too, said I wasn't well. I was going home to sleep for the rest of the day. Anything of importance could surely wait until Monday, I reckoned. She sounded unconvinced, and flatly unimpressed.

30

Pick up the phone already

'George? George! Why have you not been picking up your phone?!! Really missing you. It would be lovely to talk. Just want to see your face. Maybe we could Facetime. Or anything. Please call.' It was my second voicemail. He would also have something like seven missed calls, and two texts. No reply. Again and again, no reply. An hour passed, then two. No reply. I knew he was busy, and I had at times suspected trouble at his business, when he looked worried about an incoming mail, but shrugged it off unconvincingly. But this was something else.

That couldn't have been his car, disappearing around the corner, could it? He wasn't even in Yorkshire. Unless he was, of course, planning a surprise romantic visit. And that old habit of kissing Terry on the lips, tenderly, like we always used to do, had scuppered George's plans and ruined both our lives. No, no, I told myself. Impossible! It's just paranoid thinking. He probably is ill, or his dad is, or his business is in trouble. He's not perfect but he's conscientious. He would surely tell me if there was anything I had done. I mean, there *was* something

I had done, but ever so tiny, and he couldn't possibly have known, which means it doesn't matter, doesn't it?

Why does he think total silence improves things? What's he trying to say, by saying nothing? How can it be helpful so pointedly to say nothing; not merely saying nothing but refusing to answer messages. It's like if you are in the same room as someone and they say something to you, you don't ignore them completely. How is that any different when you're ignoring someone via the phone? It's no different at all.

I was mad with him. Well, unless he had been in a car accident or was at his dad's deathbed, in which case I was sympathetic to him. But I preferred being mad. In any case, if anything really bad had happened, a message would have got through to me by now. So, he obviously had dumped me, or was about to; he had probably found someone else, someone so bloody smooth and southern, a university-educated ballet dancer with a posh accent and legs longer than his car. Jessica, she'd be called, or Samantha maybe (not 'Sam') and her daddy was a TV producer, and her mummy wrote cookery books, and she got interviewed by Alex on *The One Show* about the pressure of being in the public eye, and what were the Camerons really like, and how was it performing with Darcy Bussell and tell us about your six-bedroomed mansion by the Thames and who's this secret entrepreneur you're rumoured to be dating. Bloody Jessica. I hated her already.

You know when there's someone else, you just kind of know it. Unless that person was me. Had I been cheating? That kiss by Terry – or was it by both of us? – actually in front of his girlfriend. It was just an old habit, a gesture, friendly, really; but I had felt an exhilarating kind of tingle, perhaps more so as it was forbidden. But that was history, my history; my and Terry's history. It had nothing to do with George and me, obviously; nothing at all. It was almost a memory; the reminder of a memory. Nothing to do with the present day at all. And anyway, he couldn't have seen us; although if he had, if he had...

No, it was his fault; him and that scheming, horrible Jessica. I was imagining her lying languidly on his king-sized bed in his Surrey mansion, warm and naked, with a flat stomach and legs so long that her delicate toes brushed gently against the low footboard at the end, saying summat like: 'Oh, darling, have you still not dumped that northern girl yet? Can't we go to Bermuda? Just hire a private jet and we'll be on our way. Two weeks of sunbathing and making a beautiful baby. I'm twenty-six and ovulating, don't you know.' They were probably on their way already. That's why he hasn't texted to dump me yet – he couldn't get a signal at altitude, and he was too guilty and embarrassed to admit it all to me yet; what a coward.

These were my thoughts, all weekend. I had two shifts and then another on the Monday, then two days off in the middle of the week. A shift in a dead-end job actually varies in terms of how tedious and horrible it is: if you've got hope for something – a new love, a new job, your child's performance in a play – then the time passes agreeably enough. But if all hope is snuffed out, it is like a nightmare from which you know you can never awaken.

On the Monday, it seemed that things were about to take a bad turn at work. 'The boss wants to see you,' said Keke, my friend and shift partner, in her sweet Nigerian accent. It didn't sound like a warning, and she gave me a bit of a smile, but it didn't sound like I was to be offered a pay rise either. Her tone was neutral.

'What's that about?' I asked, alarmed.

'I've no idea, love,' she said. 'He just said "I need to talk with Karen." Cannot tell either way.'

I went straight away, to get it over with. Graham had

receding hair, a bit of a paunch and a habit of always looking tired. He wasn't a bad boss mind, considering. He sat behind a small desk, largely taken up with a PC, in his small office with a tiny window.

'Come in, Karen,' he said. 'Take a seat… The thing is…'

'Oh no,' I responded immediately.

He looked up, alarmed. 'No, no! It's nothing bad. Hear me out. The thing is, the company's been getting a bit of a bad press lately. You might have seen something in the *Yorkshire Post*.'

'Can't say I did.'

'Front page of the Business section. Reports of low pay, long hours, poor working conditions. Quite exaggerated, in my view, but rather than get mad with the paper we thought we'd do summat about it.'

'Article passed me by, I must say.' I was puzzled. Why on earth was he telling me this?

'Anyway, the bosses are under pressure, and they reckon some standards could be improved. So, what they're trialling, beginning in our department, is a new vocational training scheme, and more career development options. Reckon it'll improve standards and bring staff turnover down.'

'We've certainly been losing folk recently,' I said.

'Right, anyway. I've been asked to select people as suitable candidates to be supervisors, with a view to becoming trainee managers. And I think you'd make an excellent candidate.'

'Oh, thank you. It's just difficult, as a single mum, to find time to study. I'd love to in theory, but…'

'Well, we've thought of that, and we've come to an arrangement with a local private nursery to provide free places. Plus, we're offering all trainees a thirty per cent pay rise, fifty per cent once you qualify.'

'Well, there's not much to say no to, I guess,' I replied,

feeling rather more proud and hopeful than I would have expected. It was the first time that I had been singled out by a boss or teacher in a positive way since Miss Smith in junior school told me I had a nice way with words. I felt an inch taller already.

'You'd learn all aspects of facilities management. Not the most exciting qualification ever, but looks really good on a CV. Would open up all sorts of opportunities in hospitality, events and exhibitions, and so on. So, what do you think?'

'Well, duh! I mean yes. I mean thank you, Graham.'

'Pay rise is with immediate effect. You start next Monday.'

That was unexpected. The pay rise would come in handy. We had identified an art tutor for Bronte; now we could afford her. Terry and Astrid offered to do so for free, but that might have complicated matters. During the weeks of dating George, I had insisted on a pretence of equality; he paid for most meals out, and a few gifts for the children, but I never asked directly for cash. It would have been vulgar, wrong, sort of distorting the whole relationship, or so I thought. The money thing was always rumbling along, underneath our relationship, but I tried not to let it bother us. A pay rise and a management post might make me feel just a tiny bit more equal. I still missed him so, and it was him who I missed, not the car or the treats or the luxury home down south or the promise of a spectacularly comfortable marriage some way down the line. I missed his kindness, humour, lying my head in the crook of his shoulder after sex, pretending to do telepathy, developing our own in-jokes. I missed him so much, and felt a burning sense of loss, despair and jealousy at his imagined new love. I tried a last, despairing text, sounding pathetic, on the Monday night. It turned out he had been having trouble at work – not that that excused his complete radio silence all weekend. I expressed my sympathy, said I wanted to hug and reassure him; I really thought we were connecting again, and then he dropped the bombshell.

31

The menacing silence

'The partners have called this meeting.'

'You can't do that. It's my company.'

'Actually, it isn't any more. It's owned by the partners. You're a shareholder and the current CEO.'

'Current.'

'Just stating facts.'

It was the ice-cool Susannah, a long-standing consultant and partner, who was delivering the difficult message at the hastily arranged partners' meeting on the Monday morning. Luke had clearly ducked out of this duty, the coward. He was there, but remained silent, outwardly calm. Unless, of course, it was Susannah who was the main instigator of the coup. Nonetheless, I at least respected her for having the guts to speak out openly, and despised Luke all the more. Both, however, were enemies. 'George, there's no easy way to say this,' she continued. 'But your behaviour in recent weeks has become a business issue. We've started to lose reputation and custom. More specifically, we've had a couple of complaints.

First off, Legal have got a seriously threatening letter from Derek Cooper, chief executive of a company called Swish FM, that you've been chasing for business.'

'It would be in their interests…'

'That's not how he sees it. The letter complains of persistent, aggressive sales techniques, naming you. They are inches away from applying for a restraining order. There's worse. He says you've been briefing against them to the business editor of the *Yorkshire Post*, giving them negative publicity over their working practices. Says he has proof. They are actually talking about libel action. Not a problem if the reporter got facts right, but he's talking about coming after us. Do you have any idea how disastrous all this is for our reputation?'

'Look, I'll apologise; it was just overstepping the mark on one occasion,' I said, cursing myself for being so clumsy that I had looked up the company's CEO on LinkedIn, a system that lets you see who has viewed your profile. The *Yorkshire Post* journalist was obviously a contact of mine, as he had profiled me previously. It wouldn't have been difficult for Derek Cooper at Swish to connect the dots; the evidence was circumstantial, but damning. 'These things can be sorted without getting lawyers involved.' I probably kept my voice calm, but my cheeks were burning. The humiliating accusations were all true. I went too far because of Karen. Is that what love does to you?

'But there's more, isn't there?' Susannah continued. 'Sudden, unexplained absences, disappearing off to the north country for a day or two, and no one knows where you are. And the last contract for which you were the client-facing consultant has also resulted in a complaint: Technik UK reported two occasions on which you were late for meetings, another where you nodded off during a meeting, and they are unable to report any performance improvements from your intervention. They want their money back.'

'Look. I created this company. I'm the boss. You don't get to give me appraisals!'

'Actually, we do,' she said. 'It's a partnership. You're the founder, no longer the boss. Everyone's wealth, career and reputation are on the line. That's true of all of us.' She stayed ice cool. Susannah, from a moneyed, international family, with jet-black straight hair; not beautiful but with the indomitable assurance of family wealth behind her. Despite my anger at her words I had to admit that everything she said was true.

There was a long, prickly pause. I didn't know what to say. Luke still said nothing. His silence was more menacing than anything that was uttered. It was like being in court as the accused; your counsel had assured you before the hearing that there was nothing to worry about, but then a prosecution witness pops up and places you at the scene of the crime and puts the murder weapon in your hand. Our boardroom had little natural light, and I lamented that it was not a room that faced over the river; its claustrophobic feel seemed to cause our discussions to be hemmed in with limitations. At that moment I wanted to gaze out at the moorhens and the boats. Instead I just studied the wood patterns in the highly polished board table. I had spilt a large drop of mineral water just before setting down my glass on the coaster, and it magnified the grain patterns in a manner that I suddenly found fascinating.

At length, Tony spoke up: 'Look, Susannah, Luke, everything you say is true, but it's such a partial, biased, limited truth that it amounts to a distortion. Worse than that, it's a betrayal; not just of George himself but of the company's principles. He's had a dodgy couple of months, after a long run of success. Let's get some perspective. George encouraged the move to a partnership because he believes in sharing the wealth. If we repay him by stabbing him in the back, it kills the ethos, which kills the company. I'm against what's being said. I'm against this meeting even being held.'

What an ally. I could have hugged him. He had sent me a text that morning, saying:

If only you'd come in Friday, we could have headed this off! But don't worry. I'm on your side. Worked all weekend to shore up support. Not sure how effective. Tone.

Teresa Ruiz, the Latina whose Spanish was worse than mine – her Mexican parents had raised her in Enfield, speaking English only, with the mistaken idea that this was necessary to prevent her picking up an accent – spoke on my behalf. 'I'm with Tony,' she said, matter of fact. 'George still has, what you call in family business circles, the emotional ownership, or a majority share in it.' Her words were clear and sincere; she did not catch my eye, but that could have been to avoid giving the impression that she was taking the cue from me, so it probably helped that she was cool and professional in manner. It suddenly occurred to me that I knew little about her; I had heard that she wrote rather racy fiction as a sideline, and one of her novels had been published, but she was always cool and proper at work. She, like me and Tony, was from a modest background, having worked her way up from state school and university. It was starting to feel a little like the posh set was pushing us out.

And yet, maddeningly, Tony's and her speeches were met with silence from the other four partners. I waited. We all waited. Was it really four against us three? The mood in the room had swayed, but because of other people's intervention; my own influence seemed to count for nothing, and I was struggling to articulate anything of substance to say; highlights from the previous year's achievements would have sounded banal and defensive, I felt. As the implications of this sank in, I decided to say nothing, just rose from my seat and walked towards the door, not saying a word. Every pair of eyes followed me. No one said a word until I reached the door, at which point Susannah asked: 'Are you going to reply to the points we made? Where are you going?'

I paused and said: 'Thanks for your words of support, Tony. You are without doubt the finest Chelsea supporter in the country. Teresa, you are an absolute star, and I will finally buy and read your novel. Now, excuse me, everyone, I just need a break.' And then I opened the door and left the boardroom.

Just before it closed, I heard two comments. Susannah said: 'He's not coming back, is he?'

Then Tony said: 'Absolute idiots. The lot of you.'

It was curiously liberating, as I walked out into the street. I didn't have the car in town that day; I had come in on the train. I walked from the City-based office to Covent Garden, watched the living statues for a while and then walked on a little further, generally northwards, through a couple of the neat squares in Bloomsbury, to St Pancras. A trip to Paris, perhaps? Brussels? No. I didn't have my passport. I carried on, crossed Pancras Road at the pedestrian crossing between stations, and entered Kings Cross. Leeds would have been too obvious, and too close to Karen, and Scotland too far. I settled on York. Purchasing a last-minute, first-class ticket was deliciously expensive. I also bought a copy of *The Economist*, an egg and cress sandwich and a miniature bottle of malt whisky. If only the journey were longer than two-and-a-bit hours.

There was another text from Karen, more desperate this time and, despite my continued state of annoyance, you might call it a sulk, I began to sympathise.

Honey, I dont know what Ive done wrong. It must be something but I really don't know. Please call even if its just to end it cant go on like this. Or maybe your ill or ur dad is. Love you K xxxxxxxxxxxxxx

I drank a glug of whisky before replying:

Hi K. Sorry for the silence. I've had a lot of problems at work. Fact is, they've moved against me and I've been ousted from the company. Need some space to think. Love G x

She texted straight back:

Thats awful and outrageous! They cant do that its ur company!! So sorry luv wish I was there to giv u a big hug. Pls call soon xxxxxxxxxxxx

I replied:

Well, it's not my company any more, so technically they can outvote me. But it's a big change and I have to rethink lots of things x

My phone went ping! once more:

U can always talk to me about anything. Really want to see u again soon. Sending much luv & hugs xxxxxxxxxxx

I nearly softened completely, but instead replied:

Well, maybe you and I need a bit of time apart; some space, just so much to think through. G x

She didn't respond.

32

Have your 'space' if you want it

He needs some 'space', some 'time apart'? Without even saying why, or telling me face-to-face? Oh, no, George, you don't get to make that call. You can't bail on a relationship, not like that. He was so obviously with someone else, that bloody Jessica or whatever her name was. I didn't reply to his devastating text. I then awaited his imploring emails, calls and texts begging forgiveness, so that I could ignore those too. But none came! That was maddening! How could you pointedly ignore someone who was already ignoring you? It was obviously my prerogative, my turn, to be blanking him while his role should have been to get on his knees and say sorry and implore me to want him back! How completely and utterly selfish of him!

Unless, of course, he was on his knees, but with Jessica, as she lay languidly on a fold-down bed in his executive jet, pulling down her panties and initiating her into the Mile High Club. 'Oh, George!' she'd be saying. 'Do it again! Higher! Faster! Better! I bet your Yorkshire lass was never classy or rich enough for this plane! Am I better than her? Oh, say I am,

George, say it, say it!' The image would not depart from my brain. Maybe, by thinking about it, I was making it less likely. No! That was a silly superstition! Thinking about it doesn't make it more or less likely! The reason I was thinking he had started a new relationship was that he was behaving exactly like someone starting a new relationship: avoiding me much of the time, suddenly lukewarm in the few communications we did have; obviously avoiding any long conversation as he knew he'd have to 'fess up and he didn't know how to.

All Tuesday was miserable; even the sad songs on my iPhone just made me feel more sad, when they were supposed to have provided some sort of consolation. I listened to Adele and Amy Winehouse and a few others all through my boring cleaning shift, conscious that I had to try to put myself into a more positive frame of mind for when my training started.

Heartache is as bad as grief, and worse than illness. The pain is something physical, deep in the gut and in the soul. It stayed with me at every step, haunted me with every thought that I had and everything I said. It was an effort to do stuff. I felt tired at every step. Often I just did what I knew was necessary, for work or for the house or for Bronte or Danny; just did the tasks, without much feeling, almost like I were in a trance. I would lie down when I got the chance but most days I didn't.

At least the pay rise had started, so it was nine-pound-something an hour not seven-pound-something, and I should keep my tax credits, and maybe I could start saving. Maybe I could let myself into George's house and find something valuable to sell. That would serve him right, I thought, though this was only a stupid revenge fantasy, and I didn't want to do anything to stop him coming back, assuming he would want to, one day.

Still, I reflected, there was zero chance of my ever coming across Jessica if I let myself in, or indeed anywhere on our street; dearest darling Jessica would only be seen in Chelsea or Surrey or the stage at Covent Garden, or her parents' mansion out in Oxfordshire near David and Samantha Cameron, darling. I was getting more and more detailed in Jessica's back story. When I was a girl, sometimes I had an imaginary sister, or female best friend. I had a brilliant brother but sometimes I wanted a sister. Back then I never thought that one day I would have an imaginary enemy. Wow, had my life really turned out that bad? Was I some sort of psycho monster, these days?

But then, don't blame me. Blame George. It was obviously all his fault. And Jessica's as well – I mean, it takes two, doesn't it?

It was difficult, really difficult, to be happy for Bronte and Terry when I was disintegrating inside. I didn't even let them know that my relationship with George had broken up; of course, in truth, I was not quite sure that it had. The two of them had another meeting that week, during which he took her to Astrid's studio. When she came back, she was full of it: 'It's so cool, Mum! She does these amazing paintings and montages – you know what a montage is, don't you? – and they showed me some techniques and said I could use them during art A-Level if that's OK with you!'

I smiled, and said I was pleased, but probably my eyes were not smiling, however hard I tried. Terry was friendly and normal. He said nothing about the kiss, and didn't lean in again, even for a peck on the cheek, so his failure to do that was sort of a communication, an acknowledgement that it had been an error, even if it had been a bit of a turn-on for his girlfriend, rather than prompting a jealous rage. Oh, what a mess.

The first training session as a manager was not what I expected at all. I was expecting it to be quite dull – just learning about shift rotas, and types of cleaning product and where you got your supplies from, but it was all kind of personal and a bit more interesting than that. They wanted to know what sort of a personality you were. I wasn't sure how that made you better at running a load of cleaning shifts, but it was fun and quite interesting. Anyway, after a long questionnaire about what I prefer, how I make decisions and so on, I came out with the initials 'EFSP', which means I'm outgoing, friendly and chatty, which I already knew, so I wasn't sure how it would take us further forward, but the trainer, this lovely, smart woman who introduced herself as Sue Clark (we all got name badges), organised us all into groups to talk about the results and what it meant for our management style and we had some interesting conversations. I also worked out that George was classic INTJ – not so talkative, and keen on the scientific evidence. It shed light on how to deal with him; shame that the insight had come too late.

She was really nice, was Sue, and I started to think that I was more interested in doing her job than a supervisor's. The other trainees were friendly too; there were about fifteen of us, from all parts of the company, including people I hadn't met before. There was a tall, young guy trying so clearly not to flirt with me that it was almost excruciating. But he was nice. Danny even had a fun time at the free nursery, and we went back home together in the evening, both having made new friends. He was so tired he just slept for eleven hours, which was a relief.

If I was going to be heartbroken for the rest of my days, and never have sex again, at least life was going to be a tiny bit more comfortable with a bit of a career ahead of me, and some supportive colleagues; all the more so once Bronte started providing for me as a famous artist.

33

People want decisions

'Oh yes, I'd forgotten that. When you've had a major setback at work and a crisis in your main relationship, the best response is to hide away and sulk for days on end,' Joy told me with crushing sarcasm. 'Always helps. Funny the life lessons you learn, but then forget again.'

'It's the only thing I can face doing at the moment.'

'And how's it working for you?'

'That presupposes there is something that will work,' I said.

'Well, at least try honest and positive communication, then if it doesn't work, you know why. You can move on.'

'I don't want to find out. I don't want to communicate. And I'm not sure I want to "move on". That's such a cliché.'

'Saying nothing, when you're in a relationship, *is* a type of communication! And quite an aggressive type!' she replied, raising her voice and slightly alarming me as she did so. We were talking on the phone. I had ignored all pleas for a face-to-face meeting. In any case, I was holed up at a country hotel between Wetherby and Knaresborough, and she was in her big house in Broxbourne. I paced about the suite, in and out of the small living room area, returning back to the huge bedroom, with the view over the lower Yorkshire Dales. I had always liked Knaresborough, ever since a school trip there when I was about eight. I made a wish in the wishing well: that I would play football for the school team. That never came true. It's just as well I didn't wish to become a wealthy business owner. I booked a suite for a whole month, paying in advance for a discounted rate. It was a week or so after the dreadful Monday with the attempted office coup, the train ride north and the final exchange of messages with Karen.

There had been several communications from work, including the HR department and the lawyers. 'People want decisions,' was the gist. But Tony and Vicky were the only colleagues I could face talking to; they and Teresa were the only ones I could trust. As an interim arrangement, I was signed off for three months with 'depression', and Tony persuaded the partners to delay any vote over ownership or my role until the end of that period, while he acted as temporary chief executive. 'He who wields the sword rarely takes the crown,' I quipped to him in one of our few conversations, as I expressed my relief that Luke or Susannah was not taking over. I thanked him effusively, and promised that I would do everything I could to make the post permanent upon my return; though he and Teresa still wanted me back. At least someone did.

The days passed quickly, and silently. The seasons nudged their way around. The scenery was rolling green farmland and drystone walls, but I didn't look out much. Sometimes I just lay on the bed, not reading – not even looking, for an hour or so.

I had hoped to hear from Karen, but there was not a word, rather confirming my fear that she had resumed her relationship with Terry and was simply finding a way to tell me it was over. My last message to her had been about wanting some time to myself; nonetheless, I had hoped to hear from her. It was vaguely satisfying, if somewhat cruel, to have ignored her pleas for love and hugs and contact; but, now that these pleas had ceased, I felt worse than lonely – almost humiliated. She had given up even wanting me, or fighting for our love. I pictured the four of them, the perfect nuclear family, on a day trip to York or somewhere, father and daughter bonding over their intense spiritual and artistic thing that they had going; mother putting together a packed lunch and whistling as they got in the car.

I didn't do depression, I knew that. Depression was for other, less entrepreneurial people. I was different; I always had an imaginative response to problems; I was infinitely resilient. I never got weighed down by oppressive situations or rules because I always created my own. I was aware of the concept of Mindfulness, and getting-in-touch-with-your-feelings, but I knew I was skilled at this, without professional help or weekend supervised retreats. I didn't do depression. I didn't see it as a weakness, I had just worked out how to avoid it. I would make these points to someone if there had been someone to make them to, which there wasn't; and if a need arose, which it didn't. My trusted sister was on the line with me, but I felt uncomfortable about confiding too much in her, as she had counselled against the relationship in the first place, so there'd always be the 'I told you so' in the background; in my head, even if she didn't say it. No, there was only one person I would have been prepared to divulge the really personal stuff to at that stage in my life, and that person was dead. Mum came to me in dreams, and her face and voice were clearer in my dreams than in my conscious memories. Each time I awoke I felt that I had lost her again and over breakfast I sank to a very low place. She was the only one I could talk to and the only one who got me. Anyone else could clear off, thank you very much.

From experience, I felt that, often, the best response to feeling low was to get on your feet and achieve something new. This feeling right now wasn't depression. I had just experienced some setbacks and I was taking stock. First world problems, I told myself. There was something, though, that was chipping away at any feeling of solidity; at the inner resilience and buoyancy of spirit that I had previously taken for granted. When I thought about what had shaken this inner core, some of the findings surprised me. It wasn't only about Karen, and the feeling that she was out of my league and already moving away from me. There was something about the trivial incident on the pedestrian bridge after the match the other week, feeling jealous of the easy-natured banter between Terry and his two friends, and how I had volunteered an opinion, hoping to be invited into their friendly ring. He was one of the lads. I had never been 'one of the lads'. In one entire term at school, no one spoke to me at all during the break period or at lunch. At university I studied, staying away from the drinking crowd with disgust; similarly, as a junior consultant, I slaved away for my clients and bosses, and never went to the Friday night pub sessions. Then I ran my own business. The boss-owner can never be a team member. Perhaps I had secretly always wanted to belong – to have peers. I used to envy the school team players, hence the wish in the wishing well in Knaresborough, but I was hopeless at any ball game, and a sluggish runner.

I was well versed in all the psychological literature about group behaviour; the harmony and hypnotism of a high-performing group where everyone is lifted by that buzz, that team spirit. It can be felt in sports, or in a choir, or in a crowd at a sports stadium, or in the army. I had tried to nurture that at the business, and at times it felt we were achieving it; but I was always the boss, and always slightly removed. I was always on the outside of this imagined communality of other people, and my commercial success confirmed this isolation; the fear that every friendly overture was a manoeuvre and every flirtation a calculation. I only came close to this sense of belonging when at the football. This deep, inner psychological drama was the real reason, I realised at that moment, that I sat in the stands and never hired a hospitality suite at the stadium; this desperate desire to belong; to have peers. It was sad.

And there was something else. Walking away from the business, my business, was liberating, yet also disabling. Terry had found his baby; I had lost mine. As a young human, unless you've been abused, you become aware of the astonishing power of your own consciousness. As an adult you can experience the most humbling sense of futility at simply being a sole being. You may have your superpower, as Karen put it, but it may be worthless, depending on context – like arriving as Superman from another planet, with the ability to fly, only to discover you're the size of a bumblebee. What I was feeling wasn't depression, I wasn't prone to that, but it was something.

What would it be like, I wondered, to give it all up completely? Quit the business, the job, Karen, the UK, divide my wealth evenly between cash, property and gold, and live on a beach in Bali, or somewhere? Learn how to surf. I had always assumed that dropping out would be boring, but what if it wasn't? What if the stupid, crazy working world is all a bit pointless, a bit inauthentic, and what we really ought to do as humans is eat, drink and splash about in warm water with dolphins? And make love, we need to be able to make love, though; that's where it gets complicated. Prostitutes? Ugh no; it's being fancied that matters.

So, am I stuck with it, this life? Uncomplicated and

despairing on my own, or connected but panicky and insecure with someone? Futility or anxiety: is that the choice? Actually, anxiety comes with both options.

In any case, if I lived in a surfing paradise, I would only start to spot errors and missed opportunities with how the surfing companies were run, or how the accommodation was promoted, and how their websites were designed and where they ranked on Google; then I'd get chatting with one of the owners and propose a new approach to marketing and customer service, put up some capital and be offered a business partnership. I would end up making money again. It's how my brain is wired.

I was not like other people. I was different, more enterprising. But that has its downside. It's a gift. It's also an illness. And now I was signed off for three months with it.

'Hello? Are you still there, George? Don't hang up on me!'

'Sorry, Joy. I was miles away.'

'Have you seen Dad?'

'Of course. I'm just round the corner. Though he just wants to talk about Karen.'

'Well, go figure.'

'I will talk to her. But I'm not ready yet. You know she's back with her ex, the father of Bronte?'

'No, I don't know that. And I very much suspect that you don't know that, either. You've just got a hunch, or a fear. You're all for facts and the evidence base when it comes to work, why not for relationships?'

'It's different.' I felt uncomfortable. My disinclination to talk to Karen felt close to a phobia, linked with feeling inadequate, unfanciable, asocial, like my fifteen-year-old self. It was deeply irrational, but I wasn't ready for therapy. And Mum was still dead.

'Self-fulfilling prophecy.' Joy continued. 'She's not ending this relationship; you are.'

'Yea, well, I'll think about it.'

'OK, sermon over. It's your life. Call me again this week.'

'Will do, little sis. Ciao for now.'

'Yea, ciao, big idiot brother.'

34

Imaginary love rival

My dreams had become savage. Horrible. In one, I was stuck in a room in a large building, like a hotel, but also with offices. I had this urgent need to get up to the next floor, but the only way to do so seemed to be to clamber up onto a ledge, then jump up to another one, then crawl through a narrow space. I was thinking 'Surely this can't be the way to the room on the next floor! The building must have stairs, or a proper lift or something.' But onward I struggled, feeling lonely and scared, my clothes getting torn by the jagged stone I was crawling on. I could hear the murmur of cultured people, at an artistic event or something, but always somewhere above, somewhere just out of reach, taunting me. I did hope Bronte wouldn't paint this. I'd have looked a mess.

During this time, though, I decided to try to educate myself a little more, reading up about metaphysics online, having been told I had a gift for it. It was an experience where some aspects would be really clear while others were completely incomprehensible. But there was a difference this time, compared with earlier learning experiences: when I came across something I didn't understand, I wanted all the more to learn about it, instead of feeling intimidated and giving up. I guess that was the influence of George and Terry and Astrid, not just their example of being educated themselves, but taking me seriously. And Bronte too, I guess.

It was a strange thing, being both happy and heartbroken. New opportunities were opening up for me, and more so for Bronte, and I really did feel some of her joy when she came back from a morning at the studio with Terry and Astrid, and told me about what she had learned or worked on, and especially when she was able to show me a new painting or little sculpture. They always looked beautiful and clever to me, but of course I was biased. Sometimes, I wanted her to notice that I was hurting so deeply inside, and to ask after my feelings, but in those first few weeks of getting to know her dad, quite honestly, she did not, so caught up was she with this new dimension to her life. It's so hard not to feel selfish; you can act unselfish, but it is so hard to feel it. She must have cared little for George, with him having not honoured his promise about the professor; now she had two real art tutors, one of them her dad.

So, I would have a little weep on my own, or I could talk to Sharon. I thought endlessly about George, especially on the work shifts or when I woke up in the middle of the night, reached out for him and he was not there. Was he reacting any differently? Are men less emotional, more rational? Do they 'move on', as the saying goes, without much pain? George is rational, I reflected. He's probably not hurt at all, just sees being with me as having been a social experiment, with some great sex. Do rich people have feelings? Do they hurt? How much does having lots of money and a nice house ease the heartache, supposing that he felt any for me at all? How much does it soothe any emotional pain to have a beautiful house, with a designer kitchen and a garden that's like a mini country park? But was he feeling lonely in all that space? Except that, of course, he probably wasn't alone! By now he would be lying in the arms of Jessica, or whatever her name was, back in with his sort of people, back home, thinking up girls' names and boys' names, deciding how to decorate the nursery. Men are just so weird, impossible to fathom, especially quiet men, which is most of them.

When a love affair ends, and ends so suddenly, you can look back and wonder why you had not appreciated it more at the time. 'Just three weeks ago I was happy; happier than I realised at the time,' I would say to myself. 'The time has gone and it's never coming back. Just four weeks ago; I was happy even when he wasn't at my side, and I was just going to the shop, to buy something for our dinner.' I tried concentrating fiercely to capture those moments, to recall every detail that I could, as accurately as my memory would permit, and the feeling of lightness and quiet euphoria that accompanied them, and scoop up what scraps of happiness I could on my time travel and try to carry them back with me to the dreary present.

If there was one thing that I had gained from knowing George, it was a sense of putting my life back in my hands again, and not being so passive. There was something about his attitude to work and life that had rubbed off, which was undoubtedly why I had taken up this chance of training and promotion. Given the pay rise, I would have had to anyway, but I decided to be enthusiastic about it, like I had something to prove. The trainers were nicer than I had expected, and I was doing better than I had expected. Sue Clark the trainer became something of a role model: she had that wonderful combination of being authoritative but kindly, like a good schoolteacher.

At times I stopped looking back, and projected forward: five, ten years. I would be a senior manager, with a nice house in the suburbs; Bronte would be exhibiting at a swanky gallery in London, and George would turn up to the event, all curious, without having told me. I'd be dating a famous photographer by then; he'd be all over me. Jessica and George would be icy with each other, owing to a dalliance he had had in Buenos Aires and the fact that their third child wasn't sleeping through the night. I would be able to note the weariness in the lines around her eyes. George and I would exchange a deep look, and Jessica would notice, feel jealous, and tug at his elbow to move him along. Then she and I would exchange a knowing look; I would be all calm and superior. The fantasy ended. Did having a fantasy make a good outcome more or less likely to come about in real life? I often wondered about that. If you declare that you want a really good thing to happen, and you plan for it, people say you're jinxing your chances. But that's just a superstition, isn't it? Things never work out how you anticipate, but that doesn't mean good things can never occur. Maybe George had been a good thing; he came into my life just to jolt us out of this weary resignation that I had fallen into. My head said this, repeated it to myself day in, day out, but my heart was still in pieces, and my soul felt heavy and low.

The next time Terry came round, he was on his own. Bronte was at a friend's; he had gotten the wrong day. This was not unusual for him, as he could be dreamy and in his own world. If he was working on something major, he would genuinely forget which day it was. It was bad enough when he was at school, but now that he worked for himself he was even more at sea, not distinguishing weekends from other days.

He stayed for a cup of tea. It was around 8 p.m. and I had just put Danny down for the night. He was exceptionally tired after a long game of football with Jayden and had crashed out.

'You and George are finished?' he asked. He looked genuinely concerned.

'It would appear so. He said he wanted some time for himself, and he's ignoring me.'

'Oh, I'm so sorry, babe. I hope it's nothing to do with me turning up again.'

'I don't see how it can be, Terry. I mean, he won't have seen us together, and we're not back together.'

'Well, there was that kiss. Sorry, by the way – old instinct.'

'Don't apologise. Anyway, he was in Surrey.'

'Which makes it all right.'

'Well, even if hypothetically he saw us via Google camera or summat, it was nothing; we could have talked about it,' I reasoned. 'I know he's having big trouble at work, but that makes no sense either, that that would be a reason for dumping me. I offered to hug and comfort him, etc., etc.'

'Yea, that doesn't make sense. There must be something else.'

'Or someone else, like that Jessica, for example.'

'Who?' he asked, puzzled.

'Oh, this ballerina. I'm pretty sure he's started dating her. Accomplished, highly educated, trained by Darcy Bussell, long legs and perfectly fertile, beautiful and with highly connected parents. Mind, she did contract meningitis as a five-year-old, which shows that bad stuff can happen to well-off folk. But her loving mother knew the tumbler test for the rash, and got her down the hospital in time. And after that she took her to London for a weekend, with two visits to the Royal Ballet at which point she fell in love with dance and decided that that would be her career. And she reached the summit of the ballet world, despite missing out on the collaboration with the Bolshoi because of her injured foot in 2012.'

'Wow. How do you know all that?'

'Well, I have made guesses and interpretations based on...
on...'

'Quite limited information?'

'Well, more a hunch, really. I mean, it's obvious he's got
someone new.'

'Um, Karen, this Jessica...'

'Yes?'

'She doesn't really exist, does she?'

'So, what are you trying to say? That I'm the only person
in the entire world who creates an imaginary love rival with a
back story all worked out?'

He thought for a second, screwing his face up a bit, with a
gesture of real affection, before saying: 'Um... how do I put
this? Yes? I think it's just you, Karen.'

'You make me sound neurotic when you put it like that.'

'Weeeell...'

'I suppose it is a bit paranoid, thinking about it,' I admitted.
'Saying it out loud. I blame you, mind. We always used to
think up back stories for all sorts of folk, even the birds on the
roofs.'

'Yes. However, I tried not to let them affect major life
decisions.'

'Did you ever have an imaginary friend as a child?'

'You're kidding, right? I was one of six in a three-bed house
in Chapeltown! I used to have imaginary solitude. I could
always escape in my head, but it was away from folk, not
towards them. Until I met you.'

'Oh, Terry, don't.'

'Don't what?'

'Try to start things; restart things.'

'I didn't think I was. I was just reminiscing.'

But he looked at me deeply in the eyes. 'Maybe we could,
you know,' I said, spontaneously, the years melting away.

'I didn't hear that...' he said, but then his eyes caught mine, and time slipped away again. He began to lean in to kiss, and I leaned fractionally also, but we both pulled away. What would it have been like? With more passion perhaps, and less guilt, given that George appeared to have left me, and Astrid seemed to think an open relationship was cool – though I may have over-interpreted what she said on that point. Yet, a mistake, all the same.

He looked directly at me: 'You broke my heart, you know. Just dumped me without saying owt. I thought your family were racist or summat, that I was like the lover but could never be the regular boyfriend. Or that you'd found someone new.'

'I'm sorry. I'm so sorry.' I looked down, feeling ashamed. 'It was nothing like that. I was wanting to spare you the burden.'

'Bronte's not a burden! She's a... well, an angel.'

'I know, but I didn't know that at the time. I was young, so young, and frightened and I just turned to my mum.'

'Well, you hurt me. You've no idea how much.'

'I'm sorry, Terry. I'm so, so sorry.'

He took a deep breath, pulling himself a bit further away. We had been sat on hard chairs, at the table, on the same side. He looked at me again, and then down at his teacup. 'Maybe everything's happened so fast, and it's difficult for all of us,' he said. 'Sometimes, the heart cannot catch up with events. The main thing that we have to concentrate on is Bronte. What's best for her.'

'Absolutely, and it's wonderful the way you are with her. I am genuinely happy for her. It's best if you and I are friends; like, you get divorced couples who become best of friends and are great parents. Let's be like them.'

'Yes,' he said, breathing deeply once, looking down. 'Let's be like them,' he replied. But then he gave me one of those looks again. I said he had better go.

35

We're all an odd mix

'Where's that Karen? Have you patched things up yet?' my dad asked. He forgot everyone's name except hers. It had become customary for him to greet me in this way. He was looking paler and weaker, though there was still some spirit in the eye.

Joy was with us, and replied on my behalf: 'He hasn't yet, but I'm working on it, Dad.'

'I don't know where he gets his stubbornness from,' said Dad. It was impossible to tell if he were joking.

'It's a mystery,' replied Joy, sarcastic, deadpan.

'England are doing well in the test matches,' he said. 'Beating South Africa. That Joe Root, he's the best since Hutton. I met him in a pub, once.'

'Glad you've got your Sky Sports then, Dad,' I said.

Afterwards, Joy invited me for a swift half in the nearby town.

'Thanks for visiting some more,' she said. 'I think it means a lot to him.'

'It's hard to say,' I replied. 'I run out of conversation

sometimes. But I think that says more about me than about him.'

'We're going to have to talk about, you know, finances and the will and everything,' she said.

'I thought everything was sorted. The will is up to date, you have power of attorney, and so on.'

'Oh, yes, there's no crisis, that I can think of. I'm just conscious I have to be transparent with you. He's still got savings, and he's agreed to leave something to Aunty Alice, which is only fair. She'll probably outlive him and we're better off than she is, even though she's in a relationship now. Never saw that coming!'

'Seriously, Joy, don't worry. Just make the decisions, whatever they are. I have everything to worry about except money. I don't want Aunty Alice to be struggling. I should visit her more often, actually.'

'Just as well you and I have done well. It's eased all his worries. He used to fret so.'

'Yea? We had a comfortable upbringing, didn't we?'

'By the skin of our teeth.'

'What do you mean?'

'Well, I've probably never told you this before, George, but Dad was actually not that good with money. It reached a near crisis when you were at uni. So, I sat down with him and sorted it out.'

'Really?'

'Yes. Well, GCSEs were hardly stretching, so it was a good exercise. He had various hire purchase arrangements, a credit card debt and was going overdrawn most months. So, I sat down and went through it all. But it turned out he had over ten thousand pounds on premium bonds on the basis that it might produce some winnings some day. So, I used that to pay off most of the debt...'

'*Most* of it? It was more than ten thousand pounds?'

'Yes, though not much more. Then I looked up some better mortgage deals, and encouraged him to stay in the company's occupational pension scheme.'

'All when you were sixteen.'

'Fifteen, actually. He was very grateful.'

'How peculiar. He always appeared sensible and well organised.'

'He's an odd mix. I guess we all are. Do you know he believed in mysticism?'

'*What?*'

'Well, for a while. He got into it after Mum died. He tried to get in touch with her using an Ouija board. It had been all the rage in the 1920s and 1930s, so he learned. Sir Arthur Conan Doyle was an advocate, and you know how much Dad was a fan of his.'

'That's so poignant. I mean, not the Ouija board itself, but the trying to get in contact with Mum. So sad.'

We rarely talked about how much we missed Mum. Of course, in Joy's case, she had no memories. I did not tell her that I had been yearning to talk with Mum about my relationship problems; that it seemed like she was the only one who got me, because it would have made me sound like a six-year-old, and because I may have sounded superior; my saying: 'Oh yeah, I had a relationship with her, you didn't.' Once, when we had been very much younger, Joy asked me to describe Mum for her, and I struggled and became upset. She didn't ask again for many years.

Joy left that evening, returning south, and I returned to my luxurious but lonely suite. But the month was coming to an end, and I had to decide whether to rebook the suite in the hotel, or return home, wherever I decided home would be. It occurred to me that the Surrey house may want a bit of care and attention, with the central heating and the deluxe wood-burning stove fired up for a day or two. It may, of course, need selling or renting out to help furnish me with an income, I reflected, though if the partners did want to buy me out of the company they wouldn't find it cheap; booked revenue and goodwill amounted to millions, and there was no debt.

Pat, the local woman in Surrey who did the cleaning, had a key, and had let herself in a couple of times, to tidy up. She reported that all was fine, but I concluded that it was time for a visit. As for the Leeds home, the 'caretaker' was Karen, so contact was out of the question. It could have been flooded or burgled by now, or just very dusty. Or perhaps she was using it for trysts with Terry, away from the children, I reflected. I played with the painful fantasy in my head as one might wiggle a rotten tooth. Perhaps they would be using my house, sleeping in my bed, the perfect love nest next door, to which she still had a key. The thought tormented me.

I had had my birthday alone, and it was nearly Christmas. I had arranged to spend Christmas Day and Boxing Day with Dad. Joy would surely join us too, so it seemed to make sense to spend a week or two back down south before returning north for the holiday. So, I began the journey home. As the signs for the M1 appeared, multiple lanes filtered off from the A1. I briefly contemplated the south-westerly option, which passed close by the south Leeds home, so that I could call in on the property and perhaps catch a glance of Karen, either happily ensconced with Terry, or red-eyed with grief and heartbreak over me. Was the latter actually possible? There was a period of a mile where the lanes respectively for M1 and A1 ran in parallel, and I moved consciously between them, changing my mind a couple of times before settling on the more easterly route. I did not stop until I reached Peterborough Services, some two hours later.

I drove the long way around the M25, over the perilously high Dartford Crossing, jetty lights, ship lights and power stations illuminated on the wide Thames estuary, arriving on the gravel drive well into the evening.

There was a pile of mail, mostly flyers and other junk, that Pat had thoughtfully arranged into separate piles and placed on the smooth polished occasional table in the hall. The smell in the entrance hall caught me by surprise. I had been away long enough for it to prompt a deep feeling of nostalgia. Every house has its unique smell; it is never a combination of identifiable fragrances, but exhales its own distinct flavour. There was little left of Penelope and Amelie in the atmosphere; even so, I thought of them. Among the few personal items, there were two envelopes, from their stiffness each clearly containing a card, and each with my name and address in rounded, girly handwriting. The first was from New York, a birthday card from Penelope and Amelie; intriguing that their faces should have appeared in my mind just before opening the card, though, given that this had been their home, perhaps the coincidence was not so great. There was only a short message, but it was sweet and sincere. That was unexpected. I wondered whose idea it had been. The other was postmarked Leeds LS11, dated ten days earlier. My heart started thumping. Ten days. Enough for her to have raised her hopes, then given up? I paced up and down the spacious hall, clutching it in my right hand. I waited for a minute, nearly two, then ripped open the envelope, letting the torn paper fall gently to the polished wooden floor, where it reluctantly settled, after being chased briefly by a floor-level zephyr. It was not themed to Christmas, or any event. It may have been for my birthday, but there was no printed message inside or out, just a print of a watercolour pastoral scene on the outside. Inside, she had written a short note:

229

George – I hope this finds you well. I'm very unhappy with how things are between us. It feels like I must have done something wrong, but you won't say what. If it's over between us, I want to know for sure, and I want to know why. If you're unwell, I hope you get better soon.

Lots of love

Karen x

The pain behind the words was evident; the strain that lay behind the words that were unsaid so evident also, emotionally still present, as they hid behind the carefully chosen phrases that did appear. She had avoided accusation or self-pity, and I had to acknowledge her maturity, and feel a sense of shame that my own was lacking. I had to call now.

36

This has so not gone how I planned

I had sent him a card. I had thought long and hard about it. Technically, it was my 'turn' to contact him, as I hadn't replied to his last text, some weeks earlier; but as that message had clearly indicated his wish for some 'space' (what a dishonest form of expression, making it sound like you're just seeking a bit of liberation when in fact you're telling someone to clear off, someone who had given her heart!). I decided not to be all vengeful, or too sorry for myself, just to state that I deserved some sort of explanation and that, if it was over, to know for sure and to know why. For more than a week he did not reply. Perhaps he hadn't received it; perhaps he wasn't even in Surrey, I reflected. He could be away on business – or on a romantic holiday with Jessica in the Maldives or Bahamas. I thought about little else in my quieter hours, and even in some busy ones. Or perhaps Jessica had gotten to the post first, after slipping downstairs to make the coffee and toast in her soft cotton slippers, her pale blue silk dressing gown gently flapping against those impossibly long, perfect legs, and she noticed the female handwriting on the single item of post, and discreetly destroyed the card, waiting for the gurgling noise of the cappuccino maker to drown the sound of the paper shredder before putting together the breakfast tray for her husband-to-be. Or, perhaps her faithful cockapoo Bolshoi had torn it to shreds, keen to defend the territory and mate of his beloved owner.

It was mid-evening, and I went to bed early, as I had a 6 a.m. shift, and management training after. I felt exhausted. I had not even begun Christmas shopping, and my list of things 'to do' was too long for one side of paper. At least Christmas was more affordable this year; not only did I have my pay rise but Terry had started contributing child support, at times generously, making up for lost time. He had explained that his freelance income was irregular and I thought 'Here we go', but then at the beginning of December he received a windfall after getting exhibited somewhere and selling some more photographs, and he sent £500! Plus, we began discussing Christmas presents for Bronte, as he had his eye on some artistic equipment for her, and I delicately pointed out that we had to bear in mind that Danny could feel left out, so he offered a Scalextric set for him, who wasn't even his kid. Not that we were like a couple, or anything, just divorced-but-best-friend-parents, like we agreed.

I had the House Dream again; better than ever, which is to say, worse than ever. It was ever more vivid, but ever more out of reach. I was with a girlfriend, a little like Sharon but a unique person in her own right, who was asking me why I had never tried the shower in the en suite bathroom off the bedroom on the very top floor, as it was the best in the house. I replied that I hadn't even known that it existed! And we giggled. 'But it's your house!' she replied. So, I removed all my clothes, and put on a thick, white towelling bathrobe, and began walking upstairs. As I began showering, I noticed that there was a man watching me. To begin with I was alarmed, then I realised that he was my new boyfriend, and I began to feel turned on. He was quite unlike either Terry or George, he was a footballer who had just gotten in from the game, with muscly legs and a kind smile. I washed the dirt from the pitch off his toned thighs. I loved the way his long fingers moved all over me in the shower, from my cheek down to my breasts, down to my hips... oooh, the way he stroked my hips, the most underrated erogenous zone in the body! This female body at least...

I woke up to the familiar reality that there was no luxury bathroom, no top floor, no hunky, caring boyfriend, just a long list of chores.

It was then that George finally called, nearly two weeks after I sent my card.

'Hello, stranger,' I said, trying to sound serious and not sarcastic, trembling with nerves. My heart was pounding so furiously I was convinced he could hear it, down the line.

'Hello,' he said. 'Thank you for the card.'

'It was all I could say. I think I'm owed an explanation after all this silence.'

'I'm sorry. I lost my business – well probably. Technically I'm off for three months with depression, while we all figure out what to do. I had been losing it, I mean, my performance at work was off. I have to admit that. Something had to change.'

'Still no reason why you wouldn't talk to me, George. I mean, if you want to end things, then that's your privilege, though it would break my heart. But you've got to tell me! You've got to say something!'

'Well, I lost my business, and it seemed I had lost you too, so I just wanted to have time in my own company, to let the wounds heal.'

'You hadn't lost me though,' I started to panic. He sounded

angry. He seemed to be referring to something that I knew nothing about. 'What are you even talking about?'

'I just think that you and Terry and Bronte have lost time and need to catch up. It's obvious you still have strong feelings for each other, and I'd just be in the way...'

'Oh no! You don't get to play the martyr! You're not being all goody here. That's all fake. You're breaking my heart! How dare you try to pretend you're the good guy! I never asked you to get out of the way. George, that's horrible!'

'Well if I'm horrible and fake, why do you want me?'

'Well, you don't have to be!' I protested. 'It's a choice! We can go back to how we were!'

'I saw you, you see, kissing Terry. You're not just co-parents, you're lovers too. It's obvious the feelings had never gone away. I had already felt the chemistry when you met on the street that day and he saw Bronte. Then I came to make a surprise visit. I had bought you some gifts and everything. I had brought a present for young Danny and I had news about the art professor – when she was going to be in London next and could meet Bronte. And there you and he were, snogging on the doorstep. I just did a U-turn in the car and drove off.'

Oh, God. He'd seen us. 'We weren't snogging. It wasn't like that. I thought you were in Surrey; I mean it wasn't a real kiss. Just a peck goodbye. Just old instinct.' I protested loudly down the line, but my cheeks were burning at the recollection.

'*What*? Cheating is OK for you if I'm in another *county*? Is *that* what you're saying?'

'NO!! I wasn't *cheating*! Oh, God. Look, I'm clumsy with words, but, George, you have to believe me! I'm begging you. Pleeeease!!!'

'It's just... There's this side of you that's not sweet; that's selfish. Like letting yourself into my house and bedroom and making yourself at home before we'd even got together...'

234

My heartbeat suddenly sounded very loud in my ears. 'I'm sorry. *What* are you saying?'

'I saw you. In my bedroom. Before I turned the screen off.'

'You had a *camera*? Spying on me?'

'That's not spying. That's my home! Not yours! Any case, I turned off before the end.'

'The *end*? Oh what! What are you saying? Why bring that up?' Oh my God. He really had been watching. My humiliation was complete. He sounded cool and judgemental on the call, not wanting to listen to my side of the story at all. I did feel terrible that he had brought the present for Danny, and lined up an interview for Bronte. That came as a surprise, and I felt guilty and ashamed.

'Because it's another indication that you don't care for me,' he continued. 'Not me as a person. I'm just an access to nice properties while you're free to flirt with anyone else.'

'That's not true. That's so not true!' I protested. I was drowning in tears by this stage. 'Oh, God! This call has so not gone how I planned. What a nightmare! One little kiss and my whole life is ruined.'

'I'm sorry, Karen, the trust is not there. I hope you and Terry will be very happy together. He seems like a great guy.'

'We're NOT TOGETHER! We're just not! I don't know how else to say it.'

'Goodbye, Karen. I'll arrange to sell next door. Goodbye.'

37

Don't be naïve, George

It was either late winter, or early spring. Cold. There had been little snow but the wind was relentlessly cold. I had not sold the Leeds house, not even called the estate agent. Christmas and midwinter were bad times for selling, I reflected, so I could wait until after Easter. At work, the three-month cooling-off period came to an end. Negotiations with the other partners were more protracted, but less hostile, than I had expected. I consulted my lawyer, but did not need to involve her directly. After a couple of weeks of conversations, facilitated by Tony, someone both sides trusted, we came to an ingenious solution: the social responsibility work, the Living Wage consultancy, would be spun off and owned by me. The other partners would be left with the corporate work, which had begun to bore me in any case. Luke allowed himself a smug smile at the one face-to-face meeting we held, which I let him enjoy. He had never fully understood the business, and did not appreciate that helping an employer lift their staff out of poverty was lucrative, as well as socially beneficial.

I had been living in Surrey for the duration of the talks, but as they came to an end I was desperate to return back north, back home. I had decided to base the new business in York or Leeds, so I could live near Dad. In due course, I needed to start viewing potential offices, but I was in no hurry. The business transfer would still take a few weeks, so I had moved from being on sick leave to being on holiday – or between jobs, as the saying goes, but with a substantial capital gain on the way.

To begin with, I decided just to return for a week, staying in a hotel in the city centre. I travelled up on the Friday, noting with pleasure that there was a home game on the Saturday afternoon. It is a short cab ride from the Queen's Hotel to Elland Road, and I arrived at around 2 p.m., a full hour before kick-off, to savour the atmosphere and enjoy the build-up. I sauntered around the club shop, even though I had no desire to buy anything, then I wandered out, and circled the statue of Billy Bremner, the club's legendary late captain, his fists pumping the air in a familiar victory salute. It was the sentimental heart of the club, and was invariably adorned with scarves and in memoriam wreaths for deceased fans. People waited their turn to have their photo taken with King Billy as the backdrop. I had not previously taken part in such touristy activities, but on this occasion, spontaneously, posed in front and took a selfie, carefully positioning the view such that only my and the statue's face would fall within the cropped image. As the synthetic 'click' of the smartphone's camera sounded, I could hear a voice calling out my name. Its tone was earnest, and friendly.

'George! George!'

I looked up and around me, unable to detect the caller.

'*George!!*' It came again, and I noticed that the voice was from across the road. I could make out Terry, and he was smiling at me. He called out again: 'Wait! We'll cross! Want to get to the shop anyway.'

He was accompanied by three others. 'George! Great to see you. This is Craig, Johnny,' he announced, half turning to his left to introduce the two white lads whom I recognised from the brief encounter on the footbridge. 'And this is my big bro Don,' he added, turning a little to his right to introduce an older, more rounded version of himself, with similar, though less piercing, eyes.

'Where have you been? Karen's been missing you, you know. Something terrible. You should call her!'

'Well, um, I thought you and her... You know...'

'No!! We're just friends, co-parents to young Bronte. Seriously, we're not an item. She's crazy about you. Won't get over it; can't even get her to talk about it any more. Well, not now. For a while she would talk about nothing else.'

'Well, I didn't get the impression that she still wanted me.'

'Seriously. Anyway, good to see you for the game. Let's grab a quick beer.'

'Have we got time?'

'Sure. It's ten past, we've got half an hour or more. Which stand you in?'

'East.'

'OK, we're in the South. That's OK. Still plenty of time. We'll go to Billy's bar, there's an offer.'

'Beer in the Peacock's better.'

'OK, we'll go there. Back over the road! Traffic's stationary.'

The five of us squeezed into the large pub on Elland Road, opposite the South Stand. The other three occupied themselves talking about music, leaving Terry and me to have our chat.

'She adores you, mate,' he said, without preamble. He had an admirable directness of manner, something that I had always lacked, at least on personal matters. 'She misses you. She talks about you, all the time. Well she did, until she reckoned you two were done for good. Now she won't, but I can tell it's still all eating her up inside.'

'Why won't she pick up the phone and talk to me?'

'Oh, you know why, George. Don't be naïve.'

'Why? Why?'

'Because of the money thing, obviously. You pretty much accused her directly of being a gold-digger in your last conversation, according to her.'

'Oh.'

'Did you?'

'Um, yes. I might've said something accusing her of having her eye more on property than on me.'

'So, if she called you it would look like she was just after a nice house and a quick registry office do without a prenup.'

'But I thought you and she… were back together. I mean, she denied it of course, but, well, I suppose I'm a more insecure person than I look. She's out of my league…'

He interrupted me. 'Look, we never did get back together! Seriously. Look,' he took a deep breath, and then a deep swig from his beer. 'It would be in my interest too. I'm with Astrid, she's an artist, we're strong at the moment. Karen, if she wants anyone, wants you. She's lost without you, she seriously is. And it would be good for Bronte. At least give Karen a call.'

He looked so eager, so sincere, so full of enthusiasm, that I could not protest. I had come across people lying before, especially in my professional life, and this was not an example.

'Hey!' said the taller, heavier-set of his two friends, interrupting us. 'Sup up! We'll miss t' kick-off.'

'All right, Johnny, right with you.'

38

The artist's studio

With the pay rise, and with Terry's child support, I was at least getting on top of my finances, eliminating debts and even making overpayments on the mortgage. I was heartbroken, but solvent, in those bleak winter weeks of the new year. I arranged a meeting with a mortgage adviser, and it went even better than I expected. I was young, the salary was as secure as you could get, and there were no more personal debts. The big semi-detached houses in Horsforth were still out of the question, but a tidy three-bedroom place near my parents with a garden – a garden! – was now within reach.

'Can this really, really be mine, like actually mine?' I asked the estate agent. It was a light evening, the first week after the clocks had gone forward, but cold. Even so, the garden looked like the paradise of Eden, as far as I was concerned.

'With the deposit you've set aside, and your salary, and no personal debts, then yes. The sellers are moving into rented, so no upward chain. You could be moving in within six weeks.'

'Great!' I said. An additional reason that attracted me to the property was a modern, fairly large outhouse, that I thought would make an artist's studio for Bronte. I had mentioned this to Terry, who loved the idea, and was all keen to help kit it out, making me feel pleased but all anxious at the same time, reflecting selfishly that he would look ever more like the husband, complicating my quest for a real one. I mean, I didn't *need* one; just wanted someone. Sex, companionship, shared planning; what is life without these?

'I don't want to tempt fate, but it should be all straightforward from here,' the agent said. She was a nice, mumsy sort of estate agent, who might have been better suited as a social worker. The next time I visited, I took Sharon with me. We had to explain that we weren't a couple. I felt slightly awkward about the matter, despite priding myself on having modern opinions. Sharon had no such qualms. 'Well, if I ever were to get bi-curious, you'd be first on the list for a snog,' she cheerfully informed me as the two of us sat in the garden. She was on the swing, rocking gently, and I was on a bench nearby.

'Oh well, that's a compliment I guess,' I said. 'Don't be offended but I'm not on the lookout for a wife. Mind, I'm running out of options when it comes to husbands. And Terry being back in Bronte's life is a mixed blessing, really. The better he gets as a dad, the further away I ever get from having a relationship again. Any bloke'll just see him with Bronte and think Terry and I are an item, or will be again soon.'

'Well? Is it a possibility with Terry? I know he's got a girlfriend,' said Sharon, pausing suddenly as though she were going to add something but had changed her mind.

'Oh, I've thought about it. I mean, there's still a spark, when he looks at me in a certain way. We even talked about it one evening.'

'Did you?' she asked, eyes widening at the scandal. 'Did you kiss?'

'None of your business!'

'I'll take that as a yes.'

'No, we really didn't, but we came close. Oh, I don't know. I want George back, really. We had this language, this understanding, this sense of humour together. But I'll never see him again, I just feel it, deep down. I know I did something that was out of line for him, but his reaction feels over the top. So, there's something else, or someone else. Or both.'

'Can't you call him?'

I just looked at her.

'What?' she asked.

'Oh, I can't. It would look like I were completely mercenary, just after him 'cos of his money. I just can't.'

'Boyfriend who's too rich. Nice problem to have.'

'Well, he's not my boyfriend. He's dumped me.'

'Oh, come on, you had a bad row. Folk say things in the heat of the moment. They say stuff to hurt, it may not be true. I'm sure he loves you. He were crazy about you.'

'Well, he'll have moved on by now. And moved in with Jessica, I imagine.'

'There's someone else?'

'Well, there must be.'

'You've got a name for her, and you've just made her up?'

'Well, just being realistic.'

'Dear me. Takes all sorts. Well, come on, let's head back to yours.'

'Right y'are.'

'Haven't you got a coat?' she asked, as we thanked the estate agent and made to leave. 'It's right cold now.'

'Oh, I just forgot, I were in a hurry,' I said, wrapping my cardigan around me.

'Here, let's go back to mine first, I've got a spare one. It's a bit old but nice and warm. Then we'll walk over back to yours via the park.'

'Can we go via the cemetery? I want to see Kevin. Tidy up the flowers.'

'Of course, love, though we can't be too long. It is on the way.'

A couple of the flowers on Kevin's grave were brown and needed removing. I tidied the rest. It was clear Mum had been there at the weekend.

'I used to fancy him,' said Sharon, a small tear appearing on her cheek.

'I know,' I said, smiling. I looked up at my fair-haired friend, petite, smiley and buxom, and I thought of the two of them together. 'You and Kevin would have made a great couple. I can imagine the kids you'd have had.'

'That's all we can do. Imagine.'

I stretched forward and traced my finger over his name, in a well-practised gesture. 'Bye bye, big brother. I'll be back again soon.'

Secretly, I hoped that there would be a light on in George's house as we walked past it, but there was none. I might let myself in later, I reflected, just to tidy up. At least there wasn't a 'For Sale' sign, though there was one outside mine.

As we walked through the front door, Danny leaped up from his toy train and shouted 'Mummy!' which was nice, as he was a little boy's boy, not openly affectionate, most of the time. He even wanted a hug. I felt bad that I hadn't spent enough quality time with him, and promised myself I would make it up to him. Sharon didn't get such a warm greeting from Jayden, but he was nice enough.

'I see George hasn't put next door up for sale yet,' said Sharon.

'Probably just not got round to it yet,' I replied.

'Hmmm. It may not be over yet, after all.'

'Well, if it's not over, it can only get worse.'

'My, you're a little ray of sunshine, aren't you? I think he still loves you. We'll see. He'd have sold up or rented out if he were wanting to be well away from you.'

'Maybe he's not the right one, anyway. There's something a bit secretive about him at times.'

'You don't believe that.'

'It's what I have to tell myself.'

'Well, like I say, we'll see.'

39

The gifts

Despite Terry's plea, and the couple of beers inside me, I had not resolved to see Karen, or even call her, but as the Leeds home was just half a mile away, I thought that I would pay it an overdue visit. I could decide later in the evening whether to knock on next door, or I might bump into her in the street. It was a change of mind. I had jumped into a cab just outside the stadium after the match – an unexpected and depressing 4–1 defeat, after having taken the lead, against one of the division's mid-ranking sides – with the original intention of returning to the Queen's Hotel. The mood of the home crowd after had been somewhere between shock and embarrassment.

'Change of mind, turn left here,' I said to the driver. I paid him the full fare to the city centre, plus a tip, so he had no cause for complaint.

The first thing that I noticed entering the familiar street was a 'For Sale' sign close to my house. As I neared, it became clear that it pertained to Karen's. This was not a good sign: so firmly over me that she could no longer bear to be next door, even if I was an absent neighbour. I was exceptionally nervous as I slowly turned the key in the lock. I even stopped for a moment, withdrew the key slightly and thought about leaving, then reflected that I didn't have my car. I would have to call for a cab anyway, and it's more comfortable to do that sitting down indoors. May as well enter, I reflected.

If she had not been in at all, there would be a mound of flyers and other types of junk mail behind the door. The key reached the maximum point of its turn, and I gently pushed the door inwards. It slid smoothly open, with no resistance. Potentially, this was not a good sign; she had been in, and perhaps using it for trysts with Terry. Then I recalled the look of absolute sincerity on his face just a few hours earlier. I looked down the hall. It was surprisingly clean, almost gleaming. I had expected a coating of dust, and possibly even mouse droppings. I ventured into the kitchen. Karen had laid the items of post neatly on the circular table, which shone with recently cleaned brilliance. They were only utility firms, and all bills were up to date, so nothing urgent. There was a fresh stack of coffee capsules by the cappuccino maker. I was touched by the gesture, but my mood turned sharply to anxiety as I worried again if the home had been the love nest for her and Terry. Tentatively, I opened the fridge door, fearing a couple of pizzas and a half-empty bottle of Sauvignon Blanc. There was a bottle, but it was Sancerre, one of my favourites, and it was unopened. There was no food, and not much milk. Hmmm.

Before entering the sitting room, I ventured upstairs, to confront that demon first. I opened the bedroom door slowly, as though demonstrating such deference to the space would persuade it not to reveal any horrors, such as crumpled sheets or a used condom in the bin. It opened and I peered inside. My silk bathrobe was neatly arranged on the bed, the letter 'G' on the left breast prominent, alongside a bath towel folded into a perfect square. Again, everything was scrubbed and vacuumed or dusted and polished, even the bottle of cologne on the tiny shelf, and she had bought a fresh, new one, and placed it alongside, of the same brand. I walked around the small space; nothing was out of place, and some thoughtful things had been added, such as a copy of GQ magazine on the bedside table. I left the room and walked downstairs, and into the sitting room. Everything was as orderly as the mess deck before the admiral's inspection, all was gleaming and bright, including the thick, still-new polish on the wooden floor. The fronds of the rug were immaculately combed and parallel on both ends. The CDs were in alphabetical order. There was a vase of freshly cut flowers on a tiny side table. How many had she arranged in the months since my last visit?

On the coffee table were three unfamiliar books, shiny and brand new: a history of Yorkshire Cricket Club, a history of Leeds United Football Club and a copy of *The Ninth: Beethoven and the World in 1824*, by Harvey Sachs. I picked up the Beethoven book, and just held it in my right hand, stood still for a minute or so, before slowly opening the cover. She had written a short note inside, just *To George, thinking of you xxx*, and noting my birthday. It had been there for four months. I picked up the others in turn, to discover that each had a similarly loving note, respectively dated Christmas and Valentine's Day. I sat down with them on the settee, leafing through them without reading, caressing the firm, new covers and crisp printed pages, my hands slightly trembling with wonder, as though the gifts were supernatural. All these months, she had been thinking about me: every big day, and every small one. Me. For the first time since Mum died, someone had devoted her waking thoughts to me. I began to cry inside, with both sadness and joy.

After about half an hour motionless in stupefaction and wonder, I fumbled for the phone in my pocket, and began a text. I simply typed:

Karen. I'm home. I'm next door. Thank you for the gifts. I've been a fool. I love you so, so much. G xxxxxx

She was there within minutes, nervous, radiant, hopeful; bold and shy at the same time.

'You look well,' she said. 'Lost a bit of weight.'

'Only through nerves, I think. You look beautiful.'

'Thank you. I've missed you.'

'I love you,' I said. 'I'm such an idiot. I used to think I was intelligent, but that was an illusion. You're the smart one. I got you wrong. I got everything wrong. I am so, so sorry for not trusting you, for not believing, for being such an idiot. I've put you through so much.'

'I love you too,' she replied. 'I always did.'

We kissed, passionately, deeply, then pulled away. 'But we do have to talk. Let's sit down. Thank you so much for the gifts, the books. So thoughtful. They blew me away.'

'I never stopped thinking of you, George. I thought about you all the time, wanted to keep the house tidy, remember your birthday, and Valentine's. It was only you. Look, I can't deny there were still feelings for Terry, and it's great Bronte's got her dad, but we never restarted things. It was just a kiss. You should talk to him, get it straight from the source.'

'I already have.'

'What?'

'I bumped into him at the game this afternoon. Well, he spotted me actually. Came over and we had a pint and a chat. He's a good guy.'

'And he assured you there was nothing between us.'

'Well, as much as anyone could.'

'It is complicated, George, but only up to a point. Everyone's got a relationship history unless you're fifteen. But it's history! I mean, first love, you can't completely extinguish those feelings!'

'I know,' I said, calmly.

'And anyway, at least we know a bit about my past. What about yours? You're so secretive in your mansion, with your business and your London life. What about *your* first love? Why don't you ever tell me about her?'

'Because she's you, of course! *You're* my first love!'

'But that's crazy! I don't believe you! Flattery! I mean, you've been married and you're like... well, nearly fifty...?'

'Well, forty-three, actually. I did tell you once.'

She looked suitably appalled with herself, but recovered. 'Oh. Sorry. Well, you look authoritative, that's OK in a guy. But, well, my point is, surely you've been in love before!'

'Really, honestly, Karen, I haven't. Not 'til you. Only you make me do crazy things, send my feelings off the scale, cause me to lose concentration at work, get me so hyper-aroused with desire and love and lust all mixed up into one. I become like a weird, different person! Only you. Just you. Bloody you!'

'Well why didn't you bloody say so?'

'I thought it was obvious,' I replied.

'What, by hiding away? Hurting me?'

'I... well. I...'

'*What??!!*'

'Didn't think I deserved you,' I said. 'Terry has the looks, the artistry, the youth, the confidence.'

'How many times do I have to tell you? We're not an item. He has a girlfriend.'

'I know! I know! I know that now. I'm so sorry.'

'George?'

'Yes?'

'Did you seriously not fall in love as a teenager, or in your twenties?'

'Seriously.'

'That's so sad.'

'Then stop smiling.'

'I'm not smiling!'

'You're looking at me all emotionally mature and superior. Beauty plays tricks.'

'Oh, take me upstairs and fuck me already!'

And I did.

40

Strange, the things you hope for

The books had done the trick. I mean, it wasn't a trick – not a gambit. I just wanted to buy him something on his birthday, Christmas and Valentine's, and, with his birthday being in December, the three dates were close together. I had cleaned the house twice a week, which was a real busman's holiday, as I earned my living as a cleaner. But it did mean that I was very good at it. I even polished the bottle of cologne in his bedroom and bought a new one. I wanted him to know that, even if we were finished for good, that I had loved him, that my feelings were real, that they had shaken me to the core, and that I would have loved him still, just as much, if he had lost all his stupid money, even had minus money. I hadn't given up on Darren because of the debt, but because of the lying – also, he had more given up on me, and Danny.

I knew something of George's tastes and interests. I knew which sports teams he supported, and that his favourite music was Beethoven's Ninth Symphony. I chose some books; nice, hardback, gifty books, and just arranged them on the coffee table, with a little note written inside the cover. I didn't wrap them or anything. I even dusted and polished the books themselves every week, and replaced the flowers in the vase. It all looked nice.

He must have let himself in, for the first time in months, just beyond the point at which I had begun to give up. So much for my telepathic powers. Everything I hoped for, concentrating fiercely, stayed just out of reach – until I had abandoned all hope and only then did he contact me. The news came in the form of a text message. I had expected a knock on the door, as he would surely only make contact after going to his Leeds home and seeing the presents and all the cleaning. And I had expected a further round of bloody negotiations and difficult conversations and accusations, but there weren't any. He called himself a fool, and just said he wanted me. I was there in nanoseconds, washing-up soap still clinging to my hands, calling over my shoulder to Bronte to please keep an eye on Danny, and she had just grinned, saying; 'Lover boy's back then!' with her usual cheeky grin, but I didn't care.

He told me that I was his first and only love, which was magical to hear; I mean, he may have been lying, but it would have been a thoughtful, inspirational lie. In any case, there was something about what he said and how he said it that was convincing; how I was the only girl who had caused him to lose concentration, do crazy things, forget himself at work… maybe that was how it was going to play out; I would be such a distraction that he would become hopeless at his business, lose all his money and then, at last, we would be equal and fall in love properly, and money would never be a problem between us again! Strange, the things you hope for.

We talked about some stuff, such as how he met Terry and that was cool. I can't remember what else. Then I practically ordered him to the bedroom, where we made feverish love for several minutes, or hours, I wasn't sure which, or didn't care. Time obeys different rules when you're crazy in love. Then we dozed, and then woke up. I fetched him a cup of tea.

'So, if we're back together, how are you going to break it to Jessica? I mean, she gave up ballet for you.'

'Who?'

'Oh, don't worry. I made up a whole back story for my imaginary love rival.'

'And I thought I had mental health problems.'

'It's just imagination – creativity. You should take it as a compliment, really, that I went to so much effort. Did you know, she survived meningitis when she was five, and had her heart broken at age seventeen? Despite her privileged background, she's had some tough things to overcome.'

'It's an inspirational story, for girls and young women everywhere.'

'And anyway, you did behave like you had someone new. I don't know for sure that you didn't, and I thought maybe you'd only come back because that Jessica – that is to say, whoever it was – dumped you so you thought you might as well go for the Plan B with the sad single mum up north, desperate for anyone with brass.'

'Well, I didn't. You're my Plan A, my Plan alpha.'

'This being in love thing, it's, like, better than a drug, isn't it? It's worth everything. Even heartbreak. This euphoria you feel on the days when you're floating inside the soul of another person, and even chores are fun to do – everything is. You grow up listening to love songs and how wonderful it's all supposed to feel, but no one prepares you for how it really is, which is even better.'

I traced my forefinger over his hairy chest as I said these words. I was lying on my side, close to and touching him, as he lay on his back. I wanted to add: 'Which is how I feel with you,' just to make absolutely clear that I wasn't thinking of my first, teenage love, but of course the risk in saying that would be giving the impression that I was thinking of Terry, and just saying that as a cover. Words can be very misleading, including when you're telling the truth.

Fortunately, he just sighed with pleasure, eyes half closed. 'Let's never break each other's hearts ever again,' he said. That was good enough for me.

'Absolutely. Let's never. You feel it physically, right here, don't you? Love, I mean.' I pointed just below my breasts. 'It's a physical thing, like an illness, but in a good way. A positive illness.'

'There?' he asked playfully. 'Or down a bit? Up a bit? Or is it over there a bit?'

'Stop making fun! Where do *you* feel it?'

'Here, in the chest, in the stomach, and all over my skin.'

'Fingers and toes?'

'Most of them definitely.'

'What were you thinking about, when you were away from me down south, assuming you weren't with Jessica?'

'I was missing you. I was feeling down. I was assuming you'd moved on. I wasn't down south the whole time anyway. I was in Knaresborough some of the time. I visited my dad a lot. He kept asking after you.'

'Where did you stay?'

'In a hotel suite.'

'My, it must be nice, to have so much money you don't have to worry.'

'It's a source of comfort, but you can get bored, and it doesn't fix your relationships. It's a compensation, not a way of life. I guess what I've learned in the past few months is that I can't rely totally on career and business and savings in the bank. Being rich is not a spiritually enhancing experience.'

'Neither is being poor, honey.'

41

Which direction now?

The engagement party was just a few weeks later. It was late spring, perhaps, or very early summer, and a light Saturday evening, but chilly. It was to take place at Karen's parents' house, as it was a bit larger, and had a garden. Only the smokers and a few hardy lads would be outside, in this weather. Karen was still at the Holbeck house; she had pulled out of making an offer on a larger place in Beeston, as we had begun looking for a new place. My new business was going to be headquartered in Leeds.

I drove her there from the hairdresser's, even though it was only a mile. I wanted her to drive, but she resisted. She didn't want her hair messed up, she said, but, really, I think she wanted to get out of the Mercedes in front of her schoolfriends.

Her mum and dad opened the Prosecco as soon as we arrived.

'Just one for me,' I said. 'Driving later.'

'Not for me thanks,' said Karen. 'Lemonade, please.' The three of us raised an eyebrow, but we all moved inside.

There was quite a crowd: Terry and Astrid were there. So were Craig and Johnny, whom I had gotten to know, even though Karen hadn't. Joy had come along – I was thrilled that she accepted the invitation – and she fitted in quite naturally to her new friends, which slightly surprised me, as she could find meeting new people difficult. She wasted no time in getting to know her future sister-in-law. I was taken aback by her first conversational topic: 'So, I understand you have an interest in metaphysics, especially the concept of first cause?'

Oh no, I thought, but Karen replied swiftly: 'You mean the philosophical point put forward by Aristotle and Thomas Aquinas?'

'The very same,' said Joy. 'And you're right that it's neglected in life sciences.' And they were off, the two of them, chatting earnestly. Mmm, interesting, I thought. She'd been swotting up without telling me.

I turned to my new friends. I was one of the lads, finally. Craig and Johnny were older than Terry, and had gone to different schools. I had even gone along to one of their gigs once, and pretended to like their music. Terry was an occasional vocalist whom they kept trying to persuade back full time. I was introduced to their wives: Petra, a sporty, tomboyish, friendly young woman with cornrow hair and formidable biceps, who was with Johnny; and Debbie, gentle mannered, petite and buxom, who seemed to fuss over her Craig to a remarkable degree. They chatted about bands and albums I had never heard of, and I did my best to follow.

'Do you remember when Terry auditioned for us the first time?' asked Johnny, reminiscing for my benefit.

'It were, like, gruelling,' Terry replied, then turned to me. 'Before we'd like played a note or anything, Craig asks: "So, what's the best Jam album?" and I say, "*All Mod Cons*". And he just says "You're in." So, Johnny goes: "Oh come on, the last vocalist was good. Aren't we at least going to have an audition?" "But he preferred *The Gift*," says Craig. So, I had to, like, persuade them to test how good I was before I could get in.'

'Standards,' said Craig, deadpan.

There was a pause. 'What about Leeds, then?' I asked. 'Looks like Evans is on his way out, from what he said at the end of the last home game.'

'Yea,' said Craig. 'He were all right but not sure about selection. Botaka should have played more. Best technical skills in the squad.'

'I dunno, he makes bad choices sometimes,' said Johnny. 'Tries to take a defender on when he should pass.'

'Still deserved longer run in t' first team,' said Craig.

'I'm a fan,' I replied.

Karen had sidled up to me, having interrupted her chat with Joy who had gone to the bathroom. Karen was listening to us, curious, intertwining the fingers of her left hand with those of my right. 'You know,' she said. 'It is a bit funny, you footie fans, the way you talk all admiringly about fit young men. I mean, it is a bit, well, gay isn't it?'

Johnny bristled a little, but the rest of us were relaxed. 'I guess Jordan Botaka is quite pretty, when you think about it,' I said, just to wind her up. 'Nice pony tail.'

'Typical!' she says. 'I'm on to significant other number three before I'm thirty-five and he turns out to be gay!'

There was a ring at the door. 'Can you get that, Karen, love?' asked her mum. 'I'm busy back here.'

The front door was just a few steps away, and we could see her look of shock and consternation as she opened it, paused briefly, and then cried out: 'Darren! Who invited you?'

His reply was partially audible to us inside, but it seemed clear that he was unaware that a party was taking place, mentioning having called at her place first and, remembering where her parents lived, decided to try there as an alternative.

'Well,' she said, uncertain. 'This is awkward, but you might as well come in.'

He did so, a cheerful enough, handsome-looking guy of around thirty, tee-shirt and jeans, looking about him, recognising a few of the faces. Little Danny looked up, curious, then smiled as he spotted his own eyes looking back at him.

'Well, I've got some good news, Karen, actually,' he said, as he patted young Danny on the head, who had stood next to him.

'So have I,' she replied confidently, and pulled me towards her with her hand. 'This is my fiancé, George, and this is our engagement party.' The others retreated to other conversations, and it was just the three of us.

'I'm really pleased, really pleased for you – for you both.' He looked at me directly, and seemed most sincere. 'You're a lucky guy, George. I was just immature. I realise that now. Let her slip through my fingers. But it's all right, Karen, I've got someone new. And I owe you an apology. And lots of money. For child support. How has Danny been?'

'He's doing all right,' she replied. 'I'll reintroduce you properly another day, though he seems to be bonding to you already. If you're going to be in his life consistently, that is. So what's your good news?'

'Well, you may know that I've given up the gambling, and cut back on the booze. I've got a sponsor, and everything. I'm getting my life together. The turning point was a couple of times I was so drunk I didn't even know what I'd bet on. There were in-game bets, all done online. But the thing is, and I don't really deserve it but...'

'But what?' she asked.

'Well, absolutely the last time I did that – placed bets while drunk – was last August. I was so pissed I couldn't even recall what they were and forgot about them for months, while I tried to get straightened out. My mate Dave reminded me this February. It turned out I'd placed three ten-pound bets at five thousand to one each. One was Tony Blair to become the next Pope, another was Lord Lucan to be found alive in Africa and the third was Leicester City to win the Premiership.'

'So why are you telling me this?'

'Because Leicester City have just won the Premiership.'

'What?' asked Karen, incredulous. I just chuckled. 'But that's daft,' she continued. 'How many teams are there in t' Premiership?'

'Twenty.'

'What? Only twenty, and you got five thousand to one? Some folk at t' bookies need some arithmetic lessons, I think. The world's gone mad!' She looked around her, wide-eyed, baffled at the strange world of men.

'That's as maybe,' said Darren. 'But I'm quids in. I owe you two and a half years' child support, and then some.'

'There's no justice! There's no justice,' was all Karen could say. 'The world has gone mad.'

'But you'll take it?' he asked, hopefully, then turned to me. 'I mean, it'd help you both out.'

'I don't think we need it, thank you very much,' said Karen, smartly.

'Actually, Karen,' I said to her. 'It's not only about you, and Darren's trying to do the right thing here. The money could be a college fund for Danny – pay for his apprenticeship or uni, or whatever he wanted to do.'

'I don't believe it. I don't believe it!' was all she could say. 'All those years of poverty, all that suffering, and all the windfalls come at once. It's too much. Well, have a drink, you might as well stay. You might as well meet Terry, Bronte's dad.'

'Cool!' said Darren, as the two of them were introduced.

'Hey!' called out Craig. 'Look at 'em. One fiancé, two exes. All in a row! Two of them dads.'

'Well, maybe three actually,' said Karen, placing a hand lightly on her stomach.

'You what?' I asked, as everyone turned to look.

She blushed. 'Well, it's too early, and I shouldn't have said owt, but I am five weeks late and puking most mornings.'

'So that's why you're on the lemonade!' I said as I went over to give her a hug. There was cheering. The emotion surged up within me, stronger than expected, stronger than anything I had felt before. My eyes became wet with emotion. A child! Someone would want my child!

'Get a room!' said someone, from the back, as Karen and I began kissing.

'Got one booked. A suite actually,' I said, after breaking off the kiss.

'Get away, then, the pair of you. Make it twins.'

I had booked a beautiful hotel in the Dales, where we were going to either take some wholesome country walks, or just stay in the suite and make love for four days. Probably just the latter. Before long, we were back in the car.

'Well, I assume we can afford this,' she said, as we joined the motorway and I opened up the throttle. I said nothing. 'Why are you smiling?' she asked.

'You said "we",' I pointed out.

'I know. It feels good, doesn't it? We can look for a house.'

'We can do whatever we want.'

'Still have to be careful, mind,' she said. 'And another thing.'

'Yes?'

'Well, just to clarify things, I'm now assistant trainee manager on a regular salary, with prospects, and you're basically unemployed with, not to put too fine a point on it, some mental health issues.'

'That appears to be the case. I shall get down the Job Centre.'

'Well, all I'm saying is, just as well one of us has steady earnings, for when we apply for a mortgage and stuff.'

'Female breadwinner. It's a growing trend. You wear the trousers.'

'Trousers? I'm not even wearing knickers.'

The car swerved a little in its lane. 'Behave!' I said. 'You'll cause a road traffic accident with your wanton sexiness.'

'Brazen hussy, that's me.'

I ran the fingers of my left hand over her thigh, up to the hem of her short skirt.

'Do you know which direction we're taking?' she asked.

'Are you talking about this journey, or our lives together?'

'Well both, I guess.'

'As regards our life, we make it up as we go along. It's a creative project. As regards the journey, I have a mostly reliable satnav.'

'*Mostly* reliable?' she asked.

'Well, a near-faultless record, but sometimes messes up big time. Once, on the way to the Leeds ground, got it wrong completely – sent me way off course. On the other hand, maybe it wasn't an error, maybe I was being guided expertly. Artificial Intelligence has come a long way. Thanks, Maggie,' I said, tapping the dashboard.

'Who the hell is Maggie?' asked Karen, curious and alarmed.

I glanced up. She was pouting with an annoyance that was pretend. At least I think it was.

Ah. And so begins married life.

Acknowledgements

I must thank my development editor at Unbound, the amazing Kia Thomas, for her insights and advice; also the wonderfully gifted Shannon Kyle, for insights on prose, character development and what it's really like to be a single mum. Thanks to the inspirational editor, my friend Dina Aletras. Thanks, also, to Katy Guest for taking on a relative unknown at the house of Unbound. I would like to thank my fellow Unbound authors and, of course, the sixty-eight people, not all of them known to me, who made the most generous pledges to make this book reach publication. Thanks to Sue Jennings for her support and everyone at Castleton Mill. Thanks also to Andreas Loizou and all at the Margate Bookie for their amazing support. A very special thanks, as ever, to Charlotte, and to Adam. Thanks to my amazing siblings: Cathy, Andrew, Felicity, Anne, Peter and, in spirit, Michael and Mum. Thanks to Dad too for his encouragement and support. I would like to give a very special thanks to my amazing siblings-in-law, whom I've known for decades: Paul, Ian, Nicky and of course David, who inadvertently gave me the idea for *A Love of Two Halves* when describing where he parked when taking Felicity to Elland Road. David: your Merc is always welcome in Beeston, and always safe #crossesfingers.

P. J. Whiteley, July 2019

Unbound is the world's first crowdfunding publisher, established in 2011.

We believe that wonderful things can happen when you clear a path for people who share a passion. That's why we've built a platform that brings together readers and authors to crowdfund books they believe in – and give fresh ideas that don't fit the traditional mould the chance they deserve.

This book is in your hands because readers made it possible. Everyone who pledged their support is listed at the front of the book and below. Join them by visiting unbound.com and supporting a book today.